Charlotte's End

CHARLOTTE'S END

Veena S Rao

Vitastaa

Let Knowledge Spread

Published by
Renu Kaul Verma
Vitastaa Publishing Pvt Ltd
2/15, Ansari Road, Daryaganj
New Delhi - 110 002
info@vitastapublishing.com

ISBN 978-93-82711-91-9

Typeset by Vits Press
Cover Design by Geetali Baruah
Printed by Vikas Computer and Printers

Dedication

To
My husband YS Rao, who endured the late nights with lights on
My daughter Nishta, whose school examinations with their domestic silence started this novel

My mother, Sita Devi, and my father, the late Brigadier Sri Ram, who would have enjoyed reading this book

Acknowledgements

Indian writers of my age and background have normally been influenced by the world of British literary fiction with which we grew up and the real world of India in which we lived, more so in my profession which was deeply linked to ground reality of India. In this work of fiction, I am reflecting the former.

This novel has remained dormant for about two decades, developing during 'domestic curfew,' very common in Indian homes when children's examinations are on, and periods of lesser professional demand. Finally, it emerged. My grateful thanks to Ms Renu Kaul Verma, Managing Director, Vitastaa Publishing, for her faith in the manuscript, and her confidence that we could make an entry into the exclusive world of British literary fiction. Thank you, Renu.

A big thank you to Ms Veena Batra, who edited this manuscript in the most supportive and positive way, improving it with her suggestions.

I would also like to thank my brother Suraj, a former naval officer, but better known in the artistic and literary world as the cartoonist 'Eskay', for helping with fleshing out details of naval warfare in the Atlantic voyage chapter.

I am grateful to several of my friends who read the manuscript as it evolved, and gave me very valuable suggestions.

A lot of information regarding the `drole de guerre', the Battle of the Atlantic, the convoys, and about wartime England has been referred from the *World War II – Time-Life Books.*

It was June 1945 and the war had just ended. We had to organize our lives afresh, but were exhausted and drained. We had won the war, but everyone had lost so much.

Summer had been limping along, battling clouds and rain, giving us all seasons of the year in a day.

But today was a beautiful summer day. The sky was a clear turquoize blue, with not a wisp of cloud. The earth was opening up with plants and leaves, dragon flies were buzzing around and the birds were atwitter. There's a very special feeling on such days—a feeling of hope and happiness, when windows hitherto shut are opened, when heavy woollens and blankets are aired and put away and light cottons brought out, when the woods put on their finery and beckon you for long walks, smelling of adolescent leaves and birds, and you want to embrace the heady air in everything you do.

Raymond was out on the estate with Henry, supervising the planting. Alexandra was at school and would be back for lunch. I had finished my morning chores in the lawns and the garden and was about to go to the children's cottages when John came into the study with a grim face.

"What is it John? You look worried."

"Ma'am," he said, his face extremely agitated, "Miss Portner is here. She insists on seeing you. She isn't taking no for an answer."

I could see John was still as nervous of Miss Portner as in the past. "Miss Portner? What on earth is she doing here? I thought she was in some institution."

Her name evoked no specific reaction in me. Too much had happened, too much had been compressed and crammed into these past five years to provoke any feeling, this way or that, at the sound of her name. I didn't feel threatened, I didn't feel intimidated—the woman had no power over me anymore. That much was certain. The only thing I did feel was an irritation at having an unwelcome visitor in the middle of my day. I wondered what she wanted. Perhaps she had been released and had nowhere to go. Well, she certainly was being presumptuous if she thought she could come here, after all the destruction she had wreaked in our lives. I started getting angry too. Just who the hell did she think she was?

"Well, I wonder what she wants. Send her in John."

And then, for no real reason—perhaps, because I did not want her to defile Lanverndel again, I said, "No John, I'll come outside and see her at the landing. I don't want her inside the house."

"Yes Ma'am."

I waited for him to leave, and then went up to my room. I examined my face; it was now a little filled out, my hair was styled, and my head was positioned with confidence and poise. My clothes were practical and chic, and I think I looked quite in charge of my domain. How far I had come, I thought, from the nervous, gawky, frightened girl who had walked in here seven years ago, and been terrified of her. Miss Portner meant nothing to me, except a damned nuisance right now which had to be got rid of. I wondered how her mental condition would be. Perhaps she was more stable, or else she wouldn't be roaming around freely.

Should I call the police, I wondered. But what for? What would I say to them? I would only end up appearing very foolish. I could still tell John to send her away, but deep down within me, I think I wanted her to see me as I was today, changed and grown, the mistress of Lanverndel in my own right, mature and confident, and the mother of Raymond's child, something Charlotte could never be. Yes, I would see her just to show her, if nothing else, that we had won, Raymond and me; that for all her viciousness and evil, she had not been able to destroy us, and that the final triumph was ours.

I walked down the stairs, composed and undaunted. I would face her as I had faced the world the last five years, and flaunt before her that she couldn't ever annihilate me again. I crossed the hall and reached the landing.

She stood there shrivelled and shrunk, her beady eyes sharp and piercing as she glared at me with hatred. She looked like an apparition from a morgue.

I looked at her directly and coldly. "What do you want, Miss Portner? Why have you come here?"

She looked malevolent and she looked insane.

Her words were like the hissing of a snake. "I was passing through madam, so I thought I'd just drop by and give you my greetings. I keep getting news about Lanverndel and how you're doing. Charlotte tells me about it everyday. I've always missed Lanverndel so much."

She kept staring at me malignantly. I didn't know what to say. A creepy feeling was slowly coming over me, but I wasn't afraid. I thought I'd just gaze back at her coldly until she left. I'd rub it into her silently and deliberately that she no longer had any power over me.

But she had her own intent. "So now you think you've taken Charlotte's place, have you?" She spat out her words. "What a fool you are. If you only knew how she mocks you when she talks to me every night," she shrieked like a witch. Then her voice again turned soft and malicious.

"And I hear there's a child in the bargain. What happened to Tom Camlin, Charlotte's uncle? How did he disappear from the face of the earth?"

And then after staring at me with more hatred, she continued her imprecation, her voice like poisonous velvet.

"And now you think you are mistress of Lanverndel. What a fool you are! Laverndel shall always belong to Charlotte." She spoke and stared at me as if she was trying to overpower and mesmerize me, like she had tried to do, in an age long passed, and had almost succeeded. "You know, she has never left it."

But I still did not cower. That was enough, I decided. I would ask John to send her out. I had no business at all to listen to this.

"You'll never be like Charlotte, you village upstart, with all your fancy clothes and manners. Upstart, that's what you always were." She spoke with that devilish low toned chant.

I kept my composure, though my anger was rising uncontrollably.

"If that's what you've come to say," I said with deliberate coldness, keeping my dignity, assuaging my rage, "you may leave now. You know, Miss Portner, nothing of what you say affects me at all. You have no influence over me anymore. Don't you understand? So just leave, before I ask someone to show you out. You have caused enough harm here."

Her eyes blazed hatred. "Where is Mr de Villiers? Does he still yearn for Charlotte, my Charlotte whom he adored, who could never be his? Or has he set up another home somewhere? How could you ever believe that he would remain with you? You, an uneducated, common village pretender." There was more venom.

My blood was boiling, but I would not lose my cool. I would remain dignified and would call for John to send her out. Miss Portner looked pale. She was trembling and there were beads of perspiration on her forehead. I saw her opening her purse to take out a handkerchief, I thought. She looked so deathly ill. I rang the bell.

John came and I turned towards him. I would ask him to show her out. And in that split second, I heard a crash like the clap of thunder, and something penetrated my left side causing excruciating pain. I heard John shout and for some inexplicable reason I saw Miss Portner turn into a huddle on the ground. My legs were giving way, the pain was spreading and my eyes were losing sight. I thought I was dying, as a wave of darkness swallowed me.

Chapter One

It had been a beautiful day. I had discovered it was my birthday. It was my first visit to the opera…so grand and opulent…and Raymond had said I looked lovely.

I was slipping into a procession of images…a war had been declared…I was walking along a familiar cobbled driveway…I saw the hedges lining the drive, standing like silent sentinels dressed up in a riot of colour, rich and luscious cherry blossom, rhododendrons, daffodils…the walking paths criss-crossed by little streams and rivulets, connected by beautiful little curved garden bridges and arches dressed with flowering vines, clemantis and wisteria, some bold and flaming, some gentle and sober. The gate was open and the drive meticulously clean and distinct, its pebbles glowing with a pearly sheen, as if a giant pair of shears had scissored it from the earth. Like a satin band deliberately twisted into serpentine form.

I sensed a welcome even in my dream, from the tall, stately trees of many forms and clans—the maples, the chestnuts, the oaks, which lined the drive—some scattered here and there, now in groups, now in neat little rows. I saw the flowering trees screaming their colours, explosions of blood red and orange and royal purple, like untamed lanterns, from the crape myrtles, setting the woods aflame with brilliant anarchy; and the pastel, shy mimosas and magnolias—clusters of misty pink and mauve and pale lemon, whispering their spell softly and magically, as in a fairyland.

On and on I walked the labyrinthine path, with a sense of joy and elation. And then I saw Lanverndel, Raymond's beloved Lanverndel. The lights were blazing in the house, but the moon made gentle, mystical shadows on the lawns, and the sea shimmered so tranquilly.

And then, suddenly and mysteriously, a fearful alarm shot through, something that happens frequently to dreamers when happy dreams are turning risky and threatening, which even in deep sleep they instinctively know they must heed. And my elation changed abruptly to desperation. Something seemed so wrong, and I was trying to capture it...and then I remembered. Where was Raymond? Where in God's name was Raymond?

I looked back over my shoulder and was swallowed by sudden fear and panic. For what I saw was unfamiliar, barren landscape. Gone were the tall, stately and comforting trees. Gone were also the seductive, alluring blossoms. I was in a devastated land. But I kept dreaming feverishly, hoping with that peculiar kind of urgency which sometimes surges along so palpably, side by side a nightmare, that Raymond would be in the house. And I kept running faster and faster towards Lanverndel, panting for breath, in hope of finding him.

I reached the entrance and looked up. And then it struck me with full force, like a whip, with horror and with helplessness. Lanverndel was not there. It had vanished and in its place I saw a revenant, black darkness, and it started descending upon me menacingly, coming closer and closer, enveloping me like a fatal storm at sea, suffocating me, drowning me slowly, gradually, tenaciously. In terror, I tried to turn my back and run, but my legs became stuck and would not move. And finally with the hopeless despair of a condemned hostage I gave up and prepared to die.

And then the alarm broke the dream circuit, as often happens when dreams become too threatening and out of hand. I awoke with my heart thumping, my consciousness struggling furiously to assert itself, and a feeling of slight dizziness.

I forced myself to sit up and shook my head repeatedly to become fully awake.

I clicked the bedside lamp, and tried to focus my eyes on the objects before me, the door opposite, the door knob, the mirror, the dresser, and waited for my galloping heartbeat to turn calmer.

Raymond stirred. It was no use. He was bound to wake up.

"What's the matter?" he mumbled, sleepily.

I felt I had to wake him. I had to assure myself that he was all right, that the devil of my dream had not destroyed him in his sleep. I ruffled his hair and stroked his head lightly. I had been told as a child that it was the gentlest way to break a person's sleep.

"Raymond, I'm sorry," my whisper trembled. "I had a nightmare, a horrible one, and I can't seem to calm down....It was about Lanverndel...it disappeared and I couldn't find you anywhere...and I was going to die." My voice was breaking, but I had to prevent the tears. There must never be tears before Raymond; that promise to myself was not to be broken—ever.

Raymond was up immediately. He must have seen the terror on my face. He held me close, "Come, come, darling, try and calm yourself," and he kept holding me in silence for several minutes. I could feel his breath and I could hear his heartbeat, with my hair, with my skin. Then he faced me, very clear-eyed, very still. "There, there, don't let it get at you...Yes, I know, I know how it must be, but it's over now. I'm here with you. Shall I get you some water?"

I nodded and drank up the whole glass.

"Now, look at me," he said quietly, like an elder, a guardian.

I did so.

"You see me here, don't you? And everything is fine. So, start saying goodbye to your nightmare. And you're not afraid of it."

I mumbled something incoherent in barely audible words. I looked up at him and then I felt a smile start somewhere on my face. He eased up and I felt the dream devil's grip loosen a little.

"Come, come, try and sleep a little. God knows what time it is."

"No, not sleep, I don't think I can risk that again," I whispered. The nightmare was still with me, oscillating before my eyes now and then, like a pendulum, and I would be defenseless in the dark when it hurled itself again.

"Trust me, it won't come again," he tried to persuade me, but I was too distraught to listen.

"Even now I feel it clinging." My voice was shaking. But I kept looking at him, almost staring. He was silent. Everything in the night was silent.

His face changed. He was trying to look extremely solemn, and even produced a frown on his brow, all of it quite spurious I could tell.

"Well," he was saying, "not if one goes by what the latest research on dream analysis says." His face turned a little mischievous. "You couldn't have already forgotten all those case studies we dissected to boredom—when was it, yesterday, the day before? Apparently, nightmares never recur the same night," he said, trying to sound extremely categorical.

I don't think any dream analyst had said any such thing. But this was hardly the time for an academic argument on nightmares. I saw him smile wanly. I knew he was trying every ruse to put me at ease, to make me less terrified, including inventing fake theories. And then I smiled too.

We had been reading Freud and Jung, who were very current and fashionable at that time, and were particularly fascinated by their theories about dream interpretation and psychoanalysis. Anything was worth grasping to forget the past, be it Freud or Picasso or penicillin.

I made a tremendous effort to sound strong and rational. "Raymond, please go back to sleep. Don't mind me. I'll take some time. I'm a little shaken, but don't worry, I'll be fine. Can I leave my lamp on?"

He made no more fuss over me. I think he realized that I wanted to be awake and with some light. I wondered if he ever had nightmares. He never spoke of them.

I brought a towel from the bathroom and covered the lamp with it so that the light would not disturb him, and I would have enough to give me courage for the remaining part of the night.

I looked at my watch. It was about three o'clock, and I hoped at least some tranquility would come to me before the morning broke at Nice. It was so still and silent. The night was noiseless and dead.

I rested my head on the pillows and heard Raymond get back to sleep again. His breath grew longer and steadier, and in the dim light I stared at his face, and my eyes filled with tears.

How he had changed in these last few tormented months, receiving lash after lash from the fates. His face, always with that very patrician, outdoor, weather beaten look, now seemed so overrun with fine criss-cross lines, especially around the eyes. I don't think I had ever noticed them before, at least not in such large numbers. Shorn of the mask of wakefulness, it was all written on his face in sleep. The vulnerability, the tiredness, the resignation, like someone who had given up a fight.

We had been in Nice for just a short while. We had come on a very specific mission, a mission of healing ourselves, rebuilding our lives, and discovering some formula for happiness. Of course, I had a little secret mission too, which was completely personal, and extremely ambitious, now when I look back.

I had to change. I had to become a new me, overcome my inadequacies and fears, if I wanted to save ourselves or our sanity. Sometimes, it would seem to me that the past, present and the future were one continuous stream, all entangled with shadows and fears and lurking death, blocking out any ray of light. And we were trapped in them. How did one sever the past and throw it behind, far away? Was there any way that one could create a new present and a future?

It had been hard to make the decision to come to Nice, and finally it was I who had to make it. I, who had never before been faced with any decision making worth the name. The gauche and frightened girl who had entered Lanverndel and been intimidated by everything around. But I have come to believe that at least once in almost everyone's life there comes a moment when events hold you hostage, and you realize you've become an important little cog in a vast machine of events, very much outside your control. And a terrific jolt happens within you that you could never have imagined or predicted, and you become another person. The diffident become decisive, the shy turn bold, and the passive take on command.

On the whole, I think it had been a good decision. The change of air, the change of atmosphere had already revived us somewhat, I felt. Raymond was unwinding a bit. I could see it on his face, though there would always be some good patches and some bad. We decided we wouldn't hurry about anything; let time do it's healing at its own pace—we would be patient. I sometimes had strong spurts of hope and tranquility, that we would defeat the demons of the past. Other times, my confidence would falter, and I saw only obstacles and traps.

But right now, one thing was certain—tranquility was nowhere near.

My life, the unexpected turns it had taken, flashed before me, like a film in slow motion. My marriage, one that happens only in fairy tales, and the strange mysteries and fears thereafter...Charlotte, her skeleton surfacing on the night of our grand carnival dinner... thrown up after tremors hit the belly of the sea...bits of her jewelled gold chain entangled in her bones...the fishermen and the police... the court proceedings and accusations of murder—they all kept sliding around me with the slow, icy sinuousness of a glacier.

My mind went back to Lanverndel, charred, disfigured, blackened by smoke and fire, velvet curtains and precious Persian carpets smouldering, priceless paintings and objects of art smashed and burnt to cinders, galleries and staircases flaming and crashing, and the great fiery gash streaking and splitting the midnight blue sky of that fateful night.

Naturally, we were in a shocked and benumbed state when we drove through the fumes and confusion. I saw Raymond turn completely impassive and expressionless, and like a lifeless, automatic machine, take charge of the salvage and firefighting operations and of the countless other things there must have been on that tragic night. The entire village had gathered there, helping the firefighters, moving things out of the less dangerous or unharmed areas, or merely giving moral support.

Strange it seemed to me that my mind was still alert, in spite of the beating we had taken on that long day at London and on the drive back. When we had hovered between life and death, and the die was getting cast against us and damnation stared us in the face.

And then the most unexpected happening, and the die of damnation slowly melting away.

The visit to Mr Sommers, her lawyer, who possessed all the secrets of Charlotte's long concealed and hopeless brain tumour growing at alarming rate, her bouts with morphine, her half and incomplete will, and her life ebbing away...And the court was satisfied that there was credible motive for her suicide.

And just when we were soaking in that disturbing, robust fatigue which follows an ordeal which one believes is over yet dare not believe is over, came the next lethal shock—the flames of Lanverndel. But what I felt that night, the feelings that travelled in me, none were really original. I was only feeling them for him.

His home, where he was born and spent his childhood years and youth, where his ancestors before him had lived and loved and died and left their imprints, was in flames before our very eyes. Henrietta de Villiers, gracious and smiling on her canvas, who had put me through my most tormented moments at our grand carnival celebrations, scarcely a few days ago, lay burnt. The grand sea wing, with its shrouded furniture, ornate and enamelled mother of pearl hair brushes, dainty nightgowns and slippers, grand evening dresses belonging to another Mrs de Villiers...to Charlotte...all in ashes.

Was her presence, her obdurate, dark shadow also being exorcised by the flames? One must not speak ill of the dead, but was the fire finally transporting whatever lingered of her with us to the great unknown? In the midst of all the confusion, I tried to read Raymond's face. It was still and devoid of any expression. What thoughts travelled through his mind, I could not tell. Other than that, I had no feelings of my own that night; I was only getting deeper and deeper inside his tragedy, and feeling vicariously what I thought he felt.

I can remember the constables later interrogating the servants, Bede, John, the porter, the scullery maids and the cooks. I remember Bede telling them about Miss Portner, the housekeeper always fiercely loyal to Charlotte and full of silent hatred for me. Someone had driven her to Lanverndel around ten that night, and thereafter she had been moving around the house, quite aimlessly. They had kept an eye on her, since they did think she was behaving rather strangely, but also a safe distance, being accustomed to her usual churlishness and ill-humour. Then Bede suddenly got a strong whiff of petrol from inside the house and by the time he reached the hall to check, the flames had already erupted upstairs and were spreading with demonic speed.

For twelve hours the fire raged, for the petrol had been sprinkled from the stores, through the kitchen, the dining hall, and up the stairs to the bedrooms. Not expecting us for dinner, the kitchen servants had gone home early, and this had left the place clear for Miss Portner. By some quirk of fate, the fire did not travel to the morning room and study. Perhaps Miss Portner panicked as many criminals do and forgot to douse this wing, and just as well, as the dogs were saved, and so too some of the priceless china and curios and furniture.

Miss Portner was arrested in a bus bound for London. Whether she was fleeing or merely travelling, no one could tell, as her state of mind appeared to approximate insanity.

When I saw her some days later, I could only come to one conclusion—she was possessed by the devil. Her small screwed up eyes were corpse like, her face blank, and her speech ranged from low, soft monotones to shrill, high-pitched, hysterical torrents. Yes, she said, she had tried to burn down Lanverndel. Charlotte's voice had continuously been commanding her to do so to avenge her murder. And she, Miss Portner, always carried out her lady's orders as faithfully as she could.

Miss Portner was found guilty and declared mentally unsound. She was committed to an institution for ten years, under police observation.

The local papers and the tabloids went berserk. Once again in the span of hardly a week, the speculations of Charlotte's death, the discovery of the skeleton with her tangled, tattered gold chain; murder accusations by Tom Camlin, Charlotte's uncle and lover; the inquest; and now Lanverndel's inferno, were recapitulated even more sensationally than before.

Those were days of dread and fear when my first battle of the day would begin at waking—dodging the morning papers, hiding them from him and then reading them clandestinely; he doing the same thing, and then both of us battering ourselves with that armour of pain and terror and silence.

The inferno has become an indelible landmark in my life, but ironically enough, in those rare moments, when for some reason or other, I am constrained to look back upon it, all I can recall are impressions of an inexhaustible collage of confusion.

It isn't only because this is one of the things that I so desperately want to forget and erase from my mind, which must be why I have locked it there in some deep chamber. But also, for another very simple, basic reason. You see, none of us had really slept much the last few nights and of course not at all on the night of the fire, and this I think has also had a significant bearing on the quality of my memory.

That night, I noticed for the first time the curious effects that sleeplessness induces. Without any prompting whatsoever, everything urgent and immediate started happening mechanically, as if an invisible switch had been turned on somewhere with perfect timing, goading me. My senses became so much more alive and electric—but the fabric of my mind gave it all away. For it remained unnaturally taut and tense, lending an impression of an airy kind of unreality to whatever was going on. It was almost like swimming in the air, high on champagne.

All our tenants and many of our neighbors were there. I had seen them scarcely three nights ago at our own grand and disastrous carnival party, the night her skeleton emerged. Patricia, Raymond's sister, and her husband Rupert arrived full of concern and love, and the fire engines worked all night.

Miss Portner had chosen to start the fire upstairs. I found it inexplicable then, but I can now understand why. For if she had started it first on the ground floor, naturally someone would have noticed it and it would have been extinguished well before it could destroy everything, as she had intended it to. And if she had started it on both floors simultaneously, she herself could have been trapped in it. Perhaps, she meant to set fire to the ground floor after coming down, but on seeing the flames gurgling demonically, devouring everything above, she probably just wanted to escape. My suspicion is that insane and evil though she was, the sight of those flames she had created must have frightened her, and by some unexpected kind of instinct, she then just wanted to get away. Anyway, whatever were her reasons, the ground floor was fortuitously saved from total destruction, and by the time the ceilings of the ground floor were burnt enough to come crashing down, the main fury of the fire was spent. The burning staircases, railings and banisters were finally tamed with the persistence and support of the villagers gathered there.

Did it not occur to Miss Portner that stone doesn't burn, and earth and iron neither? The majestic stone walls, buttresses and towers went through their ordeal of fire, and stood stoically while their limbs burnt, and when the fire was spent, the fair marble and stone were charred, angry and black, yet stood erect, as if to mock the world.

And when Raymond and I surveyed with leaden eyes and broken hearts, the grand manor, a tangle of smoke and devastation, black with soot, weeping in the dying flames and ashes, its burnt finery scattered around cruelly, its flower beds singed and lawns ravaged, it looked like wreckage in battle.

And then I passed out.

Chapter Two

On the face of it, Nice was just the same as when we were here last barely a few months ago, and yet it was so different. Last time, I had come here as au pair to Mrs Kappelhoff, and had left as Mrs de Villiers. And now we were both here seeking sunshine for our troubled minds and souls. Who was it who had said that this was a sunny place for shady people? For us, I hoped it would be a sunny place for wounded people. Last time, Raymond was shadowed by secrets which I didn't know. This time, there were no secrets—only scars and wounds. Last time I was a dazed, timid simpleton. Today, I was a woman who had gone through experiences far beyond her years, possessed by a fierce resoluteness to survive.

The Hotel le Neptune sparkled and glittered as before, and was mercifully less crowded, as the season had really not yet begun and none of the regulars had started descending. There was little difference between the colour of the sea and the sky, and the green and gray hills appeared like little jewels scattered here and there. The boulevards were spotless and shining, and one could easily see that everyone looked less harassed, preparing to meet the full brunt of the impending season. The hotel maitre de chef and concierges welcomed us with broad smiles and assured us that the best rooms had been kept for us. They remembered us only too well, as our marriage had been instrumental in getting very favourable publicity for their hotel; indeed the local papers had carried the complete story with the hotel as the central point, and this had naturally made them very happy. I had no idea if they had kept track of the vicissitudes of our lives but the thought didn't bother me in the least. What a wonderful feeling it was not to worry about what others were saying or thinking about us. It gave a sense of complete freedom to act and think as one wished, and this, I think, is what gave me that look of confidence which I had so envied others for. These were the innocuous, trivial things I was experiencing each day, in spite of myself. Confidence in the bearing did not come from the body alone, it came from one's attitude, which made the head to be poised more purposefully, the eyes steadier and the voice firmer.

I couldn't fail to notice what a different status Mrs de Villiers had in the eyes of the hotel staff as compared with the mere au pair that I was before, even if to a millionairess. No more condescension or carelessness. It was Madame this and Madame that. Was Madame pleased with the view from the balcony? Would Madame be pleased to require any more furniture, or different furnishings? A continuous stream of *s'il vous plaîts*. Even my smile was gradually transforming into something different, something bordering on graciousness and I was generally pleased and satisfied about everything. So this was the way of the world.

Raymond would sometimes give himself away. I think he found my behaviour quite intriguing and perhaps even amusing, but the important thing was that he was curious about what was going on with me. And that was what I wanted so badly—anything to take his mind off Lanverndel and the past.

"I've never before had the pleasure of witnessing a little girl blossoming into a young woman; I can tell you it's fascinating," he smilingly told me one day in his usual laconic manner.

"Raymond, you make it sound as if I'm some kind of guinea pig in a laboratory," I replied, making a face at him and chattering on. "Actually now that you mention it, you're in company. I find the experience equally fascinating myself. And what more can a girl ask for with the most wonderful, caring husband, security and comfort. I think it's high time I grew up and got a little more educated in the bargain. I don't want to be a dumb, boring wall flower. And if I carry on as I am, you'll soon be fed up of me, and I shall not like that at all. And besides, Raymond, it's not as if I'm forcing myself to be different; I'm actually experiencing quite an urge to be more intelligent and useful. To know more and be more confident, and to share much more with you, at least a part of your mind."

He looked thoughtful again. "I'm wondering, if I have a mind left at all," he said in a tired, fatalistic voice.

My heart missed a beat. It was this demon that I had to destroy. I put my arms around him and stayed close to him. I felt guilty that I was feeling so good and so free, while he remained tormented.

"Raymond, let's think of all the good things too. We've faced so much and not been destroyed. We've rediscovered ourselves and experienced so much strength. We really do have such a strong bond between us now, don't we? We, both of us, will change as time goes by but we'll change being with each other, and everything will heal. That's what we're here for anyway, aren't we?"

"Ah, for the ambrosia of youth," he said smiling, this time a little more naturally, I think.

"Ah, for the confidence and wisdom of years," I replied smartly.

"My dear girl, you're becoming quite impossible. Are you planning to end up giving lectures on philosophy in some university or other?"

"Not at all. On the contrary, I'm planning to stay put right here with you and tease you and amuse you and infect you with some of my ambrosia, as you call it. How would you like that?"

"Hmm, let me see. As a matter of fact, I would like that very much. It might just give me back my mind."

So we had done full circle. What an extraordinary figure a circle was—seamless, without beginning, without end—it could start anywhere, and end anywhere and keep continuing forever, round and round.

But now I felt a gentle, compelling warmth rise within, so soft and dulcet, begging for expression, for sharing, or else it would have no meaning. That we had come so far without mishap, in the face of all odds, it was almost like a miracle. The words tumbled out even at the risk of sounding overly sentimental. "Raymond, do you see the deep blue sea outside and the glorious sunshine? You know, that's exactly how I feel. I wish I could paint it. I have an instinct deep within me that we will be like that—so calm and clear. Don't you feel so too?"

I'm not really sure whether he caught the wavelength or understood what I was trying to express. Or perhaps, he did not want to get involved with any of my sentimentality. He replied jocularly, "And who, according to your instinct is the sea and who the sunshine, pray?"

"As always, you are making fun of me, even when I am most serious," I accused him. My eyes turned a little moist, but I continued my prattle, feigning a careless tone.

"Well, I couldn't possibly be the sunshine. What I am today and all I have is only because of you, isn't it?"

Finally it touched him, or he allowed it to touch him. He came close to me and looked deep into my eyes, "Why are you so loyal and steadfast, after knowing whatever you do? That is what I'm unable to comprehend."

"Actually, the answer is very simple—it's because I love you. You doubted me on that last night at Lanverndel, didn't you? But you were so wrong. Never in the past few months has any doubt or question ever arisen on that, I promise you. Do you believe me?"

He looked at me again with a sort of gratitude and said simply, "Yes, I think I do". And then after a moment, he took my face in both his hands and said without emotion, "No, I do."

Chapter Three

The flames of Lanverndel were engulfing me, and I was choking. The smoke was black and grey, with a devilish force. The flames were sometimes yellow, sometimes red, reaching high into the sky. I panicked and tried to breathe deeply, but the air seemed clear. I quickly shut my eyes again. No, these were not real flames. They were visiting me from some other world. I tried again to breathe deeply and open my eyes slowly, shaking myself to become alive. I moved my limbs; they seemed alright and I wasn't burnt. I breathed deeply again. The flames seemed to recede. I must have lost consciousness at Lanverndel, while the crimson flames did their dance of death around me. I didn't seem to remember anything after that.

I opened my eyes wider. I was in an unfamiliar place. My eyes hazily scanned the room. Where was I? This was not my room, the walls and furniture were different. The grey drapes were tightly drawn. With an effort I rose unsteadily and drew the curtains. I saw the lawn, with beds of roses and nasturtiums in full bloom, and I recognized the place. This was Henry's cottage, Henry Collins, our estate manager. Slanting sunrays gently brushed the lawn, shading vertical spikes of various greens that moved and shimmered with the soothing breeze. The cries of seagulls came from somewhere, and it looked to me as if teatime was drawing near.

My head felt heavy and hurt. My eyes preferred to remain fixed—on anything, on nothing. The night of blood red, orange flames started coming back and then I became fully awake.

On hearing me stir, dear faithful Jane rushed in with great relief and gave me an account of what had happened and how I was here.

"Thank God, ma'am, you're alive and well. What an awful night it's been. I mean, Lanverndel. You were standing and watching everything, and then you fell. You fainted. And Mr de Villiers got so terribly worried, and he put everything else aside and called for Dr Spencer. And Mr Collins kept saying that you and I come over here and stay. Are you feeling better ma'am?"

"Yes, yes, Jane, I think I'm alright. Just feeling a little weak." My mind shot back to Raymond. Where was he?

"Jane, where is Mr de Villiers? I wonder if he managed any sleep at all. He must be so exhausted." I was again getting disoriented.

Jane helped me get back to bed. "Mr de Villiers was on his feet all night, he was, at Lanverndel. Hardly slept a few hours..... in the morning here, and now he's out again with Mr Collins to see the insurance gentlemen and Colonel Osmund at the Police Station. He said he'd be back for tea, and I've been told to call the doctor immediately after you wake up."

I was still tired and aching, and had lost track of days and time completely. I couldn't for the life of me place today's date and was mentally empty and numb, and ravenously hungry.

Ironic as it seems to me now, this was probably the largest meal I had since coming to Lanverndel, though I scarcely remember what I ate, and that strangely enough in a room and a house not my own.

I followed the meal with a hot bath, but it did little to revive me, and I realized that I still did not have the strength to leave the room.

I stayed in bed, feeling a wee bit refreshed, waiting for Raymond to return. I didn't want to see the papers, I couldn't think coherently about anything. There was a tightness in my stomach and chest, which I couldn't comprehend, which I had never experienced before. It was as if they were being pushed higher and higher by some powerful, unseen force, and I could feel no rhythm or harmony in anything around me, only a state of perfect discord. And there was something very unfamiliar and uneasy happening within me. Like a violent pressure building up, heading for heaven knows where, something I could not give a name to.

As I remember this after several years have gone by, I try to recollect as faithfully as I can, this defining period of my life. Sometimes, the memories come effortlessly, other times I have to reconstruct them with great effort, and I wonder in disbelief that this actually happened to me.

I tried very logically and coolly to investigate what it was that was scalding and dismantling me inside. It was as if an alien presence had encroached within, and I searched hard in my mind, trying to lay a finger on it, to recognize it, to identify this interloper which seemed a stranger and yet had taken possession of me. And as I tried harder and harder, thinking, questioning, answering, all to myself, for the first time in my life, it seemed to me that the numbness in my brain started receding, and the alien which had lain in a dormant state within me stirred, and then I felt it implode inside me.

It was anger, furious consuming anger, anger which could not be suppressed, anger which had been building up insidiously for days now, without my being aware of it. I felt no urge at all to want to suppress it—on the contrary I wanted to give it full vent. The vision of Lanverndel engulfed in flames, those violent orange patterns, streaking up and down the midnight sky—evil wreaking havoc, and us standing by passively and helplessly—evil chasing us relentlessly and Raymond standing like one damned, receiving punishment, lash after lash—that is all that I could see.

I must have dozed off again. In my half sleep I heard unfamiliar sounds of a gate opening, a car door shutting and people talking. And then I heard Raymond's voice. It was a little after five o'clock when he came in. I felt I was seeing him after an eternity. As much as I tried, I was still not able to re-enter the world's flow of time. In my mind, there was a hazy mesh of the day at London, the anticlimax of the lawyer's evidence, the drive to Lanverndel and the tragedy of flames that awaited us, and I was still quite unable to focus where time stood in relation to these wretched nightmares of my life.

"Raymond, it's so good to see you. Did you manage to get some rest, darling? I do feel selfish doing all the sleeping." I stared hard at him. He looked exhausted, but alert. His eyes had bluish hollows beneath them.

He sat on the bed beside me and put his arms around me, and we stayed like that, still, for a few minutes.

"Has the doctor seen you?" he asked.

"No, but Jane has sent for him, and he should be here any moment. I don't think there's anything wrong with me. I'm just terribly exhausted, but I'm so glad to see you. What happened to me Raymond? I believe I fainted. I don't seem to remember anything. If I shut my eyes, I see only flames around me everywhere. What about you? Did you get some sleep?"

"About three hours. There's been a lot of paper work to attend to with the insurance, but Henry is now looking after all that. Then the police started interrogating Mrs Portner, and they wanted me to come along for some clarifications. Thank God, that's over, and it looks as if she's gone completely mad. They might ask you to come for some questions later. Fortunately there's so much evidence against her. Now and then she admits what she's done. My best guess would be that she'll be committed to an institution very soon."

He looked at me long, and said, "Darling, I'm sorry for all that's happened. And I am sorry for messing up your young, innocent life which could have had more happiness than what I've given you."

"No Raymond, please don't ever say that. I have suffered only because you have suffered. What is all of this to me? The only time

I was alone and frightened and unhappy was when I wasn't sure of you...when I wasn't sure of your love...and I thought you only loved...her."

I was silent for a while but I felt an uneasy chill, a tension building up. I knew I had stepped into uncharted territory, but why could I still not bring myself to utter that name? Why did I always falter and get paralyzed whenever I had to confront it? Or did we both feel safer and more protected in silence? I looked at Raymond. But he was not with me. He seemed locked in some private world to which I had no access. He must have heard what I had just said, but I don't think he noticed anything more. Thank God men restricted themselves to their five senses and never believed in perceiving beyond them.

I tried to regain my composure, and with all the sincerity and earnestness that I could command, I continued softly, "Now I can face anything; we can face anything. And Raymond, I have decided one thing quite definitely. None of all this shall happen again. No ghosts, no shadows shall ever invade us again. You told me at Lanverndel, three, or was it four days ago, that you found me changed, that I had suddenly grown up. Actually, that wasn't quite true. Do you know when I really grew up? It was yesterday, or at least I think it was yesterday, when I saw Lanverndel burn. I've decided Raymond, never, never again am I going to stand by idly and allow the hounds to get the better of us, not as long as I live. I'm not anymore going to be the helpless, defenseless little nothing. And God help anyone who tries to touch us again."

Raymond looked at me with a new interest. I thought I saw a trace of curiosity on his face. I tried to read his expression. Was it merely surprise at the unexpected, or was it relief that I was not breaking down, and was coping on my own and not adding to his burdens? Was he happy to see a new facet of my personality, shy and timid as he was accustomed to seeing me? Did I see a hint of amusement in his eyes? But he said nothing.

Jane announced the arrival of Doctor Spencer. He was the elderly county doctor, very experienced, and well loved by one and all in the villages around. He ran a successful practice at Salcombe but kept enough time each day to treat ordinary people, charging them whatever they could afford, and visiting homes. Raymond was always full of admiration for him, not only for his kindness and generosity to common folk, but also his passion for being up to date with the latest medical discoveries that were taking place at breakneck speed. His jovial personality and slightly chubby face inspired confidence even among people who had reached the end of the road.

Dr Spencer gave me a quick check up, the temperature, the pulse, the heartbeat, and confirmed that I was physically all right, and only needed some rest.

He turned to Raymond, and said with some earnestness, "You must, after your responsibilities in this unfortunate affair are over, take a short break, Raymond—perhaps go abroad. You do need a break. It would do wonders for both you and Mrs de Villiers. "

I was already feeling better, more relaxed and serene with Raymond near me.

"If there's any problem, please don't hesitate to call. I'm not prescribing anything. I think it's quite unnecessary. There's nothing to worry about. Some good rest and a change will make all the difference, and of course regular meals."

"Thank you so much Doctor Spencer. I'm sure I'll be moving about by tomorrow."

Raymond showed the Doctor to the door.

"By the way, Henry will be coming to see you shortly. He's very worried about you."

"Dear Henry, what a pillar of strength he's been. What would we have done without him?"

"Yes indeed, what would we have done without him," he said abstractedly.

His face grew cloudy and indiscernible, and his eyes once again acquired that look of defeat and hopelessness.

"Raymond," I said, "Raymond darling, we have been through hell, but we've also come out of it, alive and strong. Let's thank God for that. Let's not be defeated. Let's never again be defeated. I know you must be shattered. Lanverndel has been destroyed. Your home, the home that you loved so much has been attacked and vandalized. But we can restore it, I'm sure, if you want. And we need never allow anything to beat us down again." The new me was being tested and I think I did not fail.

There was a knock on the door and Henry came in with a bouquet of flowers. Good, loyal Henry, looking exhausted and sad but trying his best to help us overcome our dark hour.

"Mrs de Villiers, I do hope you are feeling better and are comfortable here. Words fail me. I'm still not able to recover from the shock."

"Henry, thank you so much for your support and affection. Yes, I'm much better. Raymond and I were just discussing how wonderful you have been."

Tea was brought in and I still felt so hungry. The continuous tension of the last few days had starved me. My new animation was charging me. Fragments of our lives were lying all around—they had to be picked up and put together again. I needed so much strength, and I felt so weak.

"That's the very least I could have done," Henry was saying, "I hope you're going to take it very easy. Please stay here as long as you like. I'm quite comfortable for the time being with the Sanders next door."

Then turning to Raymond, "And you too Raymond, you should take a break. The insurance documents should be ready in about a week, and the police matters from our side will be over in a couple of days. Take some rest and get back to normal. I assure you, I will attend to Lanverndel's affairs once you decide what you want to do. Please take a holiday, go abroad if you like. Both of you need it so badly."

"Yes, we have so many decisions to make Henry," said I. "And thank you so much for everything, your house, and all your kindness. I wonder how we can ever repay you."

"Mrs de Villiers, please don't mention it. I only wish things would get back to their normal, happy state."

"Yes Henry, surely they will, soon, and thank you again for everything."

Henry left, and Jane arranged the flowers in a bowl. Graceful lilies and narcissi with gentle fragrance, daffodils with brilliant golden cusps, and misty pale and pink carnations. I had forgotten what a difference they could make to a room. I think it was the plentitude at Lanverndel that had deadened my senses. I had grown so accustomed to seeing flowers in almost every corner, that I had ceased noticing them. And yet, I thought to myself, why should flowers symbolise happiness? They represent a slow death of life and beauty even as they stand amputated in our vases. Anyway, I returned to myself. A phase in our lives was now firmly sealed. What the next phase would be, what the new tomorrow would be, neither Raymond nor I knew. And nor could I tell this moment whether I was sad or in despair, nonchalant, or just blank.

Raymond and I looked at each other. I was hoping desperately that there'd be something that needed our attention, something we had to do. Having chores to attend to can be an anodyne in itself, a balm to deaden the sorrow. But we were in an unfamiliar house, a house without a routine of its own, without habitude or custom, and it could not come to our rescue. So I had to improvise, to say something, anything.

"Raymond, shall we have an early dinner and then sleep? We could have dinner in the room, and you need the rest so badly."

"Yes, anything you say." He was helpless and mechanical.

I did not want to discuss anything with him while he was in this state. Even now, I was better slept than he and more refreshed. I wanted his serrated nerves to heal first and I didn't want to push him into anything. He should decide his affairs from a position of strength, just as he always had.

We had an early dinner, and before he went to sleep, Raymond turned to me and said, "Thank you for undergoing all this with me without a murmur. I wish I knew when our evil star is going to leave us. I wish I knew how much more of our lives are to be destroyed."

"Raymond darling, don't torture yourself, I beg you. Please, please don't think that way. We shall restore Lanverndel if you like, no matter what it costs. We'll do all the things that we want to without fear of anything or anyone. But first you must recover, and we'll try to get over the tragedy, and then we'll have so much time to talk. And, if we're to be tested still some more, we'll brace ourselves and face everything and win. But, I'll never stop loving you, and we're never again going to be with our backs to the wall. That's the only thing I've learnt in this last one week."

I kissed Raymond gently on his forehead. Before going to sleep, he asked me, "Do you really still love me after all that I've put you through?"

"You know I do, Raymond," I said simply and softly.

"I sometimes wonder why," he sighed to himself in a tone so fatalistic, and then he drifted off to sleep.

Chapter Four

The days that passed in Henry's cottage now appear one big blur, except that they were days fraught with anxiety, fear and sadness. Anxiety for the unknown tomorrow, fear of the insecurity and of what was yet in store, and sadness for all that we had so rapidly lost in so short a time. When I look back upon that interregnum of our lives, and believe me, there were so many more yet to come, what is clearest in my mind is how furtively we tried to conceal from each other our fears and insecurities, the raw chilling fear of the unknown, of the vicious, invisible forces arraigned against us.

As for me, it was all so erratic and unpredictable. Sometimes, I could feel the strength pouring in from some mysterious quarter, and I would become full of hope and optimism, afraid of nothing. And then suddenly that feeling would leave me and I would again be without moorings, without answers.

I was not a very educated person. I had passed through high school indifferently and when I think back upon those days, I remember less about what I learnt at school, but more the despair at the failing health of first one parent, then the other, and then finding myself penniless and alone. How generous and kind the simple village folk had been and how patiently they had tried to restore some kind of confidence and courage in me, and bring back a normalcy to my life. The Vicar had contacted some of his friends in London, and that is how I had found myself an au pair to Mrs Kappelhoff.

What manic, restless dreams possessed me during this very incoherent phase of my life. When nothing seemed impossible, when my most compelling activity would be to reinvent myself with all my absent qualities, in images which I had secretly coveted, and then plan on how to become them. It almost became an obsession, to imagine myself another person. But nothing discouraged me. If there were gaps in my social behavior or education, I would fill them with Raymond's help. I would not be ashamed of admitting ignorance, and I would not be shy to learn. I would read, paint, reactivate my interest in music and sports, and keep Raymond alive with my youth and simplicity. After all, I was still young, and my mind and personality were still capable of being moulded afresh, if I tried hard enough. And frankly speaking, right now, today, what did my world really consist of? Nothing much, except for Raymond. Lanverndel was of course important, but only because it was his world. My mind would become clear as crystal, and everything negative would disappear somewhere. My dreams would go on and on like this.

Perhaps this is something that happens to many people...a single event occurs which so unexpectedly and profoundly transforms their life and persona.

Lanverndel was gone. A home, I thought, was almost like a third parent, much more so when it was for centuries handed down from generation to generation. I suppose they are the anchors of one's life—parents and home. I had lost all three in quick succession and knew what it meant. Apart from the grief, the void, the emptiness and loneliness that I suddenly came face to face with, I sadly became aware of other subtle changes. For when my parents went, the child in me went with them; and when my home went, my roots, my security, and in a way, even my identity was snapped.

Yes, Lanverndel was gone, and the wound was searing our lives. Perhaps we could restore it. Of course, it would cost an awful amount of money, and I still had no idea of Raymond's financial affairs, but I was sure he would find it. The insurance amount alone would not suffice, I knew. Raymond would possibly have to sell some of his lands in Devonshire, which in any case were getting harder and harder to manage. I wondered whether he was sentimental about them? I had so much to find out, but I shouldn't rush him into anything.

Patricia and Rupert came often to see us, almost once in two or three days. They offered us use of their house, but Raymond always repeated that he wanted to be close to Lanverndel. One day Patricia took me aside and asked me whether we had made any plans. I replied we hadn't.

"Raymond doesn't seem well at all. Listen, why don't both of you go for a short vacation. If you don't want to decide about Lanverndel right away, leave it alone. But Raymond's condition is worrying both Rupert and me. It's not just his physical health. It's his face, his eyes. He's so unhappy and unsettled."

She was his sister, and she had read him right.

"Yes, Patricia, we must do something. I've been meaning to, but have been waiting for the right moment, which doesn't seem to appear, and I'm worried sick myself, though I try so hard to hide it. You know how disturbed and disorderly everything is right now, and I don't want to make any move or suggestion which might make it worse."

"Don't wait too long. I'm glad you're showing so much strength and fortitude. I've been asking myself these last few days, why, why is he continuously being hounded by one misfortune after another. Raymond, who has lived his life with so much honour and integrity and principle...I really think you should get away from all of this.

Henry and Rupert will look after this place or any other problems that might arise."

"Let me see, Patricia. I'll try and talk to him soon, when I find the right moment. And thanks so much for everything."

Good old Patricia, exuding confidence and energy. She could bring optimism into the darkest scene, and even Raymond who normally was a little impatient with her frank and forthright noisiness, looked forward to her visits eagerly. I think she gave him a feeling of the familiar, and a sense of security that at least some cornerstones of his world remained intact.

I was very certain in my mind that the phase of fleeing and hiding was over, and I would have to, as tactfully as I could, prevent Raymond too from slipping into retreat. We should face the world together, he and I. The worst was over, and it was now up to us to rid ourselves of our devils, and garner the remains. We would face people boldly, not avoid them. There were several people who respected and admired Raymond. I would have get togethers for them, not flippant, fashionable ones, where everyone appeared casual about everything in order to be modern and trendy, but cozy, comfortable ones, where Raymond could pick up threads of old friendships and discuss subjects that interested him—cricket, farming, philosophy, the arts.

And come to think of it, what was there to hide from? Lanverndel was burnt. Could we hide from that? It was for the world to see. Charlotte's death? That had become the personal property of every newspaper, tabloid and magazine in England in the last few weeks, and possibly even abroad.

No, hiding was no answer. We just had to somehow come to grips and take possession of our lives again. And start afresh.

I often wondered about Raymond's personal dilemma. Our last night at Lanverndel would constantly recreate itself before my eyes. I would see the library, the heavy shining writing table, the rows of books lining the walls almost to the ceiling, the great open fireplace, the long elegant windows looking over the circular, terraced lawns reaching the sea. And I would feel again the numbness, the shock, the relief of that night, all leavened by fear, rising higher and higher...... "and then I pulled the trigger ... and that was it ... she was dead ... near the creek ... where the cabin is." The words would reverberate in my mind like scorched whirlpools and I would try and drown myself in their blackness.

But I would see instead the creek on that dark night, the cabin there with all its fishing paraphernalia, and Charlotte, bejewelled and bewitching, mocking him with her triumphant, exquisite, evil smile... listing out her lovers to him...at London, at Lanverndel....I would hear the gun shot, and see the blood splattering on the floor...flowing like a crimson rivulet, making hideous, garish, abstract patterns.

I would see him drag the body to the damaged fishing boat and pushing it into the sea with its motor on, the wind howling with the rain, and feel the terror slowly creeping, like sharp little needles, like stinging nettles, from my heart, from my stomach, from my throat, and then I would desperately command myself to stop, breaking into a cold sweat and wanting to scream in that, meaningless, feverish panic that seizes you even though you know that the mortal peril is over and you are safe. And then I'd stop and reassure myself with whatever strength I could command that we had truly left it all behind and we were safe. And slowly the terror and panic would loosen and give way to a warm, engulfing relief, however warped and wicked...he did not love Charlotte...he had never loved Charlotte.

He had told me on our last night at Lanverndel that he felt no remorse or guilt. I tried to recreate his conflict in my mind, and think like him. Perhaps he believed that dealing with her evil did not fall under the cover of any law ordained by man or God, something he had to take on himself, with all its risks and consequences. Like a primitive settlement of dues into which no third force can intervene.

But we were in twentieth century England, where primitive settlements were prohibited by law. I wondered whether he was ever racked by guilt or fear? Or was the inner dialogue which had funnelled his decision so powerful that feelings like guilt and fear got extinguished. Sometimes, it seemed to me that he was at peace with himself, and was morally unperturbed. He believed, I think, that when all else fails, evil has to be wrested with both hands, head on, and dealt with. Might, they say, is right, but sometimes, right can also be might, right as opposed to wrong. People may have suspected, but surprisingly luck was on our side. It was like an action in self-defense, beyond the pale of criminal law courts. This was also, I think, silently acknowledged by many of Raymond's loyal, honourable friends who may have guessed the truth.

But this apart, I also saw the reality of our situation. Raymond was broken, and his soul torpid. He was always a very reserved, private person, and such persons are poised and attractive when the mysterious mechanism which balances them inside holds smoothly. But now I could see the disintegration set in slowly, day after day. Was it pain that couldn't be endured?…was it an insidious despair after all that had been lost?...or was it just simple resignation to fate and losing the will to fight? It was nothing to do with his actions or his speech or his demeanour. It was the expression in his eyes, one that I had never seen before, not even in the courtroom in Salcombe, nor on our last night at Lanverndel. It was an expression of defeat, that the fight was over, and he had lost.

But now there were decisions to be taken, problems to be tackled, and almost always I felt I was just not equal to the task. Raymond had given instructions that the household staff would continue in his service, and that they should not be put to any trouble. The formalities with the insurance companies had been completed meticulously. Our involvement with police matters was over, though Bede and John had been summoned to give further evidence.

Strangely enough, Miss Portner did not recognize me when she saw me at the investigation, and I don't think she was posturing. It was just that she was so mentally ill. Anyway, it saved me a lot of energy, all of which I had specially accumulated and conserved for the occasion, expecting that this would be a test for all my grand and ambitious resolves—whether I would live up to them, or buckle down and get intimidated as usual.

But even with her in that witless and unseeing state, a test it certainly proved to be. First, that peculiar kind of unexpected shock which sometimes happens even at an expected event. Then, the momentary flicker of fear, an anger rising, slowly regenerating me and giving me strength. But all the while that her dead, screwed eyes stared at me uncomprehendingly, I remained cool and controlled. I didn't flinch, and most importantly, I wasn't afraid. I answered all the questions put to me with dignity, and then, after it was all over, as if by the flick of a magic wand, she was erased from my mind completely.

I saw her again only many years later in a world that had become so changed, and on that day too, I remained true to my resolve. But by then, I too, like the world, had changed so much.

The harvest was through and all the sales completed. Raymond was attending to everything with a totally detached accuracy. But when the day's work was done and he was alone with me and with his thoughts, the wounds would become exposed, and despair and helplessness would overcome him. We would make ritual conversation, but I could see that we were shutting out the real issues. He would refuse to talk of Lanverndel or of any plans for the future. It seemed as if he was living in some silent, still world within himself. What thoughts went through him those weeks, what gnawed at his soul, I would never find out. I think this was his private battle such as we all have to face sometime or other in our lives, unaided and alone. Fear, I knew, is always a powerful foe, and I felt sure that in his solitude he would face it squarely. But it is one thing thinking soothing platitudes in abstraction, and quite another when one is hoping apprehensively, waiting for them to come true.

I think he felt more protected and secure in Henry's cottage. The past was burnt and he didn't want to think about the future. It shattered his fragile feeling of security, and kindled the threat from the unknown. How different from the person who hadn't ever in the past delayed a decision by as much as five minutes.

I finally plucked up enough courage. It had to be sooner or later, and in any case, how long could we go on living in Henry's cottage. Raymond was withdrawing deeper and deeper into himself, and instinctively I felt that I had to do something about it.

That night, after dinner, he was smoking his cigarette in silence as usual. His eyes had that distant, slightly puzzled, glazed look. It had suddenly started raining in the evening, and I could hear the rain beating against the windows. And in the silence of the room, I could hear my heart beating too. I said a prayer and looked at him with great tenderness.

"Raymond, let's go away for a while. We both need it so badly, and you're not looking well. Everybody says so. Let's go to Cote d'Azur, the place we first met and get some sun and rest. Just for a month or two. I want us to go so badly."

I think he looked relieved that I had asked.

"Yes, you're right. I'm not myself."

He was silent for some time and then hesitatingly looked at me and said helplessly and sadly, "I'm afraid, afraid of losing you to my jinx, more than what I have already. Every move of mine seems ill fated and I'm afraid of what further agony I've yet to put you through."

"Raymond, please don't, please don't be so fatalistic, so unhappy. Please... can't you also see how fortunate we've been to have survived this together? Once we get Lanverndel done up again, never mind how, you can sell some land, or even just get part of it restored, we can go back and live there. I'm not afraid of anyone anymore, and I don't mind living in just one wing of the house. It's you I want well and happy, and peace for both of us. Let's tell Henry tomorrow and let him make the arrangements for the restoration and let's leave as soon as we can."

"Is that what you want?" The tone was different, a little abrupt and unnatural.

"Yes, let's get away for a while, please—away from all this confusion and despair. We'll go to Nice or anywhere you say, enjoy a breath of fresh air, and leave this behind us. If we have to talk, we'll talk; if we have to forget, then we'll try and forget. We can decide what we want to do with Lanverndel and then we'll come back, and start our life afresh. And Raymond, I'm not afraid of anything anymore."

"I wish I could tell you the same, but there are fears ripping me apart which I have never known before. I've been like a curse on you ever since I met you. I'm afraid of this dark curse stalking me like a shadow. First I sully my hands and scar my soul. Then I marry you hoping for happiness and end in disaster again, this time ruining your life as well, giving you nothing but misery and anxiety. I have a pain deep in my heart, and now they've destroyed Lanverndel. They want to destroy everything I have. I'm not a superstitious man but I seem to be losing everything I have. I'm afraid of losing you, and you're the last thing I have."

His voice was getting softer and was collapsing. He sat on the chair, his head in both his hands and before I knew it, his body was racked with convulsive, soundless, sobs. I came and knelt beside the chair and put my arms around him and took his head on my breast. His sobs continued faster and quieter. I had never seen a man sob like this before and there was a horrible tragedy and pathos in it; my husband whose face I had desperately been searching for some signs to read these last few days was saying it all, but not in words. He kept repeating, "Why...why are we fated for this?"

"Darling…I'm sorry…I knew this was coming...,"he managed to say. "I…tried hard to control myself, but...you must forgive me ...this has never happened before."

I was torn to pieces by what I was witnessing. I could have burst into tears myself, but I remembered the role I had to play for our survival. With moist eyes and a tightness around my heart I whispered, "Raymond, Raymond, darling, don't fight it. Tell me your fears, your sorrows, your pains. Tell me everything, if you can."

The sobs continued and I sat holding him in my arms, on my breast, like a mother does a child. I could not utter another word. What could I do to stop the flow of his pent, accumulated sorrow? What was hitherto the infallible pillar of my life was crumbling in my arms and the image that formed in my mind unbidden was that of Lanverndel, the mighty manor burning helplessly. And then my anger swelled in me again. No, I was not going to let this happen, I was not going to let this happen to us. I was young and I was strong, and I would fight to the finish, fight for myself and for him against anything.

I said softly, "Raymond, I know what you're going through, and what you feel. I feel for you—what you suffer, I suffer with you. You'll not lose me, I love you too much. Let's start from the beginning. Let's tell Henry to restore Lanverndel. Let us use the money from insurance, and if necessary you can sell the Devonshire land. Or let's not do anything, if you don't want to. We'll go to the south of France and spend some time there and get back our sanity. As soon as our wing is ready, we'll return, however long it takes. I don't mind living there even if there's work still going on. And Raymond, I'm not going to run away or hide from anything. I'm certain about that. We're going to face everything, face people, face whatever happens. We have nothing to fear, and if there is a jinx, as you say, let's destroy it this very night."

"You've been so admirable and strong. You've given me all your loyalty and love. How can I ever make it up to you?"

"Raymond, you're all I have in this world. And how can I see you suffer like this? I'm going to tell Henry about taking care of Lanverndel's renovation. When shall we leave? Shall I ask him to make arrangements for next Monday? That gives us a week to tie up loose ends. Oh Raymond, I do so want to go away with you, away from this nightmare and most of all I want us to heal and comfort each other. And when we return, this shall be our Lanverndel, fresh and new, and we shall recreate it as we want. We will have children, I'm sure. But first let's get away."

Raymond smiled, part paternal, part childlike, and kissed me. "Aye aye, ma'am. It shall be as you wish," and with his right hand gave me a mock salute with an indulgent and slightly amused expression on his face, which I was seeing after an age. Thank God, that at least was still intact.

That night I slept with hope and with the joy of a bride.

Chapter Five

I can still remember what a lovely day it was. Somehow, we both woke early with the sounds of pigeons outside our windows. The sky was a clear blue with a few wisps of pure white, feathery clouds streaking it in quaint, linear formations. Today the world appeared different—perhaps I was seeing it through different eyes. The load that had been weighing down my heart had lifted and I felt freer than I'd felt for a long time. I looked at Raymond and he kissed me gently.

"Slept well, my good luck charm?"

"Hmm, and you?" I said lazily stretching myself.

"I was out like a light, and the next thing I knew it was morning. It's been a long time since I slept like this." He smiled again.

I tried to read his face. Was he also happy like me...unburdened…? But I was still too inexperienced to perceive these things with any clarity. I still had to rely on outward gestures, or an intuitive feel rather than the direct evidence which a wife learns to read after a while. I looked into his eyes, and I was certain I saw some light in them, maybe even a faint glint of hope. He kissed me warmly, happily, and we went on with the ritual of the morning. After breakfast, when we were alone, he said, "I take it we've decided to go to France. I'll be going out now with Henry to make an appraisal of what's to be done here and have a look at the accounts and finances. I must also see what's going on with the police and the insurance, and have to think up all the instructions I must leave. I have no idea how long we'll be away. Now the one important thing I want to ask you—Do you want to restore Lanverndel? Think hard, for it's probably going to be the most important decision you're about to take, maybe even more important than accepting my proposal of marriage," he smiled.

"No, you are absolutely wrong," I decided to lighten the situation. "The most important decision which really changed my life, I suppose, was when I agreed to work for Mrs Kappelhoff. For that's what brought me to Nice and to you and our marriage and to Lanverndel and its restoration."

"Okay, okay, whatever you say. So it's going to be the third or fourth most important decision you're going to have to take." He raised both his hands in mock exasperation and started shuffling some papers around on the desk, filing them neatly. He put them all in his briefcase, and continued seriously, "Take all the time that you want darling. Now, I'll be off and try and wind up things as soon as possible. There's so much to be discussed with Henry. You really do want to go to away for a while, don't you?"

"Yes Raymond, I want to go to Cote d'Azur. I want to stay at the same hotel, visit the same haunts, drive along the same coasts and mountains, only this time it will be with freedom, happiness and a certain victory. Last time, I was so unsure, so scared and quite dazed. You too would like it there, wouldn't you? And we do owe this to ourselves, don't you think?"

"And so it shall be. I hear Henry's car coming. Now we'll be off to attend to business. You could start organizing whatever you want to take. Actually, we could stop by at Paris for a while and you could pick up whatever you like. You've never really given yourself any treats have you, and I'm quite sure I haven't given you any either." His voice dipped for just one small second, and I guessed the association that must have formed in his mind. Charlotte, the fashion celebrity, constantly photographed in the Parisian world of haute couture, featuring in all the leading fashion magazines. But he collected himself immediately and the danger passed. "You could get yourself a nice wardrobe for Cote d'Azur, and then let us see what life has in store for us." He seemed to be far away again. "And darling," he continued, focusing consciously, "please don't forget the decision."

"Why do I alone have to take the decision? Don't you have anything to say about it?" I didn't mean to sound demanding, but I think that's the way I came through.

He said softly, "Not about Lanverndel. It's too painful still to think about. No, I can't take any decision about Lanverndel. I can't even look that way without feeling a wrench in my heart. Every step, stone and wall is a crucible of memories for me—some good, some bad, some happy, some sad...no, about Lanverndel, I still can't think, so that must be done by you. Oh yes, ring up Patricia, please, and tell her our plans. Would you like to visit her before we leave?"

"Yes Raymond, I would like that very much."

"And thanks again, thank you for being such a rock. I love you." Both his hands held mine.

"I love you Raymond, and come back soon."

I ran through everything and churned it in my mind, and said a silent prayer thanking God. I knew I was not imagining it. His step was springier, and his face looked more happy.

And he had said that he loved me. Just as he had said the first time on that last night at Lanverndel. When the dice had rolled at us and we had gambled with our lives. When our world was slipping away into an abyss and we didn't know whether we would live or die. But today it wasn't said to buffer pain and defeat as it was that night.

Today, it was said simply and spontaneously, with happiness, and I shut my eyes gently and felt blessed and fulfilled.

I phoned Patricia and told her our plans, and that we'd like to visit her before we leave. She was delighted. "Wonderful. I'm so pleased you were finally able to speak to Raymond and persuade him."

"Well, Patricia, I think I was lucky to have selected the right moment. And it breaks my heart to also tell you that the right moment came in a very sad way. But anyway, it came, and we were able to get over it."

She was silent for a moment, and then continued, "Since you never believe in giving yourself any credit, let me do it for you. But I would much rather give it to you in person. Both of you must come and dine with us on Friday night."

"Thank you Patricia. Of course, we would both like that very much. Actually, I really do want to see you soon. I have so much to talk to you about. And I need a lot of advice from you about several things—Lanverndel, shopping, Paris. And I know it would mean a lot to Raymond. He always feels so happy being with you."

"Splendid. So then we see you on Friday evening. Goodbye, my dear and good luck." Patricia hung up.

I felt an urge to go towards Lanverndel. What a beautiful autumn this was, with leaves of every colour and hue waving at me. It was wonderful to notice nature once more. The birds were returning to their nests. The fire had caused a migration, and now they too, like us, had recovered some confidence and were returning. Some trees were singed and the lawns and the rose garden were trampled and black with charred remnants of what were once things of beauty and art.

I wanted to have one last look at Lanverndel, standing there in its tragedy and desolation, and I thought to myself how strange it was that I, a complete stranger really, was to decide its destiny. I reached the point at which I wanted to stop, and gaze upon its blackened remains, uncertainly but with a strange sense of curiosity—the kind of curiosity we reserve only for familiar things that seem no longer familiar, my thoughts wandering off in all directions. Should we defy the secret ghosts and phantoms and take them on, or should we retreat behind pillars of unknown buildings in unknown lands? Such dilemmas were alien to me and I counselled patience to myself, bade a silent farewell to Lanverndel, and with sadness in my heart but a lightness in my step, I started walking back to Henry's cottage. I think I was beginning to make up my mind.

The week passed quietly but was full of activity. It was still difficult for me to understand or guess what was going on with Raymond. Sometimes it appeared to me that his fatalism and resignation were receding; sometimes I imagined I saw a streak of happiness on his face; and other times that puzzled, helpless expression would return and cloud his eyes. Those moments I would fight hard to keep my tears back. I would hold his hand and smile at him and silently remind him that he was not alone. Sometimes his mood would change soon; sometimes it would linger on for hours.

We were happy to visit Rupert and Patricia for dinner. They had a beautiful country house, Cranmer Hall, towards Thurlestone, about an hour's drive from Lanverndel. It was built on a little hillock which gave a grand and commanding view of the countryside and the sea. Rupert was very proud of his garden and meadows that had been laid out by a brilliant landscaper who had specially been called from London. The little streams running through the woods surrounding the mansion were connected to a beautiful natural rock pool far on the southern side of the house, which ducks and swans had also made their habitat. Like in all country houses in these parts, the mystery and aura of the past was deeply etched upon the buildings and architecture, on the age of the walls and woodwork, in the exquisite furniture crafted by hundreds of unknown hands through centuries, in the giant size ancient trees with thick trunks that ruled the woods.

Patricia was a complete outdoor person, and not in the least obsessed with having the best home or garden in the county. But one couldn't miss the easy, lived-in warmth of her home, mainly because she was such a natural and warm person herself. As usual, the food was splendid. Courses of the most innovative mushroom soup, watercress salad and crisp garden vegetables, salmon, venison, exotic creamy dessert and weightless chocolate soufflé. Raymond and Rupert discussed their estate affairs and the new farming techniques while Patricia and I spoke of whatever came to our minds.

"Do you have any idea how long you'll be away?"

"Not really, Patricia, but we're not coming back until Raymond is something of his old self again, until his health improves and he gets some peace of mind. I hope it doesn't take too long, and I hope I'm of some use to him."

"Don't underestimate yourself, my dear. You've been a tonic. No one could have been stronger or more understanding. And to think that you're hardly a little older than a child. In fact, to tell you quite frankly, both Rupert and I have been full of praise for the kind of maturity which you have shown in handling this whole unfortunate thing, bless you. Now I'm truly assured that dear Raymond is in the safest hands."

"Thank you, Patricia, I've been meaning to talk to you as you're the only one I can tell this to. I've changed so much in this short time, that very often I feel a stranger even to myself. For one thing, I'm not a snail any more, retreating into my shell each time I'm scared." Patricia eyed me with a thoughtful kindness.

"Yes dear, I've noticed that and am quite delighted, let me tell you. Rupert and I had a little wager about it," she added thoughtlessly.

I didn't mind the thoughtlessness at all.

"Patricia, I don't want to sound boastful, but I'm determined I'll be whatever Raymond needs me to be, to help him out of this. In a sense I'm seeing everything so much more clearly now. I think I'm going to have to work very hard but I feel the world in so many different new colours. It's hardly a nice thing to say after the terrible tragedies we've been through but, it's so strange, for the first time I feel I don't have to live up to any role, that there's no one watching my every step and passing judgment, no fear of anything. I don't know if I'm making any sense to you. Sometimes I don't make any sense even to myself. It's like being given a second chance, with the world before us. Do you understand what I'm trying to say?"

"Not a bit, my dear, but I can see you're pretty positive, and I wish both of you all the happiness from the bottom of my heart."

"Thank you Patricia, for all your help and friendship. And believe me, I shall not fail Raymond. "

She hugged me warmly. "Oh, by the way, I was in London and returned yesterday. My usual checkup. I picked up some things which both of you could use in France."

She took me to her room and started opening up the cardboard boxes—beautiful dresses of crisp cotton, slacks, shirts, swimwear, hats, all for me. Some evening dresses, simple, elegant and expensive, I could see.

"Patricia, this is really generous of you. You didn't have to get me so much. In any case, I was planning to ask you for advice about where to shop in Paris. All these are so beautiful and so expensive. You shouldn't have been so extravagant."

"Darling, this is not much. You deserve this, after all that you've lost. And may you have happiness and luck with them."

The dresses were of the latest fashion and design; I had seen them in magazines, with bright, large floral prints, worn usually by film stars and fashion models at the French Riviera. The slacks and shirts of perfect size, the evening dresses, one black and one white, both Channel, perfectly simple and exquisite. The white, full length with a tiny row of sequins on the neck and arms, and the black, knee length and off the shoulder. I had never owned such luxuries before."Patricia, thank you, thank you so much."

"I'm asking James to put the boxes in your car. There are some things for Raymond too—trousers, shirts, jackets and so on. I always find men's clothes so boring to select, no colours, hardly any styles worth comparing. But after being married so long, I think I managed fairly well. And if there's anything you don't like, just send it back." She called the butler, and the boxes were loaded on to our car. Dear, tactless Patricia, how sensitive and caring she really was.

"You know, those dresses would suit you really well. You must wear them, and..." She stopped suddenly and started eyeing me rather seriously with a frown.

I froze in fear and was a little startled at her expression of disapproval. Now what had gone wrong? Surely I hadn't dropped a brick or embarrassed someone or made some foolish mistake in these past few minutes?

She continued, still serious and frowning, "And you could change your hairstyle a bit. You know, right now, the best of your face doesn't stand out, because your hair doesn't help. Perhaps you could cut it shorter and fluff it out a little."

She stuck her fingers into my hair on both sides of my head and surveyed me. "Much better," she said after some contemplation.

I laughed loudly after my heart recovered its beat, "Yes, Patricia, I promise you I will. The next time you see me, you won't recognize me."

"And the last thing, take this please, they belonged to mother. She'd have liked you to have them." She handed me a delicate enamel case. It contained a string of pearls and a bracelet to match, pale and mellow with age. I stared at them speechless with emotion and felt my eyes go moist. Patricia too looked strangely sentimental, so uncharacteristic of her. Perhaps she had remembered her mother... her step accompanied by the rustle of taffeta and a cloud of perfume, removing her gloves and ermine after a Lanverndel ball...carefully putting the pearls away on the dresser. But she recovered herself hastily with an abrupt, "Come, let's see what the men are doing."

Raymond was calling for us from the study. They were finishing their brandy and cigarettes. I could see that the evening had been a success.

"So what have you two been discussing? Not Buddhist philosophy or theories of Fate as we have?" asked Rupert.

"No, we've been discussing dresses and fashion and hairstyles. Always that great divide," I laughed.

"Ah yes, while you ladies discuss them and tear them apart with your fastidiousness, we indeed have the pleasure of viewing and admiring them on you. What do you say Raymond?" Rupert blushed at his risqué.

"Raymond," I said, "You'd never believe the wardrobe Patricia has assembled for us. She spent a whole day in London yesterday shopping. Of course, her taste and selection are impeccable. She knew exactly what to get for both of us. And here I was, planning to get advice from her about shopping in Paris."

Raymond didn't say anything. He quietly walked towards his sister and kissed her. "Pat was always a roguish little angel," he said finally after looking at her with gratefulness and affection in his eyes.

We thanked them both profusely. Rupert shook Raymond's hand heartily. "Don't worry about anything, old chap. Henry and I will be in touch. As soon as we hear from you about Lanverndel, we'll get started. Just go and enjoy yourself, get some rest and have a good time and come back a new person."

"Thanks Rupert. You'll hear from me soon, and Pat, as always you've been so wonderful, so understanding and noisy."

I enjoyed this teasy banter. It was a healthy sign, a sign of progress. One day surely we'd also have children, and they'd be like this.

Patricia pouted at Raymond, and laughing we drove off waving to them for as long as we could.

There was only one day left to organize and tie up loose ends. I gave instructions for the care of the dogs. Jane was sad.

"Is it true ma'am, that Mr de Villiers is selling Lanverndel?"

"No Jane, that's not true at all. Who told you that? Is this a rumour going around the village?"

"The people in the village were talking about it last Sunday."

"You can tell them quite clearly that it is not true. Mr de Villiers and I are planning to go to France just for a change and to get some rest. We will definitely come back to live here again after we get it restored. You must look after Pluto when we're away. Will you do that?"

"Yes ma'am, I surely will. How long will it take for the restoration to be over?"

"I don't know much about these things, Jane. I would imagine anything from six months to a year, perhaps even more. I'll ask Mr de Villiers today."

And then I realized that this decision which I had to take in France, that was to shape the rest of our lives and destiny, had already been taken by me without thought, without debate, without even any effort. I was flabbergasted at its smoothness. I couldn't understand how or why I had told Jane what I did. I had certainly not considered anything of what I had said, and nor did I say it to mislead her. It just tumbled out of my mouth so casually, as if I was discussing the weather or the garden. I had a feeling of great relief and with that I dwelt no further upon it.

Raymond seemed happier and in better spirits. I think he too was looking forward to the next chapter of our lives just as I was.

That evening, after the day's work, Raymond and I were sitting in Henry's study. It had become something of a habit. Raymond would have his whiskey and soda, and I would have a glass of wine, if I felt like it. He would sometimes tell me about what was going on in the estate or the county. Normally, I never asked him any questions, but today I decided I would ask, quite directly, without beating around the bush.

"Raymond," I said, "are you feeling a little better? I'm sure getting away even for a while will be so good for you."

He didn't answer. He just looked at me and smiled.

But I persisted, "Aren't you looking forward to France? I really am."

He looked at me seriously but continued to smile.

"Since I must be honest with you, I can only say I really don't know. But one thing I do know is that I would like to go to make you happy."

"Oh, Raymond, what a lovely thing to say. Yes, I really am happy. Going far away from this whole nightmare, with just the sun and the sea and ourselves. I'm sure we'll find some peace and some of the answers."

"You know, sometimes I wonder whether you're the same little waif I married who was so totally innocent of the knots and tangles of life. It's almost as if you've shed one persona and donned another. Sometimes I feel I can hardly recognize you, you're so changed and so grown up." Though he was looking at me, his eyes were far away. "You're no longer the shy, retreating little girl who never wanted to give an opinion on anything. You know, it's just the look on your face. Yes, I've got it. You look now as if you're quite in charge."

So he had noticed, and I was glad for it, for I wouldn't have to explain.

"Yes Raymond, I feel it too. It's been coming gradually. We have to survive, we have to forget so much, and I have to be strong. Don't you like me anymore?" I asked with curiosity, but also to lighten the moment.

"I don't want to sound patronizing, but you've coped so magnificently, with me and with all the ill-fated events that we've gone through. You have the fierce, determined look of a lioness protecting her cubs. As for liking you, I'd like you anyway, but I do miss the little girl you've left behind."

I thought I should speak and tell him more. "You know, my life before was very plain and simple. Nothing really ever happened in it. And then, suddenly so much happened. I saw how you were tormented so relentlessly, and the only emotion that consumed me for days and days was anger, and that's what set off everything, like a trigger."

He kept looking at me curiously. "And don't forget another thing Raymond," I went on, "I really never had an opportunity to grow, or to develop. My childhood was lonely, with sick parents, worries about money. I could never think of myself or do any of the things I wanted to. I realize now how dull and boring I am, and I want to learn so much. I can't even take part in the conversations you and your friends have because I know so little. I have no talents or learning. Will you help me?"

"Of course I will," he said warmly, but with a slightly changed tone.

Did I discern a hint of anxiousness? Was he getting a little uncertain that I was changing too fast and becoming someone he wasn't accustomed to? Maybe I should slow down. We would have so much time to talk at Nice.

Raymond poured himself another drink, and just then the phone rang. It was Henry wanting to discuss some last minute arrangements. My glass of wine was nearly over. I rose from the chair thinking I would browse through the books on the shelf. I looked up, but slowly, a blurred, nebulous shape was creeping before my eyes.

No, this was not the wine. I shook my head repeatedly. There were locks of beautiful black hair flying before my eyes, diamonds flashing brilliantly, blinding me. But there was no face. I shuddered and shut my eyes.

I could hear Raymond saying something on the phone about his bank manager.

No, I would not let her overpower me. Raymond had never loved her. There had never been anything decent or honest in her. The only time she had any power over me was when I had thought she possessed Raymond's heart and soul. Today, after knowing her truth, I'm sure I could quite easily confront her anywhere, and stare her coolly in the eye without being perturbed, despite her fabled beauty, poise and brains. Her power over me was a thing of the past.

Raymond was still on the phone, now telling Henry something about the arrangements at Nice. I opened my eyes slowly and stared at the blurred form. It was dissolving, and for a fleeting moment, Miss Portner and Tom Camlin flashed past me.

But I wasn't shocked, and wasn't afraid of them anymore. She was totally insane, and he completely unscrupulous. She would be committed, and I swore to myself that if Camlin ventured within speaking range of us, I would simply phone the police and file charges of blackmail. I thought of all the journalists, the sleazy publicity and innuendo that we had gone through. But it really didn't matter anymore.

There was a silence in the room. Raymond's phone call was over, but I hadn't been listening. I found him staring hard at me.

"Everything okay? You seemed to have been in another world, completely oblivious."

"Yes, darling, I was. But it was good. I scored a major victory."

"Would you like to tell me anything about it?"

"At Nice. Provided…."

"Provided what?"

"Provided...you also tell me some of your secrets in return."

Raymond put on a look of disapproval for my benefit, and we both laughed loudly.

Chapter Six

There was yet another difference quite perceptible in glamorous Nice, even to the most frivolous tourist. This time everyone was talking politics. At the cafes, at the hotels, the clubs, even at the casino, it was only politics. There had always been a floating population of politicians, princes, bureaucrats and businessmen from all over Europe swarming the south of France. And everywhere we went, we saw the likes of them seated with their ladies and mistresses, gesticulating animatedly, abusing someone or the other with some newly invented obscenity and sending the table into loud peals of laughter.

But one could feel from the sixth sense that there was an undercurrent of disquiet and anxiety which all the frivolity, the entertainment and the near decadence of the Riviera could not conceal. The same men, who had wined and dined and laughed heartily the night before, had nervous, anxious faces the next morning.

In England, we had been so involved in our own personal affairs, especially me, coping with the new life I had stepped into, the forbidding Miss Portner, and my reticence in the face of everything, that I had not taken any real interest in what was going on in the rest of the world. There used to be a lot of passionate discussion about the Spanish Civil War in all social circles, and whenever Raymond and his friends spoke of it, they ended up with the gathering getting hopelessly divided and extremely agitated. I could really never understand any of it, and quite frankly, I made no attempt to do so either. I think in England nothing really interested me except getting accustomed to my new life that I had so suddenly and miraculously acquired. And later, when tragic events started casting a shadow over Europe, we were completely crushed and weighed down by the fusillade of our own personal tragedies.

Out here, people were only talking about Hitler, Mussolini, the Anchluss, Czechoslovakia etc. Jokes circulated about them, some quite unutterable, and there was something altogether unreal and contradictory in this ambience. I tried to pick up snatches of conversation and something from the English papers and piece things together, but I could never really draw a complete picture of anything.

We spent some very happy days going down memory lane, driving the same roads that Raymond used to take me on when I was companion to Mrs Kappelhoff, supposedly taking painting lessons, if you please. We spent long, lazy days discovering little secret coves and beaches where we lay soaking in the sun and salt. I wanted Raymond to befriend the sea again and forget all her associations, but this would have to happen in its own good time.

"Have you ever done any fishing?" he asked me one day.

"No, never."

"Would you like to try it? Let's hire a boat tomorrow and go sailing. I'll teach you how to fish."

I couldn't believe my ears. What I was thinking, he had uttered aloud. I only hoped my tone would sound normal and wouldn't jolt his mind to remember what I so badly wanted him to forget.

"I'd just love it," I said, and jumped into the water, carrying with me whatever expression that had etched itself on my face. But I couldn't fool him. He came behind me and joined me in the water and said quietly, "Don't be afraid, little girl. I'll learn to like the sea and the boat again, but promise to be around, please."

This unexpected expression of tenderness warmed me up. I knew that things would be well someday.

Our contact with the other guests in the hotel was limited and polite. Raymond raised his hat for the ladies, and the gentlemen raised their hats to me. We greeted each other with a *Bonjour* or *Bon Soir* or *Bon Appetit* if they were European, and a good morning or good night if they were English or American.

There were still not too many guests at the hotel and I discovered a new interest in just observing them—how they conducted themselves and moved around, how they dressed, how they spoke, how they flirted. Some of them I had seen continuously for the past few days. Some came only for a day or two and then left, perhaps in transit or on business. Then there were the usual American holiday makers creating an animated din wherever then went. Breakfast was a time when most people greeted each other before departing for their outings for the day.

For a few days we had breakfast in the room, but I was in the mood for meeting people, and Raymond through some strange telepathy understood this. He himself suggested that we start breakfasting in the hall downstairs. The men would smoke after breakfast and discuss the usual Hitler and Mussolini business. Would there be a war in Europe? Most people thought there wouldn't. France was so well defended by the impregnable Maginot Line. England had no quarrel with Germany, Czechoslovakia was inconsequential and Poland was too far away, getting partitioned every now and then. So why should there be a war? There would be heated discussions on these issues, and the smoking room sessions would generally end up with everyone shaking hands with great gusto, then all of them donning their hats and going off.

The ladies generally spoke of the latest fashion, the social highlights, bits of scandal, either in French or in English, depending upon the constitution of the group. I rarely participated in all this—because firstly I was no authority on either fashion or high society or scandal, and secondly, because I found the men's powwows so much more interesting and lively. But I was enjoying my newfound hobby of observation!

One day I asked Raymond, "Do you really think there'll be a war in Europe like the last one?"

"I really can't say. Of course I haven't kept track of much of what's been happening the last few months. This chap Hitler, one really doesn't know what he ultimately wants and where he'll stop, but he seems to have completely mesmerized his countrymen. These are all bad signs." He became silent for a while, deep in thought. "There may be some European skirmishes which England and France should try and prevent. If they succeed, there should be no major war. Otherwise, it's quite impossible to say now what the future holds."

"But everyone here behaves so strangely. They keep hemming and hawing about unnatural things going on in Germany, and then they laugh and say that it's all nonsense and exaggeration. I can't understand it."

"That's called clinging on to a dream world. It's also known as burying your head in the sand."

"I'm beginning to hate my ignorance. You'll have to explain things to me in more detail."

That day instead of going to our favourite cove with our hamper of food and wine, we sat in our room and Raymond explained to me with maps and books from the library, about the growth of Fascism in Germany—what really was happening in the Spanish Civil War, and in communist Russia, and what was going on presently in

Germany and Austria, just next door almost. I was fascinated and I believe I even asked some fairly intelligent questions.

"Why is the rest of the world sleeping and allowing Hitler to get away with all this?"

"Good question. Maybe the rest of the world is having such a good time that they don't want to spoil it by nosing around in Hitler's affairs. France pretends to itself that it is secure behind its fortifications and doesn't want to take on problems on account of some Slav or Scandinavian country. And England feels it's really none of its business if the Europeans are settling scores with each other."

"But shouldn't England be worried if a single country has designs on so many small ones?"

"Well, it doesn't seem to feel threatened yet, and perhaps when it does start to feel so, it may be too late."

He tried to be casual and matter of fact, but there was a frown on his brow, and his jaw was tight. My recent shot at contemporary affairs and modem history made me feel very good and educated and I thought I should learn something new every day. Raymond continued looking preoccupied.

I also felt that it would help both of us if we were to be a little more sociable. But again, I had to tread very carefully and make sure that he didn't feel goaded into doing something under duress. Any wrong or ill-timed move on my part could easily ruin my entire purpose. One day I said to him, "Raymond, let's attend some of the dinners and concerts which the hotel organizes. It would liven things up, and we could get to meet other people. Who knows, they might even be interesting."

"Oh," he said with an exaggerated frown and a twinkle in his eye, "so you're already getting bored with me."

"You know that is not true and it's horrid of you to say so, but since I know you don't really mean it, I shall not protest."

"To think of formal dress for dinner and shaking hands and smiling at all that's decadent in Europe, its already making me irritable."

"You can say that because you've seen all the possible glamour and fashion and high society that there is. In fact, you're part of it, by definition at least, if not in practice. But for me, it is something totally new. Something of an adventure almost. Whether I'll like it or not, I don't know, but I'm certainly curious about it. And now that I'm stuttering and stammering less and not hiding behind columns, who knows I might even be quite a success. I shall wear the black evening dress Patricia gave me and your mother's pearls and you shall take me on your arm to dinner."

Raymond feigned a look of exasperation. "What if I should have a headache and am unable to escort you to dinner?"

"Then I shall sit by your bedside, draw the curtains and darken the room, and rub a balm on your forehead until your headache goes. But taking me out for dinner, you shall not escape."

"Hmm," he said, pretending to look thoughtful, "so you leave me with no choice. You come all the way to Cote d'Azur to be presented to the decadentia of Europe on your birthday. What better way to celebrate it?"

It took some time for his words to sink in. And then it struck me in my flabbergasted state—yes, today was indeed my birthday. He had remembered and I had forgotten completely. The new me was obviously getting a bit overburdened to remember innocuous things like this.

"Oh, my goodness, you're right, how could I forget?" I finally mumbled, looking quite foolish I'm sure.

"Well, I remembered and happy birthday. And here's something for the most promising candidate to be launched into high society." He kissed me on my cheek and handed me a beautifully packaged flat box. It contained an exquisitely crafted diamond bracelet and earrings from Bvlgaris.

"These are so beautiful. Thank you, thank you so much. You shouldn't have been so extravagant. God knows how much money you'll need for Lanverndel, and how is it you smuggled this in without me ever finding out?"

"It was easy, my dear. It was bought one afternoon when you were at the Museum, and I said I was going to get the car looked over. Something like you learning painting when we were here last," he added with a chuckle. "I've never really indulged you or spoilt you, have I? There was always so much coming in the way."

Before this could go any further, I sprang up in rescue. "That's not quite true. You've indulged me and spoilt me ever since you married me, whether I was dumb or dropping bricks. You've put up with my clumsiness and ignorance without ever grumbling, and now you're putting up with my impulsive and whimsical growing up. Of course, you've always indulged me," I pouted at him.

"If whatever you have said is accurate, which I doubt very much, it still cannot compare with what you have undergone on my account, and what you have given me so ungrudgingly. You will probably realize one day, after some years have passed, how you almost gave me a new life."

He held both my hands. "And if I could ask you something impossible, it would be this—just remain as you are, remain your unspoilt, natural self."

"Anyway," he continued, "we will spend today just the way you wish. It so happens that the Sadler's Wells Ballet is performing a brand new version of *The Sleeping Beauty* at the Opera House this evening. I believe it is based on the original choreography which Marius Petipa used when it was first performed before the Tsar of Russia, in 1890 I think. So you shall enjoy the Ballet and then I shall take you for dinner on my arm just as you want. The who's who of Nice will be there and you can have your fill of them. And of course, not forgetting your black dress and pearls to complete the event. Perfect." He smiled teasingly.

"No, I shall wear my black dress and these diamonds," I was eyeing them lovingly.

"Well, well," he feigned a sigh, "I do have to keep pace with my little girl growing up."

I scowled at him. "But where would you like to go this morning?"

"I don't care if you take me to Timbuktu, so long as you're taking me somewhere." I tried to be coquettish, but failed rather miserably.

"Okay. Then today, I will show you what in my opinion is one of the finest views on this part of the coast, but you'll have to walk for about an hour to reach it. It's quite a surprise really. Are you in the mood for that?"

"Why, of course. It must really be beautiful if you say so." And without any warning my thoughts started spilling into dangerous territory. Had he taken Charlotte there, just as he was taking me? And against my will, I kept forcing myself to think of her...like drinking a bitter medicine that you know will make you well... so that I could challenge myself that she had no power over me anymore...that she was nothing more than a malignant footnote in our lives, which mattered not at all now.

It was a beautiful day. The sky was a clear forceful blue, and the sun more brilliant than ever; the warmth so soothing to the skin just as the ubiquitous blue was to the eyes. I glanced sidelong at Raymond. I had got into this habit of giving him cryptic sidelong glances whenever I thought he was engrossed in his papers or his books, or just gazing at him when he was sleeping. A childish fancy no doubt, but each time I stole a glance I would hope for a miracle, that the hollows around his eyes had disappeared, that his eyes would have the joy and sparkle of freedom.

Today, I was certain that the grain and texture of his person were different. Worry and tension no longer masked his face, and my heart sang with joy as I saw the silent whistle between his lips. My new found fancies and penchants may have mystified or irritated him but I think they also entertained him, and as far as I was concerned, any distraction at this time was a boon.

My birthday was a real surprise, and it gave us a legitimate reason to get out of the groove that we were getting into quite unwittingly. And it was a lucky coincidence that the Ballet was performing tonight. This was to be followed by a grand dinner, and it would be my first such after our own Carnival dinner at Lanverndel. The night that had shattered our lives.

I suddenly turned very still. Lanverndel...I hadn't remembered it for so long. And very soon we would have to decide what to do with it. How abandoned and forlorn it had looked when I had seen it last. Raymond had not spoken of it either, but I knew his heart would have ached each time he remembered. Anyway, we would not talk of it today. Today would be a happy day, and we would not risk mentioning anything which might stoke painful memories or cause us any sadness. We would discuss it tomorrow. What a marvellous invention tomorrow is, so practical. Anything unwanted this day, anything which was inescapable or unsavoury could always be stuffed into it. And tomorrows happened in such an easy, lovely way. Just a few steps forward for mother earth and a pirouette on her toes like a ballerina and we had a brand new tomorrow. I loved tomorrows.

We drove miles and miles with me holding the faded, creased map. I have no sense of direction, and I had no idea where we were heading. We passed through quaint villages with hearty peasant men and women working at their vineyards, fetching and carrying, conversing with each other in loud, shrill voices. We were easy and contented and the vineyards started getting more and more undulating as we started climbing the hills.

"The road ends a few miles up and then we start walking."

"Whereabouts would we be, Raymond?" I asked.

"Almost at the fag end of the Alps down south, near the Italian border I would say."

I was purring like a cat in the warmth of his presence, the warmth of the sun; the intoxication one has when there are no shadows between two people. The wind was beating against my face, my hair flying backwards, and my hand was on his knee. He would put his arm around my shoulder whenever the road permitted.

And so we reached the point where the road stopped. It was a solitary spot and it seemed as if no one had been here for a long time. Raymond parked the car and we started walking. It was a kind of plateau made up of small hills and cols extending for at least ten square miles.

"I'm waiting for the surprise," I said looking around in anticipation.

"Patience, my dear one. Now we must take this beaten track. Sure you can walk about a mile and a half?"

"Of course I can. I'm a pretty sound walker," and I skipped and ran, embracing the champagne air and the glorious sunshine.

We walked up the little hills, down the dales on the extremely complicated track. In about ten minutes I had completely lost all sense of direction and was satisfied by just following Raymond. And then all of a sudden I saw the vast shimmering sheet of blue. It seemed like a lake set up high on the plateau surrounded by little jewel-like hills, breathtakingly beautiful. I gasped at the startling change of landscape and stood dumb in astonishment. If one were to be barely two furlongs away on the other side of the glen, this little idyll would remain unseen and unknown.

I found my voice again, "How did you come to know of this spot, and when did you come here last?" I asked, sounding so stupidly inquisitive without meaning to be.

"I think I came here exactly twenty-five years ago, which is older than what you are to-day. It was a trekking holiday in the Alps after my final term at Oxford. And naturally the Alps included spots like Monaco and Nice and their neighbourhood! I'm glad it still remains untouched by modern tourism and has not been massacred by roads and cafes. I was hoping all along the drive I'd find it. It's not often in the south of France that you can get a solitary spot of such pristine and unusual beauty."

We found a place by the lake and spread the rug. I put the hamper and the books neatly on it and then I saw that Raymond had brought his fishing kit as well. It was about eleven o'clock. There was a magical silence disturbed only by the occasional twitter of the warbler or the singing of the thrush. The air was quiet and the shimmering sheet of clear blue water danced lazily in slow little circles, and everything around us had a halo of gold and a mystical stillness.

"That is not all. Would you like to see the rest now or do you want a surprise after lunch?"

"Now," I said excitedly,

"Then come with me. We have to walk right around the lake, and go over to that hill facing south."

We started walking and it did not take long to reach the hill. What I saw from there took my breath away. There was a sharp frightening drop, about a thousand feet below and then miles and miles of terraced land meeting the sea. We could see almost the entire coastline of the Côte d'Azur interspersed with little towns and villages and vineyards, the ships on the Mediterranean, some sailing, some anchored, the promontory of Monaco. One almost felt the world at one's feet in a very intimidating way.

"My God, this is the most magnificent view I have ever seen."

"I thought you'd enjoy it. Sheer good luck that I found it."

We stood there, shoulder to shoulder, and I watched him closely. Was he also being reminded of another murderous drop from the hundred and third floor of the Empire State Building, that he told me about on that dark and desperate night at Lanverndel? Their glamorous New York honeymoon, photographed in every society magazine, the secrets and horror of which he had bared to me. The circular balcony, Charlotte leaning dangerously over the parapet wall, laughing triumphantly, and playing with his fingers, making the devil's bargain, "...how's that Raymond, we'll be the toast of English society...you'll never believe that magic I work on old castles and gardens, the older, the better...I'll turn Lanverndel into a Camelot...," revealing her dark, vile secrets, "...what a fine and gracious couple we'd be...social icons and everybody's envy...celebrities will throng to be our guests...queues of them...." I shivered, but took hold of myself quickly. He shouldn't guess what's going on in my mind... today belongs to me...why do I allow her to keep haunting me like this? And I composed myself hurriedly and looked at him.

He was drinking in the view, and said with that different voice. "But you must be hungry. Let's go and eat. We can come back later if you like." We had both decided to respect the privacy of our thoughts.

We opened the bottle of wine and ate the picnic fare—sandwiches, roast chicken and oranges. Both of us were ravenous, and before we knew it, everything was over and a feeling of languid contentment came over us.

"Would you like to relax a little now, or shall we do some fishing?"

"Both. Let's relax first, and then you can teach me how to handle that contraption."

"Okay." He stretched lazily on the rug and after a while said quietly, tenderly, "Come over here."

I went and sat beside him almost obediently, and before I knew it I was lying beside him on the sand, under the bright blue sky, embraced by the champagne air and flaming sunshine. The singing of the birds grew distant, the gold of the sun turned liquid and the blue in the sky grew hazy. All I could remember was his tenderness and how much he wanted to love me.

We drove back in silence and in peace, overwhelmed by the wonder and the magic.

Chapter Seven

We reached Nice at about four thirty, and I could immediately sense a change in the town's atmosphere. It had suddenly become sombre and restrained and there were much fewer people moving about on the boulevards. Those seated in the cafes looked worried and were huddled in smothered, serious discussion. So too in the shops, the shopkeepers and shoppers were without their characteristic lightheartedness. They looked anxious, their hands were not gesticulating with the usual vigour, nor was there any noise or laughter with the usual French heartiness. Everyone was talking almost in whispers. Obviously something was dreadfully amiss.

"The town seems strange, what could have happened?" I asked.

Raymond too looked intrigued. "Well, the greatest catastrophe that can happen here is if a film star or model has an accident, or some old Monaco royal has bid the world goodbye. I can't think of anything else. Anyway, we'll soon find out."

We reached the hotel. Here too was the same eerie silence, the usual tea time pell-mell absent or subdued, and everyone looking grim and dour, engrossed in deep conversation instead of the light-hearted chatter and flirtation. There was no frivolousness, not with the hotel staff nor with the guests. What on earth was the matter?

We could bear the suspense no longer. Raymond walked up to the maitre de chef and asked, "Is everything all right? Things don't appear to be as usual."

"No Monsieur, they cannot be as usual. Perhaps you do not know, France and England have declared war against Germany."

"Oh no, my God, so it has finally come. Well, I suppose it had to," he said almost to himself.

I was a bit dazed. The afternoon at the lake was still with me, and I had hoped I'd savour it long, and there was the Ballet and the evening dinner to attend, the dressing up and the excitement, and now suddenly everything lay scattered. There seemed to be some new guests at the hotel. Raymond had gone to make enquiries about his mail, and while I was waiting I kept myself busy with just looking very discreetly at everyone, observing their manner, and trying to figure them out.

There was a tall, statuesque lady of middle age, not beautiful in the conventional sense, but very commanding and imposing in presence. Her voice was moderately loud and rang with a tone of confidence. She was escorted by a smart gentleman who seemed to have the gait of an army officer and looked quite a bit younger than her. There were two lovely young girls with her who looked like her daughters and another young man who seemed to be escorting both of them. By now I had fitted up something of a family, and was trying to place the two men in appropriate slots, my imagination getting the better of me..."she appears to be a bright, happy person with a strong kind of presence, a natural one. I wonder whether she has cultivated it...but there is also something indefinable about her...now what is it... Ah, I know, she doesn't fit into the category of the 'regulars', nor that of the 'not regulars'. I wonder why she looks different. Yes, I think I've got it. She doesn't look married, she doesn't look single and she doesn't look a widow, and she wears so many rings on her fingers that it's impossible to tell if she's wearing a wedding band. She may be a business woman, or a member of the royalty or a simple housewife. She simply doesn't fit into any fixed stereotype....

I could have mused on indefinitely, had I not realized that the lady was also looking in my direction. She'd probably find me of no interest, I thought to myself. Perhaps she too is trying to fix me in a slot and is getting nowhere. The idea amused me. Suddenly her expression changed and quickened, and she arose and walked up to me and to Raymond who had just returned after collecting our mail.

"Raymond, this is indeed a surprise and a pleasure. It has been such a long long time." I could see that she had genuine surprise and pleasure on her face. She turned to me, and Raymond made the introductions.

"My wife, Yvette la Casas. We were together at Oxford. And I assure you Oxford was never the same after she left."

"That is simply not true," she spoke with a heavy French accent and the usual French pout, all the while looking at me with graciousness. I knew she was taking in everything about me—my clothes, my accessories, my class, my everything. I did not care.

"Comment allez vouz? Though I do not meet Raymond often, I get all news about him. I was informed about your marriage recently. Congratulations." She spoke genuinely and there was this lovely glow about her which I hoped I too would have when I was her age.

"Thank you Yvette, and what brings you here?"

"Ah, if I start to tell you the story of my life, we go on till winter. My friend with me is in the French army and we have some business here and then in Paris next week. But now with this news about the war, I do not know if we change our plans. This is so terrible." She looked over her shoulder and gestured to her daughters with her hand that she was coming. "Anyway, I hope we shall see you this evening at dinner. You are not leaving Côte d'Azur soon, I hope. "

I felt her eyes bore through me, but despite that, her good will came through easily.

"No, no, we shall be here for some time," I said. She shouldn't think I was dumb.

"So we will see you all at dinner," Raymond waved and took his leave, and we went up to our room. He immediately turned on the wireless and I lay down exhausted and angry. Why did this damned war have to start today of all days, and why should it have started at all in the first place? I remembered a few months ago, in the midst of my private battles at Lanverndel, glancing at the front pages of the newspapers. I remembered the picture of the Prime Minister being received with great applause, waving a paper saying that he had brought peace for our time. What had happened to all that? Surely the Prime Minister couldn't have made a mistake.

There was a knock at the door. Raymond was deeply engrossed with the wireless, so I answered it. One of the concierges had brought a personal letter from the hotel management saying that even though today's news had come as a shock, the ballet and the dinner would go on according to schedule and he hoped we would attend. I thanked him and said we'd be sure to come.

"What is it?" Raymond asked totally preoccupied. I told him and handed him the letter.

"Yes, they're right. Life must go on."

"Raymond," I asked, "is this also going to get out of hand and cause an awful lot of destruction like the Great War? Why do men like killing each other?"

"Alas, I really don't think I can answer any of your questions. I haven't been able to get very much from the wireless except that Hitler's armies have marched into Poland, and France and England have declared war on account of treaty obligations. But, who is bluffing whom, we still can't say. As to why men like killing each other, could it be that the beast in man peeps out periodically in history and does his bit? Anyway, to hell with the whole bunch of them, at least for today. Don't let's allow them to spoil today. We shall go to the ballet, and then on for dinner. We still have an hour and a little more to dress."

I suddenly remembered my appointment with the hairdresser downstairs. I dashed out, leaving Raymond quite mystified.

I asked the hairdresser to cut my hair shorter, fluff it out and give a trim in the front, as Patricia had suggested. The result was tremendous. My face filled out, and its entire perspective changed. I had never realized how influential hair was to one's general appearance. It could almost transform a face, arranged this way or that.

The entire exercise took longer than I had expected. Marise insisted that the style had to be set to perfection, and I could not protest. I wondered how Raymond would react. He normally appeared so unconcerned about how I looked. Well, he must have had a surfeit of fashion and style and coiffure in his life once upon a time, no doubt, and I only hoped these impulsive follies of mine wouldn't irritate him.

A little shyly and with as much style as I could muster, I walked into the room. He was still glued to the wireless and when he saw me he merely raised his eyebrow and smiled with some amusement. He said nothing.

"Well, don't you like my new hairstyle?" I asked, tilting up my chin.

"Hmm, let me see. Quite becoming I must say, except that Alice in Wonderland seems to be transforming into Cinderella."

"Aha, but with a difference. Cinderella had a terrible time after the clock struck twelve. In fact, she became quite a tragic heroine for a while, didn't she?" I felt a sudden jab within me. I knew instinctively I had said something dangerous while showing off my foolish knowledge of fairy tales. I ran out of the room like a delinquent.

I wore my black off the shoulder dress and put on my diamond bracelet and earrings. They glinted their rainbow colours, but despite the magic lights they emanate, diamonds always look cold and hard;

they lack the elusiveness and gentleness of pearls, their misty, moonlit radiance. I had read somewhere recently that pearls speak a sadness in their beauty because they are made from the suffering of a living creature. I stared hard at myself in the mirror in great anticipation, all the while contemplating the ruthlessness of diamonds and the suffering of pearls. Was that really me who I saw? I could hardly recognize myself. I darkened my eyes and put a touch of colour on my lips and cheeks and dabbed Jean Patou's new perfume behind my ears and on my neck and on the pulse spots as the fashion magazines instruct.

"So, are you pleased?" I saw him in the mirror, looking at me. His voice had a ring of amusement and indulgence.

"Supremely, and you?" I stared back at him in the mirror. I had the ebullience of a debutante attending her first ball. Thank God, my thoughtless bit about the tragic heroine was buried.

"Yes, yes, I think so. I'm learning how to be pleased and happy again." But he used a tone when his mind would be wandering in places he would not wish me to know. Blast. Why were we again slipping into dangerous subjects like being pleased or happy, instead of just being so.

He looked so striking and aristocratic in his black dinner jacket and bow, and I took his arm and walked out of the door just as I had dreamed I would do at Lanverndel.

"By the way, I forgot to mention, you look very lovely indeed, and I would be quite jealous if the young men should pay you too much attention."

Perhaps this was something spoken carelessly, spoken because there was nothing else to say, but I would be untruthful if I deny that a secret reassurance and a silly sense of triumph took hold of me. For the first time he had expressed a possessiveness of me. But I camouflaged it with a laugh and continued the flippant mood.

"That sounds familiar, considering that most of the time in Lanverndel I experienced that very emotion. Of course, I was jealous of imaginary and non-existent things."

Thank God, we were talking about these things naturally and easily. Gradually they had to be excised from the mind, and I think this could be easier done if one spoke about them casually, in a matter of fact way.

I would be seeing *The Sleeping Beauty* for the first time. Raymond had familiarized me with the dance sequences, and mercifully there was no esoteric Latin or Greek classic to be mastered to understand the plot of this great musical masterpiece by Tchaikovsky. Strange, I thought, at the heart of this famous ballet is a humble fairy story that every child in the nursery is told.

The theatre had an architectural grandeur, very baroque, and the gentlemen and their ladies were as elegant as could be. This was a different world indeed. The most expensive fragrances of the world wafted in the air, priceless jewels glittered, and brocades and chiffons swished past each other. But the smiles that were exchanged seemed moulded and practiced, even exclamations of greeting appeared rehearsed. It was a blend of the classical and the outrageous which is possible only in pampered, indolent Nice. Money glittered all the way through and I enjoyed the spectacle enormously, being part of it and at the same so out of it; the novelty and the adventure, and also the stereotype and the superficiality.

I looked at Raymond again. He belonged here so naturally, and how fortunate I was to be his wife and have his love. For my sake, today he was spending this evening like this—a drill he must have endured a million times before and which didn't interest him in the least. He was doing it for me, so that I could taste the novelty of this world which I had never known before. And I was really doing it for him, wanting to tear him away from his solitude and from the threats of darkness.

The music parted the curtains and the lights glimmered like fireflies in the darkness and after that it was pure magic; the waltzes, the famous Rose Adagio, the arabesques and pirouettes, and finally the enchanting Divertissement. It was intoxicating, all of it. The curtain falling and the encore, Princess Eugenia presenting bouquets to the artistes and the conductor of the orchestra, and then the royalty departing.

As everyone moved to the exit, the shadow of the news from Poland once again started filtering through, casting a pall of gloom on this wonderful enchanting evening.

We saw Madame la Casas and her entourage. She waved to us gaily.

"Allo again, what a handsome couple you make. All eyes are upon you."

Raymond bowed. "Thank you, allow me to compliment you and your charming daughters."

Madame la Casas certainly seemed an enigmatic person. She was wearing the most elegant and simply cut evening gown of royal blue crepe de chine, and had sapphires around her neck and on her ears and wrist, delicately set, of perfect size, striking but not ostentatious. Her figure was just right, generous without being heavy. She was not beautiful, but extremely attractive and imperial, with a vibrant glow on her face. She seemed calm, self-assured, charming and gracious, but stricken with some secret worries and anxieties. Tomorrow I would ask Raymond about her.

"Meet my daughters Denise and Melissa. Denise is studying law at the Sorbonne, and Melissa is doing Physics. Mr and Mrs de Villiers. Raymond and I were at Oxford together."

Both girls had a fresh, daisy like look about them, the beauty of youth. One was about eighteen with dark hair and dark eyes, and the other was about twenty, fair with grey-blue eyes. Both were fashionably dressed in gay, flirtatious colours and had happy, laughing expressions. Escorting them both was the young man we had seen at the Hotel, but Mme la Casas was unescorted.

"And this is Martin Conally. He's from America. He's working on Particle Physics at the Sorbonne."

"Pleased to meet you. Please call me Marty," the American drawled.

He was a pleasant looking young man, about twenty-five or so, with perfect but aloof manners. He seemed perfectly at ease with

Mme la Casas and her daughters and it was evident they knew each other well.

"It's dreadful, this news about the war. Just when all of Europe was beginning to enjoy some good times. What do you think will happen, Ray?"

So she also called him Ray, something I had not heard anyone else call him.

"It certainly looks grim. It has never been well for Europe if a single power becomes a behemoth."

"But no one can touch France, I hope. They say it would be quite impossible to break through the Maginot Line—German soldiers or anyone. And as for your country, Ray, someone has to really shake it out of its stupor."

She certainly was outspoken.

"Hullo Raymond, fancy bumping into you here." A loud cannon like voice boomed from somewhere.

Raymond turned around, and the surprise on his face transformed into a broad, happy smile.

"Hey, Dick, old chap, what a surprise indeed. What the devil are you doing here?" There was great handshaking and back slapping.

So this is what happened at typical Nice gatherings. People from all parts of the world belonging to a certain class caught up with one another.

Raymond turned to me. "Meet Colonel Richard Bromley. He's a cousin from my mother's side. His mother and mine are sisters to be precise. My wife, Mme la Casas, Mademoiselles la Casas and Mr Martin Conally." The how do yous went all around.

"So Dick, old boy, you were in India last I heard of you, somewhere in the south, if I remember correctly."

"That's right. Just finished with Mysore. That's a state in southern India ruled by a Maharajah. I'm now on an assignment to Gibraltar—on my way there."

I left Raymond and his cousin to carry on with their discovery of each other. The wine was excellent and the hors d'oeuvres delicate and subtly flavoured as only the French can make. Both were going around in abundance.

We made a strange group, Madame la Casas and me, her two daughters who were really my contemporaries, and the aloof American gentleman. Madame la Casas went out of her way to befriend me.

"This war really has me worried. Ever since my husband died two years ago, I've tried my best to give the girls a good home, a good life and education, so they are secure and can be independent. Of course, I don't believe this will be a great war like the last one, but still we do feel a little uneasy."

"You have known Raymond for a long time." I don't know whether I asked this or stated it, but I felt obliged to make some conversation, and I didn't want to talk about the war. The young ladies and the American were talking with gusto, engrossed in something.

"Yes, about twenty-five years." Goodness, that was more than my age! "We were at Oxford together. I was on a students' exchange programme and studied history like Ray. I then married an Englishman, and Melissa was born. Unfortunately, our marriage did not last, as my husband fell in love with a French actress right here in Nice, and that was the end. After that, he regularly fell in love with someone new each year. I was too young and inexperienced to put up with his infidelities. Then I married Denise's father. He was a physicist, completely involved with his work, but we were very happy. Unfortunately, he died of an illness two years ago. Now I don't think I'll marry again." She fluttered her hands and gave a warm smile. "What about you, you married some months ago, I was told."

There was no cause for fear, no cause to hide. And you can't have a better ally than wine to help you talk and face the world.

"Yes, that's right, and we've been having one misfortune after another since. No doubt, you know that Lanverndel was burnt."

"Yes, I read it in the *Illustrated London News*. It must have been terrible. My husband, Denise's father and I had stayed there once some years ago. It was truly such a beautiful place. I hope you'll be able to get it together again. But I know, times will get harder and harder."

The question was building up in me, and I had to ask it, though why, I could not comprehend. I was no longer afraid, no longer insecure, but I had to say those words.

"Mme la Casas, did you know Charlotte?"

They were out; the words which I would have shuddered to utter even till a few weeks ago, had been spoken. I think it was just the off-hand casualness of saying her name which I found so liberating, childish as it might appear. As casually as if I had been discussing the cricket score or the Garland Waltz.

Her face changed expression, but oh so gradually that it was almost imperceptible. Society tactics, I marvelled.

"Well, I had been her guest at Lanverndel, and had met her a few times, but I did not know her very well. She was a very beautiful woman, but not really my kind of person."

"What do you mean, Madame?" I persisted.

"Well, it's a little hard to explain. As you can see, I am a very straight forward person, how you call it, a very open person. What is in my head is on my tongue. But with Charlotte one never knew. She seemed to be a woman with so many masks. She could become anything she wanted to be—charming, gracious, vivacious, brilliant. Of course, she was beautiful and so knowledgeable about everything. At least, so it seemed. But one does not go testing depth of knowledge at social gatherings. I always felt, how should I say, a little lost after a conversation with her, wondering what exactly she meant. Like I said, I thought there was, how shall I call it, always a mask on her, and her real thoughts were somewhere else. But with Raymond, one knows where one stands."

She understood I was being curious, inquisitive about one who had occupied my place not very long ago. And I couldn't but salute her canny intuition.

Several rounds of wine had vanished and the crowd was happy and laughing and gay. The war was forgotten. The band was playing lively waltzes, sambas, with infectious tempo and rhythm, and the floor was filling up with couples, young and old.

"And may I have the pleasure of this dance?" I turned and saw Raymond in an absurd bow.

"I have half a mind to refuse considering I've been waiting all evening, but since I've been enjoying myself so much, I feel generous and I shall accept." The wine was definitely heady.

"My pleasure," he was still in the position of the absurd bow. We went on to the floor.

"So, are you enjoying the high society of the Cote d'Azur?"

"Actually I enjoyed the picnic at the lake much more, and the fishing that we never did even more still." I looked directly into his eyes, and he acknowledged it with a gentle movement of his eyelids.

"I wish this blasted war hadn't spoilt everything. But I wanted to experience all this too. This is really your world, isn't it, the class, the background? But I also see how external and detached you are from it. I understand now your aloofness, your individuality, but I do want to experience this world in my own detached way, because of you. You understand I think," I said very unconvincingly, I'm sure. The wine was making my words go in circles, and I was making absolutely no sense even to myself.

"Yes, unfortunately I do," he replied. I had forgotten what I had been saying. The band was playing Strauss, *The Voices of Spring,* and I was trying my best to be light and nimble on my feet. Once or twice I stamped Raymond's foot and he pretended to grimace in pain. I felt so grand in my haute couture dress, my Bvlgari jewels, and my new found confidence. I was in the arms of the man I loved so much, and I felt happy and carefree.

Dinner was announced. I saw Colonel Bromley and Mme la Casas coming towards us from the floor and we all decided to sit at the same table. The food was excellent and the wine in total harmony. Someone started talking about Hemmingway and someone else promptly continued about Eliot. And then just as a particularly enterprising guest was trying to count the number of French actresses present, a rumour went around that the Duke and Duchess of Windsor were expected any moment. Mme la Casas identified a gentleman who was a close relative of the slain Tsar Nicholas of Russia and she informed us with utmost seriousness that the only reason he found himself alive today was because he was a perpetual vacationer at the French Riviera. No one spoke of the war.

The evening was everything I had wanted it to be. Actually, I was in a state of great exhilaration, but I couldn't share the secret cause of my joy with anybody. I had finally proved to myself that I had overcome my fears and anxieties, not just in my own imagination, but even in the face of snobbish Nice glitter.... Something very strong had taken hold of me and it seemed to overtake my usual impulse to run and hide. What a disaster I had been at Lanverndel. No, I would not think about that, I decided firmly. I shall only look ahead. The wine was assisting me admirably in flitting from one impression to another. Let's face it, I thought, today I have managed to acquire some confidence, maybe not enough to express strong views about anything, but enough to follow conversations and perhaps contribute marginally. I was no longer fixated upon what others were thinking of me. Today, I was strong, determined and trying to be self-assured, and everyone was being so kind and considerate to me. No one stared at me patronizingly when I was introduced as Raymond's wife. And then it dawned upon me in a flash. The world appears unkind and patronizing only when we ourselves are gripped by fear and diffidence. Well, I had made my discovery for the day.

Coffee and liqueurs were being served and the band was playing sentimental fox-trots.

"A penny for your thoughts," Raymond caught my eye and took me to the floor.

"Actually it wasn't a thought, only a discovery. And I have too much wine in my head right now to explain it to you. Raymond, have you enjoyed yourself or did you get bored?" "Strangely enough, I haven't been bored, and watching you with your starry eyes and flaming cheeks has kept me quite entertained, really."

"Oh really, Raymond. And it's nice we met your cousin quite by chance. If we hadn't come here, you'd have missed him, think of that."

But my heart surged with a childish joy, like the joy of a schoolgirl having her first crush. He had watched me and kept an eye on me, notwithstanding all the glitter and glamour of Europe around him.

"Yes indeed, he's a splendid chap. He's just completed a spell in India and was telling me about the independence movement there which seems to be getting very strong. There's this intriguing chap called Gandhi, and no one seems to quite know how to deal with him. It's such a strange and interesting country, India."

I hadn't a clue as to what he was saying. I had ingested much too much history and politics in the last week, and couldn't possibly take in anymore, and that too Oriental. All I knew about India was that somebody had called it a jewel in the British crown, and both my parents had several relatives who had gone there, some in the army, some in commerce, and some in the missions. A few of them had returned to England, some had died there of native diseases, and others had stayed on.

"Perhaps, we shall go there someday. They've got all the adventure there—thick jungles, tiger hunts, duck shoots, polo."

"And the occasional cholera and enteric," I chipped in.

"Touche, but that's unfortunately so. Yes, that's the price of Empire and pomp and tiger hunts. Part of the deal. You must either take both or leave both."

"Fancy getting so philosophic about tiger hunts," I said dreamily.

The music was over, and there was an announcement being made by the master of ceremonies. It was in French, and I hoped it wasn't something dreadful about the war. Suddenly I heard my name being announced and then the band struck again with the birthday tune. Then there were flowers and people, known and unknown, shaking my hand and kissing my cheek with a bonhomie that can only descend on an evening as complete and perfect as this.

What a wonderful day it had been right through. I couldn't have asked for anything more. Raymond seemed happier and more at ease. I was doing well and pursuing my ambitions, and we were going to start a new life.

That night I dreamt again I was in Lanverndel.

Chapter Eight

I woke up very late next morning and Raymond was not there. There were two notes by my bedside. One read, '8.30 am. Gone for breakfast', and the other, '9.30 am. Going to the telegraph office. Will be back soon. Sleep well'.

For a moment my mind seemed splintered, and I wasn't able to quite figure out where I was and what I was doing here. For the grim aftermath of the nightmare hadn't still released me. It was clinging to me darkly, like a horrid, loose mental shroud, not allowing me to escape. Like the dark wing of death casting a huge shadow over me, following me, imprisoning me and killing my power to think. I shut my eyes and tried to find my bearings; instead I saw only a face—a face without features, without eyes, without lips, without anything except a hard, cold, evil beauty and her dark hair, cursing me, damning me, wishing me death and destruction. I was on the verge again of plumbing the depths of despair and defeat with all my extravagant resolutions and promises dissolving into naught.... Would we never be free of her? Would we never have any stretch of happiness? Were we to live all our remaining days in dread, with each interlude of happiness being followed by revengeful and accursed nightmares...? And would she finally win and destroy us...?

I shuddered in fear and turned on my stomach, hiding my face in the pillows, almost like a lamb about to be slaughtered at the altar, waiting for the axe to fall. But I made one last and supreme effort commanding all my strength, and then as if in renascence, I saw myself heave up. I quickly jumped out of bed, went near the open window and breathed the fresh air deeply several times. How foolishly and inconsistently I was behaving. I should be reinforcing my resolutions and being proud of my achievements instead of sinking again into a meaningless, destructive maze from which there would be no escape, no rescue.

Yesterday had been a happy day. Let me dwell upon it, I thought. I smiled to myself as I tried to think back and recreate it in my mind. How many different events, moods, unexpected happenings had been compressed in a mere twenty four hours. But my head still felt tangled and heavy, too much wine and dancing, the disturbed night and the wretched nightmare that I was trying to fight so stubbornly.

I tried to think coolly, maturely, logically dreams, good or bad, always came from the subconscious or unconscious, so Raymond had told me. There was nothing more to them and they were certainly not any kind of harbingers from outer space. That was reasonable and logical enough, but whatever my efforts, I have to admit that I'm always in such mortal dread of bad dreams. Somehow a belief has taken root in me that they are a sort of warning with some instruction in them that has to be decoded, and if you miss it, then a disaster might be lurking somewhere. I believe each of us is entitled to his eccentricities, and this is possibly one of mine, but the fact remains that I continue to be terrified of bad dreams. I used to dream often about Lanverndel, sometimes happy dreams, strolling in the grounds, walking in the Honey Vale, even of the creek with the cabin, and other times scary ones like getting lost in the woods and not finding my way back, or falling down the stairs. But never before had I dreamt of Lanverndel as I did last night, in the grip of fear and evil.

Anyway, it meant nothing at all, I convinced myself. I was strong, I was young and I would win, dreams or not. I sighed and hoped with all my might that all would be well, and that our life which appeared to be progressing so positively would not again be buffeted by invidious, unforeseen calamities.

I dressed lethargically, but this sense of uncertainty and discomfort was again gradually becoming a despair without reason. Raymond had written that he had gone to the telegraph office. Why on earth did he have to go there? I hoped there was no bad news. But why was he taking so long? I started getting cross, as if he should have divined my exact hour of waking and helped me through the aftermath of my nightmare. I reprimanded myself severely for being so unreasonable, and continued my internal monologue about bad dreams. Perhaps I would discuss it with Raymond. He was always reading books by or about Freud or Jung or other dream-scholars, and it was high time he started putting his knowledge to practical use, instead of merely appreciating their brilliance and trying to explain it to me.

I had barely finished dressing when Raymond burst into the room looking cool and fresh, in good cheer. He had a portmanteau in his hand, and I suddenly felt very foolish about my churlishness.

"Is everything all right?" I asked anxiously.

"It would seem so, but it depends upon how you look at it."

I was impatient and irritable. "No suspense, Raymond, please. Tell me quickly. I'm frightened."

He sensed my frame of mind, "Okay, I had a telegram from Henry saying that Whitehall wanted permission for use of whatever we can spare of Lanverndel and the grounds for various purposes which Henry obviously couldn't go into detail about. They wanted to know our plans about it, about getting it into a presentable state, and naturally Henry wanted instructions since we hadn't given him any."

I was getting tense. "What did you tell Henry? Have you already sent him a reply?" I don't think I could hide the tautness in my voice.

"Yes, I sent him the reply which others have already decided for us. If the government requires Lanverndel or any part of it for the defence of the realm, they shall most certainly have it. I presume the insurance amount has been finalized by now and it can be used to do up any wing that the government wants. And if they want to billet any part of the grounds, they're most welcome to that too. I have asked Henry to get on with the job and as soon as our wing is ready, we shall return. As far as I'm concerned, the decision that you and I were to take has very conveniently been taken by someone else, and that's quite okay by me. I suppose I'm too old for military service, but I'm certain my services will be required for something or the other. Oh, by the way, you're getting psychic. You woke me up in the middle of the night about a bad dream you had about Lanverndel, and here we are this morning discussing its resurrection."

"Correction, the bad dream wasn't just about Lanverndel. It was about you and Lanverndel. Both of you disappeared, and naturally I got alarmed. And then you gave me some mock theory to put me at rest."

He smiled mischievously. If only he knew how much energy I had expended in coming to terms with my horrid nocturnal battle.

"Well, I'm here before you, and I've just wired Henry to get on with the restoration of Lanverndel, and I take it that it meets your approval. So your dream has had a happy ending, after all."

"Yes Raymond, thank God. I'm getting so superstitious. Anything a little unusual, and I start getting so jumpy and jittery."

"And I must say, in a way I'm quite relieved that the most important decision that we had come here to take seems to have been taken by everyone except us. If Herr Hitler only knew that he was almost entirely responsible for Lanverndel's restoration. How conceited we are thinking we are masters of our own decisions," he said.

I tried to follow what Raymond was saying, but didn't succeed too well. If it was any other time, we would have settled down for a huge philosophic discussion. My thoughts were back home, and my heart was bursting with happiness—Lanverndel would live again. We would go home again quite soon, and Lanverndel would be ours, a Lanverndel without any shadows and ghosts, even if the government was using it. And I would be a different Mrs de Villiers, different from the callow, clumsy girl who had walked in there for the first time last year. The war could be damned for all I cared. Raymond and I would go back to Lanverndel. This was my real birthday gift.

And then a thought struck me sharply like a blow. How an earth would we ever go back home? Would the Channel be safe for us to take the boat from Calais to Dover?

"Raymond, how will be ever get home? Suppose there's fighting in France. And there are supposed to be so many German warships around the Channel according to the papers."

He kept thinking with that frown on his brow. "We'll have to check that out at the Consulate. I think the closest one is at Marseilles. I'll also talk to Dick and find out what's going on. He's due to leave for Gibraltar tomorrow, I think. Anyway, don't worry, we'll soon find out what we should do."

"How long do you think it will take for Lanverndel to be livable again?" I asked, suddenly weighed down with all the cares of the world.

"I really can't say. Conscription has been announced, so construction help may not be that easily available. I don't think it will take anything less than six months, judging from the huge amount of work involved."

"But, Raymond, what will we do until then? Where will we live?" My voice was getting shriller.

"That is indeed a point, but don't worry, I beg you. I'll consult Dick right away, and the Consulate as well. Monaco will most probably stay neutral, so there's no immediate danger from there. We have to see what shape this war takes, and only then we'll know the safest way to get back home."

"Well, here's an idea", he continued, mainly to comfort me I think. "We could travel wherever you wish and where it is safe. If no land war breaks out, we could go to Paris, and I could show you all that there is to see, magnificent palaces, art galleries, museums. Actually, I wouldn't mind spending some time there myself. Haven't been there for ages. We could've gone to Italy, but things seem a lot more unpredictable there. But first let me consult Dick."

Dick's advice was pure common sense. Wait. Don't do anything in a hurry and let some pattern or trend emerge. He gave us his contact details at Gibraltar, and insisted that we should keep him informed of all our plans. Do not move out of Nice for some more time, he repeated, otherwise there was danger of getting trapped on land or at sea.

Other than causing fright, the other ramifications of the war had still not sunk in, probably on account of my general ignorance, or at best my half-baked knowledge of such matters. The core of my concern continued to be Raymond, and I couldn't help but notice how well he had started looking. I was certain that some amount of tranquility was coming over him. How odd, I thought to myself, there's supposed to be a war going on in some place, and I'm busy looking around for tranquility on my husband's face.

What really kept nagging me the whole day was how we would ever get back home. Questions that I was ill equipped to answer kept surfacing. Would there be fighting in France in the near future? Should we try and get home now or should we wait? How would it tell on Raymond who had only now started regaining some of his earlier strength and spirit? Would the sight of a charred and torn Lanverndel stir up bitter memories again? What a question—surely it would. Everything seemed so distressing and so out of our control. And why did this have to happen just as we were settling down to some kind of peace and routine, I thought crossly. Damn the war, I cursed, for what it was doing to us, for what it was making us go through again, fickle as ever.

Raymond too must have been anxious, though he tried to conceal it from me. I, of course, spent the day brooding. It was getting to be evening, and he said, "I'm sure Dick will have the latest information. I'll just go and have a word with him."

He returned after about an hour. "Dick had to leave for Gibraltar ahead of schedule but I was fortunate to catch him just in time. His information is that the seas are unsafe. There have already been instances of British ships being attacked by U Boats, mostly cargo ships in the Channel and on the high seas. Dick repeats his advice and I'm inclined to agree with him. Wait here until the war takes some sort of shape. And he has quite categorically asked me to inform you that you're not to worry, and that he'll make sure we reach home safely, whether on a fighter plane or on a battleship. So now, does that make you happier?"

"Bless him, yes. At least we have someone close by to help us in case we get stranded."

Thus we stayed on, neither anxious nor merry, but time seemed to pass by quite smoothly and profitably. We enjoyed each other's company, took long drives along the coast and up the mountains, exploring old Roman secrets of Provence and the Alps. We discovered quaint little villages, ate wholesome food, drank delicious local wine, and took part in most Cote d'Azur social activity—playing tennis, dancing, attending concerts, bridge evenings, and came to be known as the English Doves, such permanent fixtures we had become.

There were still no signs of any war on land, though at sea it was quite a different story. Hardly a day passed without the newspapers carrying some gory episode or other about the bloody war at sea, or the terrible destruction caused by the new weapons of sea warfare, particularly U boats and torpedoes. Their destructiveness seemed so terrifying, and we wondered where it was all heading towards. It was already beginning to look like a determined path of no return.

England's losses were enormous. Day after day, we read of the cargo ships, of freighters and battleships, even passenger ships, being struck and sunk to the bottom of the sea. On the coastal waterways of France and England, magnetic mines were taking a terrible toll of their own, and in more distant waters, powerful raiders like the Graf Spee were setting the seas on fire with their flaming prey. Day after day, we would read their names in the papers—the Athenia, the Gipsy, the Doric Star, the Aragonite, the Royal Oak—all gone, devoured by wolf packs, as formations of U Boats came to be called. Dick was right, the waters were bloody and frightening, though here in the Cote d'Azur, life went on with very little difference.

I had restarted sketching in right earnest and decided I must make a discipline of it. So whenever we went on our little expeditions, I would take my pencil and pad along, and while Raymond read his books and papers, I did serious sketching. By the time our travels were over, I had quite a formidable collection of them with names and dates neatly inscribed. Raymond said he was impressed with my talent and that made me feel very proud indeed. In fact, he insisted that an art teacher come over once a week and give me lessons.

Raymond asked me whether we should rent a villa, since our stay here was going to be rather indefinite. It might have reduced our costs and given us more freedom, but I must confess that the thought unnerved me. I still didn't feel competent enough to run a household befitting whatever status we had been labelled with, or hiring the right kind of household staff. And now that we were no longer leading insulated lives, we would be expected to entertain at a certain level, and I don't think I could have handled that. And who knew, finally it might have worked out just as expensive, if not more, considering the costs for housekeeping and gardening, and entertaining, of which I hadn't the slightest inkling. So we continued staying at Le Neptune, and to this day Raymond has never told me the exorbitant sum it must have cost him.

I persisted in my resolve to get more educated and continued with the serious reading which I had started sometime ago. Raymond was deeply interested in contemporary literature, philosophy and the momentous advances that were taking place in medicine and science. He made it a point to be well informed with everything current, and we always had stacks of books and magazines on diverse subjects coming to us from England. I read Yeats and Auden and Eliot who were currently the rage. I read translations of Sartre and Simone de Beauvoir, and found them all so strange and bizarre, and sometimes quite impossible. I may not have absorbed very much, but I was dazzled by this new world which was opening up before me—a world of letters, the existence of which I could never have imagined had I not experienced it. I could feel the territory of my mind expand with the excitement of new ideas and images as they magnified and multiplied in my head, and I was filled with a sense of enquiry and exhilaration. I may have found them abstruse and discordant at times, I may have even thought them eccentric and pointless, but the truth was that I was fascinated and overawed.

Of course, no initiation to current ideas could be complete without a smattering of what was fashionably called the New Left, and Karl Marx. This was a name which had incited sharp divisions whenever I had heard it, whether at Lanverndel or in Nice. It seemed to have fanatical adherents and equally fanatical opponents. Raymond belonged to neither group; he considered his work an impressive piece of logic, but losing trajectory as it progressed to its final statement of ideology. He treated it critically, analytically as just another piece of literature, and certainly not the Alpha or Omega. I read the Manifesto with great difficulty, and one of my earliest literary witticisms was when I asked Raymond with a perfectly straight face whether this was the fifth gospel according to Saint Marx!

We spent Christmas at Nice, but I could see that both of us were nostalgic about England. Lanverndel may have been blocked out by the unconscious, (I was certainly getting on with Freud), but England I missed with all my heart—the snow clad villages and white topped fir trees, the clear, starry winter sky and freezing air which could change breath into mist, the sound of church bells at the fireside. Never mind, I dismissed my nostalgia. Next year we would spend Christmas at Lanverndel. We would have a lovely tree, and lights and candles and turkey supper. And this would be a new, rejuvenated Lanverndel with fresh woodwork and paint, a Lanverndel from whence the ghosts had fled and the demons scorched and singed.

As lethal as the seas were, our part of the continent appeared to remain completely peaceful and untouched. Both French and

German leaders were still swearing that they would not attack, and by now the general opinion here was that there would be no war on land, that it was a matter of time that the fighting in Poland and Norway would cease, and then it would be business as usual.

The complexion of Nice was, however, imperceptibly and very subtly changing and a new breed of visitors were unobtrusively dribbling in. They were no longer the 'regulars' or seasoned casino buffs, or those who came for health reasons or by routine. They seemed different, very civil, professional looking people, proper and suave, but nobody really seemed to know who they were or what they were doing. There was muffled talk about Monaco, hardly ten miles away from here, having become the hotbed of espionage, and these activities were spilling over to Nice as well. As they said, everybody who was anybody was supposed to be working for somebody. It was almost an open secret that the Russians, Germans, the British and Italians, all had their intelligence networks operating there. I invented a little game we would play whenever we went out. In the cafes, in the restaurants, even at Le Neptune, we would try and guess who was a spy and who wasn't, and count the number of people we agreed upon. It always ended with me having a list of suspects twice as long as Raymond's! Raymond was quite amused at discovering what he called a very suspicious streak in my nature, though I insisted it was not suspiciousness, but merely an acute sense of observation.

Meanwhile, news from England was mainly by wireless as the mail had become more and more erratic, and we were kept informed of Lanverndel's progress. One day, we had a letter from Dick through an officer en route to Malta, asking us to wait on until some firm arrangements were made on shipping routes to England. Naturally, he couldn't give more details, but he said he would keep us informed of further developments. Sometimes, I wondered privately whether we were both indulging in a huge dose of escapism and were simply clutching alibis to avoid facing a premature moment of truth… a moment that would exhume the past that we were both so terrified of. Entering a robust, unstained Lanverndel and starting a new life, we had both prepared ourselves to face, but Lanverndel was still charred and wounded, and neither of us could have withstood another encounter with that. I think we had done the right thing. If we had to risk a voyage, it was better to risk it when there would be a whole, healed Lanverndel waiting to receive us. And it was better to risk a few more months here than risk a broken heart at Lanverndel. I was pleased with my rationalization and was more or less at peace with myself, but I had to ask Raymond.

I did so the next morning just before going down for breakfast.

"Raymond, I have something to ask you, and forgive me if it disturbs you, but ask you I must. Would you like to go back to Lanverndel right away? Will you be happy? We could go back even now if you so wish."

Raymond turned his face from me and looked out of the window.

And there was a long silence. Oh God, I've done it again. I've said the wrong thing, and now he will retreat into his shell once more, just when we were doing so well.

He turned his face towards me. Thank God there was no mask on it. He looked at me very steadfastly, almost with trust.

"No, I don't want to go back to Lanverndel now, given a choice." He spoke calmly and tranquilly. "I'm happy here with you. We're getting to know each other, naturally and easily. I'm gradually getting peace of mind and coming to terms with life and its bitter sweet doles. And I think we're enjoying ourselves too, aren't we?"

I nodded vigorously but couldn't say anything.

He continued, "But we must also be practical and keep our feet on the ground. Depending on what course the war takes, we make our plans. So let's enjoy ourselves until then."

We were told it was the coldest winter of the century, so we did not venture north until March, and then we went to Paris, the city of artists and lovers. We felt quite safe there too, because there was a sizeable British military presence there called the British Expeditionary Force.

Life in Paris was so brazenly normal that it was almost disturbing. The cafes were full as always with beautiful women and their escorts, military officers and bureaucrats, laughing, talking, and arguing about European politics and their own invincibility. This was my first visit to Paris, and even though there was officially a war on and we were really killing time, we enjoyed our stay immensely. We were the text book tourists, visiting historic buildings, the architectural masterpieces, churches, museums. We roamed the Champs Elysees and the Rive Gauche, climbed the Eiffel Tower, paid homage to Napoleon Bonaparte at the Invalides and to the beheaded Bourbons at Versailles. How could one believe that the streets of this beautiful city had overflowed with blood in an age not long gone by?

Paris was indeed a city of lovers, artists and bohemians, for all of whom it had always offered something—acceptance and a roof. You could feel it in the air...the generations and centuries of accumulated art and laughter and cynicism. This was the city in which artists had converged and found succour, bitter or painful, the fire of their inspiration and the magic of their talent finally succumbing to disease and poverty. Why were most artists entitled only to posthumous fame? I must ask Raymond his opinion, I thought.

There was so much to do and see in Paris, and sometimes we felt we barely had time for it all. Day after day we would go to the Louvre and stand in awe before its priceless treasures, enthralled by the sheer power of the canvasses, being transported to another world. Seeing them in print was one thing, but seeing the original Renoirs and Gauguins and Davids, their dimensions and magnitude, just took my breath away. The Mona Lisa, eternal, enigmatic and ironic—it just defied words. Then there were grand formal evenings at the Opera that we took full advantage of—spectacular performances that we could never see in England like Bizet's *Carmen*, and Mozart's famous and delightful *Mariage de Figaro*. Music was never my forte, but Paris brought me under its spell quite completely. Except that I realised that going to the Opera and going to an examination were so similar. One had to read the story, study the libretto the night before, and if one wanted to be still more meaningfully involved, a reading of the composer's life would come in handy.

We had a glimpse of the fabled Paris night life; the life of Montemartre and Pigalle which started only after the sun had set, the musical shows, the cabarets which sank lower and lower from street to street, until they became simple, painted prostitution. We experienced the romance and ritual of French gastronomy at its best, the dead serious business of selecting the right wine and vintage best suited with the meat and sauce. What major issues in life these were, but this was Paris.

Though there were official regulations for blackouts in the city, no one seemed to be taking them seriously after the initial false alarms of this *drole de guerre* wore off. If at all, Paris by night seemed to be struck by more traffic jams than ever before. Raymond more than me, was sometimes amused, other times bewildered, by the odd character of this war which was really not still a war. He would laughingly shake his head in disbelief and despair, and say, 'Look at the traffic congestion and blazing headlights in and around Paris. Do the enemy planes require any further indications aboutwhere to bomb? This is one hell of a war!"

No visit to Paris could be complete I thought, without asalutation at the shrine of haute couture. The fashion house of Channel was putting up its fall collection as usual, and I decided to do in Paris what Parisiennes do. We went to the show as I wascurious to see one, and Raymond had to agree since he had no other option, however much he may have liked one. The only difference the *drole de guerre* had made was that instead of the usual hundreds of models, hardly thirty or forty of them walked the ramp. And the grande dames of haute couture, instead of delicately waving their bejewelled hands or their exquisite fans, were knitting socks for soldiers.

I realised that Parisians loved discussions on any subject that interested them. Discussion was the symbol of their individualism, and with it went their body language, their gesticulation, and exaggerated facial expressions. The fashionable restaurants and cafes were crowded every night with politicians, present, past and aspiring, and their vivacious lady companions, having a marvelous time sharing gossip and spreading it further after extracting solemn promises regarding its utter confidentiality, which of course was not to be taken seriously by anyone at all. Some of the most exciting subjects of the day seemed to be the future of Deladier's government, whether German spies had taken over the French Government, and whether Hitler had normal sexual apparatus. Naturally, the last would invite the most hilarious and raucous speculation.

But it was clear that people were obsessed with spies and saw them everywhere. Perhaps they were not entirely wrong, because Raymond's friends too were always talking about the spy invasion of Paris.

One morning, I heard Raymond burst into loud laughter while he was reading his newspaper, and I was going through some of my sketches.

"You must hear this one, it deserves a prize. It appears that Hitler has imported thirty thousand gorillas from Brazil to be trained for an immediate attack on the Maginot Line!" I went into peals of laughter myself.

"Well, I suppose it is quite natural at times like this. Creating and spreading rumours becomes an entertaining occupation by itself when there is tension in the air and simmering underneath. Keeps everyone occupied and relieves the tension too. The funnier, the better."

But one subject that was always at the back of Raymond's mind, which bothered him quite a bit whenever he spoke of it, seemed almost taboo in Paris. Would the Maginot Line contain Germany forever?

Much as I enjoyed every bit of Paris, I was also getting exceedingly homesick. We had a lengthy letter from Henry giving us the latest news from England. Conscription had been announced for men between eighteen and forty-one, and all reservists had been recalled.

Lanverndel was progressing steadily, the basements and almost the entire ground floor had been brought to some shape. The exterior was done and work was progressing on the first floor. He suggested that we return as soon as our wing was completed, and was confident that by the middle of May we would be in a position to occupy at least part of Lanverndel. He added a single line in his usual taciturn style that we would be pleased to see it.

"Raymond, what happiness. I can't believe we'll be going home in a few weeks. I don't care what Lanverndel looks like or how comfortable it is. I just can't wait to be back. Oh, Raymond, it sounds too good to be true. Aren't you excited too?"

"If you want to know the truth, I'm more concerned about what's ahead of us. And believe me, I'm quite certain that England's troubles havn't even begun yet. Of course, I do want to reach home as soon as possible, but its more out of worry and concern. Let me tell you my dear, have whatever you want of your holiday now, because there won't be another for a very long time." He kept whistling silently between his teeth, and was deep in thought, but I felt a strange sense of foreboding at what he had said.

I was filled with a sense of disquiet, but nothing more than that. I could never visualize the Armageddon that the war was to be for the next five long years, taking the lives of millions of people all over the world. I was born just after the Great War of 1914. My father had been a doctor at the front and he would often tell me stories about it, and I knew Raymond had been fighting at the trenches of Salonika and Corfu even before I was born. But other than that, war held no particular significance for me, and the true horror of bombs and artillery, of blood and death, was yet to come.

"What a nasty business this war is. It's a pity Europe gets uneasy every few decades and decides upon a bloodbath." He mused on and was silent for a while. "And we in England must share the moral blame for allowing the Frankenstein monster to grow unchecked and turn a blind eye. Now we must pay for it."

I still couldn't comprehend too clearly or deeply what he was saying. I thought he was being unduly pessimistic. The idea of going home gladdened my heart so much that everything else dimmed in comparison, including the dangers at sea, or the growing Frankenstein.

"We have a long way to go. The Channel is risky; too many U Boats prowling around. We'll get back to Nice and take a boat to Gibraltar and then see what Dick suggests. I'm sure there must be some effective counter measures worked out by now."

It was time to leave Paris; Lanverndel was beckoning us—a Lanverndel risen from the ashes, and I couldn't wait to reach it. We decided to bid farewell to *drole de guerre* Paris with a last lark at Hotel de Ville. I wondered when we would visit here again, and I thought romantically that one day I would recount to my children and grandchildren of how we roistered in Paris in the time of a strange and silent war. It is indeed paradoxical how some of the happiest and most secure periods of our lives are when our immediate environment is a shifting, temporary thing, when our future is more or less unpredictable and sometimes when our very lives are surrounded by danger. I felt safe, I felt free and I felt secure when the silence was resounding violently from the Maginot Line, and the seas were ablaze with bombs and depth charges and shells. C'est la vie, as they kept repeating in this beautiful city of artists and lovers.

It was another of those elegant evenings which I had come to enjoy in measured portions. I tried to take in everything—the colours, the sounds, the affectations. The Frenchmen, faithfully conforming to their stereotype, always gasconading a little, handsome and flirtatious. The women, despite the exacting standards of fashion they were expected to comply with, showed simplicity and sympathy in their characters, quite opposed to the general image they projected. Just as we were settling down for dinner, and the music was gaining momentum, we caught sight of a familiar figure entering with a uniformed officer. She looked as chic and poised as I had seen her last, only more harassed. She saw us too and waved her hand elegantly, and they both came and joined us.

"Allo, both of you again, what a charming surprise," and she kissed us both in French fashion.

Raymond rose and Yvette went on, "Mr and Mrs de Villiers, Colonel Berthier. Oh, but we've all met before in Nice, I forgot." He was the same person whom we had seen at Nice. The men shook hands and the Colonel kissed my hand.

"So you're still in my country. I thought by now you would have reached home. So have you enjoyed Paris?"

"Very much indeed." The champaigne was making my speech quite versatile, and I was a little chattier than usual. "Our home should be getting ready, and we shall be leaving soon and hopefully reach safely. What a lovely city Paris is. We've enjoyed every bit of our stay here. I trust you have been well."

She looked at the Colonel and smiled, "Well, I haven't had a spare moment really. The girls are in college, and I have my hands full." She looked at me warmly and smiled and handed a card with her address to Raymond. "Keep this Ray, please. I have a feeling I shall meet you again sooner or later," and they took leave of us.

"Don't you think Yvette was a little mysterious?" I asked Raymond.

"If you ask me, I find the whole blasted place mysterious. There's probably a lot more going on than we know about. I wonder why she thinks we shall meet again."

"Perhaps she's planning to visit us at Lanverndel," I said with strong logic and no conviction.

And Lanverndel once again touched the key which unleashed the flood of memories. I saw the winding drive, heard the gravel crunch beneath my feet and the rainbow of blossoms glide before my eyes. I tried to visualize it with fresh paint. Would it look very different? Were his memories sufficiently sealed, or would they burn again? Well, that would be a moment to conquer, and I felt my thoughts sharpen. Thank God, getting used to the changed conditions of war and handling them would keep us all busy for a long time. There would be so much more to do than be helpless captives of memories and secrets, of walls and hallways that had since been incinerated and resurrected.

"And what are you thinking of so deeply, my dear one?"

"I was thinking of Lanverndel," I took the plunge, "Raymond, promise me darling, promise me you won't fight yourself or torture yourself. We're going home, to our Lanverndel and we'll find our happiness, I'm sure of it, and we'll not let anything destroy it."

Raymond raised his glass to me, "My brave little girl, what would I do without you? And to think that I should be the one taking care of you."

We bid good-bye to Paris with a slight wrench in our hearts. How beautiful and peaceful the countryside appeared. Who could believe that we were just a few days away from the blitzkrieg which was to swallow up this beautiful countryside and put its countrymen through so much humiliation, suffering and tragedy.

Chapter Nine

It was early May and the sun was hot when we reached Nice. There was so much to be done. We had to get in touch with Dick and ask him to help us get across to England. We had to get bookings on a boat to take us to Gibraltar. We had to inform the Consular office at Marseilles of our predicament and seek their assistance. The *drole de guerre* continued in its threatening silence, and by now everyone was just about fed up and had given it up as some kind of a joke. No bombs or bullets would come, no armies would march, and no soldiers would die. Poland and Norway were too far away to interfere with the simple, vain, mundane existence here.

We had a telegram from Henry informing us that Lanverndel was more or less in a state to receive us and that our wing was nearly ready and he was anxiously waiting for us to return. Though ecstatic with happiness, I was a little tense and subdued, as the journey back to England appeared at this moment one long, complicated obstacle course, and uppermost on my mind was how we'd ever get home safely.

Raymond attended to everything briskly and quietly. We got bookings for Gibraltar on the Queen Louise for the 11*th* of May, and if all went well, we would be in England within a week or so. The spring blossoms, the smell of peat and of wet earth coming to life again, the slow, golden sunrays weaving magical patterns in the air, sometimes glimmers, sometimes gilded silhouettes, the smell of the sea on my skin—well, it was just a few more days now.

We said our good-byes to the friends we had made here, to the hotel staff who has been so kind to us, to everyone who had been so helpful and hospitable when we had made our temporary home here. We settled our finances, paid our bills and got all set for the voyage up the Mediterranean. As usual there was a sadness in my heart before yet another departure, which even the joy of returning home could not mitigate.

"Raymond," I said, "why is it every time I leave a place I feel so sad. I keep telling myself there is no reason to, after all we're going home, but I keep feeling a heartache. I think Nice has always been a milestone in my life. You married me here and in a sense we got a new lease of life here too. But whenever I leave a place, I always get this awful feeling that I'm leaving a part of myself behind."

"Well, in a sense, you're quite right. Speaking realistically, and perhaps not so romantically, we do leave so much of ourselves behind, don't we, some astral part of ourselves—our smiles, our joys, our tears. Anyway, coming back to earth, we have been able to get a fairly good cabin on the Queen Louise. It sails tomorrow evening at four and we should be in Gibraltar two days later a little before noon. Dick will be there and has arranged our stay. He also promises he'll somehow safely see us through to England."

I said a silent goodbye in my heart to Nice, to Hotel le Neptune, to the sea and the sky, the boulevards and the palms, and a thanksgiving too; thanksgiving for helping me become a companion to my husband and not just a ward, for delivering Raymond from his private nightmares, for showering me with confidence, courage and a will to go on. And what happiness, we were to leave for home tomorrow. We thought we'd go driving around the coast and have one last feast in the sun at our favourite cove. We had both become beautifully brown and had acquired better health and appetite. We decided to leave after breakfast and just drive wherever our fancy took us. So after ordering our hamper of food and drink we settled down for breakfast.

I could immediately sense the unnatural, sinister ambience, so alien to Le Neptune. The sound of the wireless making announcements in the smoking room filtered through, and the guests were crowding in there, looking shocked or stunned. The broadcast was in French and sounded grim and sombre. I saw Raymond's expression change, his jaws harden, and his eyes sharpen. He looked as if he was trying to piece together and add up everything. Obviously, something very critical and serious was happening somewhere, and he went to the smoking room to enquire.

He returned with his face looking tense. "Very bad news. The Nazi army has smashed into the borders of Holland, Belgium and Luxembourg in the early hours of the morning. Their air force has started attacking Allied air bases and other targets in northern France. It seems pretty formidable."

"Oh God, so it's the real war, it finally had to come. Raymond, what are we going to do now? How will we ever get home?"

He was still tense. "I think we'll be able to sail tomorrow. The Mediterranean is quite safe. It's guarded from Malta and Gibraltar, and the Germans have no presence here. Italy is keeping quiet, and Monaco is expected to stay neutral or at least keep up appearances to that effect, but I suspect its sympathies are really with the Fascists." He continued to think and frown.

"But what about the sea? The war at sea will get worse. Oh, Raymond, what'll happen now? How will we ever reach home?"

"Let's not worry. Worrying never solved anyone's problems. Once we get to Gibraltar, we'll find a way of reaching home safely. Dick promises he will do something. And the Consulate informed me there are many more British citizens in the same boat. Literally."

I smiled, and felt a little better. I decided I must be optimistic and it was not difficult to make a reasonable beginning in that direction. It was after all by sheer chance and our good fortune that we had met Colonel Bromley on whom so much seemed to depend at this moment.

I remembered the swagger and nonchalance of Paris and its blind faith in its invincibility.

"Raymond, but what about the Allied forces in France? Surely they'll be able to contain the German army. You don't mean Hitler will overrun all of Europe?"

"Well, Hitler has certainly taken the Allies by surprise by attacking from the least expected quarters. The Allied forces have been concentrating on the Maginot Line and in Belgium. I wonder whether they'll be able to overcome this initial surprise. From the news, it appears that there's a very concentrated troop and tank movement. There's very little we can do more than we've already done except try and keep track of what's going on."

I felt so afraid and guilty. I had allowed myself to get caught in a slough of misplaced sentimentality. We ought to have gone back to England in October right after war was declared regardless of Lanverndel's state. But it was this strong instinct to protect ourselves from the past that had kept us back. We would have had to live in alien homes, with our own still burnt and blackened, and the past would definitely have come back to us with a vengeance. It would insidiously have preyed upon us and shattered whatever little hard earned sanity we had managed to acquire.

I don't know whether I was panicking or merely getting impatient.

"Raymond, let's leave today itself. What's the point of wasting time here anyway? Do you think it's possible to change the bookings for today?"

"My thoughts exactly. Let me try. I'll call up the reservations office right away. You go ahead with your breakfast. I'll join you shortly."

I waited for him to return. How fragile all our plans seemed in retrospect. Some person hundreds of miles away who did not even know of our existence had the power to alter them. How much of our actions and future do we really control, I wondered. I was getting deeper and deeper into this riddle when Raymond appeared.

"Don't look so worried, we're in luck. I've just managed to get the most luxurious cabin on this afternoon's boat. Just as we are leaving one day ahead of schedule because of the invasion, some true blue Monegasque bureaucrat has made a cancellation probably for the very same reason. So we travel in almost royal style, perched on the highest deck. How's that for a beginning? Oh yes, I must remember to keep Dick informed of the change of plans. And, now, I don't want to see the young lady worrying anymore. Come on, cheer up, everything is going to be fine."

I thought for a while. "I'm too ignorant about this war and all that goes with it to know its horrors. I do know that wars bring death and destruction and naturally I'm afraid of that. But what I'm more afraid of is that we're not in control of our lives anymore. Unknown others in unknown places seem to be directing us what to do and that I find quite frightening."

Raymond looked at me somewhat obscurely. "Yes, what you say is right. I know the feeling. I know exactly what it means to lose control and allow assorted external events to take over."

I felt a crackle of panic. Hell and damnation. I've done it again with my clumsy thoughtlessness. I've led him again to think about what we're here to forget.

I must have looked miserable and Raymond obviously saw it. He came to me and gently put his arm around my shoulders and said, "You know darling, how much of our lives we really control and how much is controlled by circumstances beyond our reckoning, we shall never know. But I've learnt one thing. We must believe that we control our lives. We must take our decisions as if we are exercising our own will, whether or not there's any such thing."

I let the words sink in; I'd ponder over them later, preoccupied as I was now with our imminent departure and Gibraltar and the U Boats. Free will and destiny would have to wait till Lanverndel. Raymond's entire energy and mind were focused solely on the days ahead. Of course he was tense, but it was a different kind of tension, a tension which arises out of a challenge which spurs one to action and not to seclusion and despair. And I was glad and relieved for that. At this moment, I don't think he even realized that what terrified me most, more than the bombs and the U Boats, were the shards of memories which would pierce him, and what he would undergo when they confronted him again at Lanverndel. With so much to think of and to do, the memories might pass by unnoticed. But first we had to reach Lanverndel.

We boarded the Casino Royale that afternoon. News on the wireless was depressing. There was no let up in the German onslaught, and the Allied forces and the British Expeditionary Force were in disarray. The Allies had apparently planned to meet the enemy only at Belgium; it had never occurred to them that there could be a major thrust into Holland and the Low Countries. The Dutch were fighting gallantly in the hope of receiving Allied reinforcements which were never to arrive.

The cabin was indeed luxurious and very commodious with charming furniture. There was excellent service, a billiards room, and an exclusive restaurant. But we were not in a state of mind to enjoy these little luxuries. We were both anxious and nervous and were trying to conceal it from each other. The result was quite disconcerting and quixotic. We spoke about inane trivia. I thought I'd put an end to this pretence.

"Raymond, let's go to the restaurant for dinner. It seems so grand, and it would relax us." Actually I just wanted both of us to be rid of our tensions. Having dinner in a restaurant would be a drill in itself, and would take our minds off from the worries of tomorrow.

There was a knock on the door. Raymond yelled out an "Oui", and went to open it.

There was a stocky man of medium height, about fifty, with dark curly hair, a beard and moustache, standing outside. His eyes were a clear blue.

"I would like to meet Monsieur Delatres, s'il vouz plait," the gentleman said with a steady eye and a heavy accent.

"There's no such person here." Raymond sounded irritated.

"But he is here, no?" he asked without expression.

"No, there was a change in bookings which you are perhaps not aware of."

"Pardonez. Then I am not aware of this. Please excuse me, excusez moi", he said with a disarming smile, without batting an eyelid, and he disappeared.

He spoke good English, grammatically correct, but with an undefinable accent. It could have been anything, French, Scottish, German, or even Scandinavian.

"Well, what was that all about?" said Raymond. Without pinning anything down precisely, we both felt a little perturbed about this incident, heaven knows why. Must have been our frayed nerves. There was really no need to be perturbed. After all, it was just an innocuous little mistake.

We dressed for dinner and went to the restaurant which seemed very stylish and expensive. There were just about a dozen people in there. The war had cast a shadow over everything, and we were pretty lacklustre ourselves. A spot of brandy might help, Raymond suggested. The sea was calm and beautiful, the sky clear and studded with stars, and the moon pure silver. But there were no lovers, no music, no laughter. Businessman were beating deadlines, the middle aged were fleeing for home, and the youth were at the frontiers either killing or getting killed. The twentieth century with its science and civilization was celebrating its coming of age.

We ate a quiet dinner, and since we were both tired, we slept early. I touched my pillow and was out in a second, so exhausted was

I both physically and mentally. After an initial period of dead sleep, I started tossing around and found the cabin becoming rather hot and stuffy. The boat was sailing smoothly, and the lights from some town or village on the shore were blinking happily. I rose and opened the large window facing north. The air was cool and refreshing, and I felt a strong urge to go on deck and watch the stars. It was about two in the morning, and Raymond was sleeping peacefully. He turned lazily in his sleep as I tiptoed out of the door on to the deck.

I looked up at the sky. It was a beautiful silvery midnight blue, bristling with stars. The air was fresh and inviting, and the moon glowed enchanting in its three quarter form. I tried to identify some constellations which my father had taught me when I was a little girl. I found the Great Bear and its pointers to the North Star. Orion the Hunter was just above the horizon. There was a magical silence disturbed only by the smooth throbbing of the ship over the waters. I walked to the edge of the deck and stood by the railing, my eyes wandering to the deck below. Everything around me was quiet and still. Only the Casino Royale disturbed the tranquility of the waters.

I suddenly sensed a movement on the deck below; there appeared to be some shadows flitting across. The shadows became shorter and I saw two figures emerge, their forms visible, moving towards the railing. They were gesticulating and talking, their arms and heads shaking in turns. It seemed as if they were arguing rather doggedly about something and were not able to come to an agreement.

It suddenly struck me that I found the forms familiar, and a queasy feeling started building up within me. I found myself becoming uncomfortable for no ostensible reason. I admonished myself severely—what was wrong if two men felt like some fresh air at this hour of the night? After all, wasn't I doing exactly the same thing? Why should that seem suspicious? And perhaps, all men looked familiar from behind at two in the morning.

But my eyes continued to be transfixed on them like magnets. They were inaudible from where I was, but after a while I could guess that their business was over and they were calling it a day. I heard a loud laugh, which again seemed familiar, a careless, derisive, almost vulgar laugh, and the two figures turned around to leave. I got a clear glimpse of both their faces in the moonlight. There was the man with the curly hair who had knocked at our door earlier this evening, hugging and kissing his goodbye in Latin fashion. And there was no mistaking the other man, the puffy face, the bullish torso, the heavy sagging jaw. I stared again, straining my eyes in the moonlight. No, there was no mistake. This was indeed Tom Camlin in flesh and blood on the deck below us, on the same ship. I must wake up Raymond immediately.

My heart was pounding violently as I tiptoed back to the room. I wondered if by any chance I had been seen. Not likely I thought. They hadn't looked up at all, I was certain of that. But I wasn't afraid. I would wake up Raymond and tell him what I had seen. He would know what to do. And then turmoil and fear seized me. I dreaded uttering that hateful name to Raymond, a name that would unleash what I wanted forever buried and forgotten. But there are some things which can never be done right and this was one of them.

He growled sleepily and tried to open his eyes, "Mmm, what's going on?"

"Raymond, listen, I have something to tell you. It's important I think. I saw Tom Camlin. He's here on this ship."

I saw his eyes widen, and his sleep disappear. He sat up on his bed almost immediately. "What was that? What did you say?"

"I couldn't sleep and I felt hot, so I stepped out to take in some fresh air. When I went to the far end of the deck, I saw Camlin on the deck below. He was talking to the man who had knocked at our door last evening. I'm certain of it. I stared hard at them in the moonlight. It was definitely Camlin. I even heard his laugh."

I must have sounded hysterical, agitated, but I couldn't help it. At least, I didn't sound afraid.

Raymond was pacing up and down, thinking hard. His face looked so transparent. I could almost see the thoughts flitting through his head. He lit a cigarette.

"I see. I wonder where he embarked—at Nice or Marseilles. But you're sure it was him?"

"Absolutely."

"Well, I suppose he has the right to travel, just as we have. Just don't let him bother us."

"But Raymond, it just didn't seem right. There was something about it that seemed so abnormal. What was he doing at two o'clock in the morning with our curly headed visitor? Who is this man in whose name this cabin was originally reserved? A Mr Delatres I think, whom our visitor mentioned. And there seemed to be a lot of familiarity between Camlin and our visitor. They were not talking like strangers. I wonder what all this means. And why did Curly Head knock here and expect Monsieur Delatres? Do you think he had a rendezvouz with him and didn't know about the last minute cancellation? Raymond, I must tell you, however stupid it might sound, but I am getting very nervous."

"What about, dearest? Why are you getting so nervous? Just ignore him. Remember your resolve?"

I didn't say a word. I knew by instinct something was wrong, but how does one say such a thing with any conviction or logic, when there is not a shred of evidence to back it, except a funny feeling inside you.

He continued. "Let's not get carried away. There's nothing wrong if two men are talking on deck at night, even if one of them happens to be Camlin."

"Oh Raymond, do please try and understand. I don't know how to explain it to you. It wasn't right. It just didn't seem right. If only you had seen them, you'd know what I mean," I persisted absolutely irrationally, but with the finality of the sixth sense. "And whatever they were doing was very underhand. I'm sure of that. Remember all that talk at Nice and Monte Carlo about spies and espionage. It could be anything."

Raymond seemed perplexed at my vehemence. "You really do seem upset." I could see he was intrigued and that's the way I wanted it. He lit another cigarette and was silent for a few minutes.

"Darling, do stop worrying, please." He kept frowning in that concentrated manner of his, puffing away and blowing rings in the air. And then to put me at ease, I think, he said, "Let's see what we can do...maybe, we could check the passenger list from the steward tomorrow morning. We'll tell him we expected a friend on board and give him Camlin's name and ask him to check whether he's here. This way, we can find out if he's travelling under his own name or not. If he's under a false name, it would mean he has false papers, and that makes the situation full of possibilities. Now does that make you feel better? But you're sure it was him?"

"One hundred percent certain. And if you ask me that just once more, I'll just scream."

He smiled. "Pardonez, Madame, but I'm always a bit dense at this hour of the morning."

Thank God, Camlin's name set us on a track other than that of nightmares. And I would deepen it as much as I could.

"Raymond, do you think Camlin knows we're here? Do you think it's us he's following?"

"No, I don't think so. It wasn't a secret that we were in Cote d'Azur. Everyone knew we were coming here. If he had wanted to bother us, he could have done so at Nice. But don't forget one more thing. We were not really scheduled to be on this boat. We got this cabin just six hours before departure. Anyway, let's wait for tomorrow and see whether he's travelling in his own name."

"Well, there's certainly never a dull moment in our lives — wars, voyages, spies, mystery, and now the Rock of Gibraltar." I was desperately trying to make my point.

"There, you've said it all. If a chap like Camlin travels under a false name, there would certainly be something fishy about it. He could either be a fugitive from justice or a spy, though God help any agency if they've recruited him. The man can be bought with one shot of whisky and starts boasting with two. Well, the Côte d'Azur is supposed to be swarming with spies currently...anyway let's see what happens tomorrow. Let's not jump to any conclusions."

Raymond kept thinking in silence, thinking through logic and reason, and probably considering various possibilities. But he was not reliving memories or being riddled with demons, and for that I was grateful. I had given Camlin the stamp of a spy or a criminal and planted the seed in Raymond's mind. Better he be branded that, even if without evidence, rather than be remembered as Charlotte's uncle or my husband's former cuckolder.

"I don't think we should go down for breakfast tomorrow. In any case, you'll probably wake up late. We can spend the day in the cabin or on our deck. There's so much reading material we have, and we can relax, for who knows what lies ahead. And now while we have this luxury, let's sleep. Goodnight darling," he yawned with his mind still somewhere else.

God, I prayed, let him not have any nightmares or memories of torment. Why must this happen to him all the time? Let the sun rise as soon as possible. Sunlight makes everything look so much simpler.

I snuggled close to him. "Raymond, if this vermin does anything to endanger our happiness again, I'm not going to merely stand by and watch. I hope he's a spy and he's caught and hanged."

The lights were off and it was dark. Raymond didn't say a word, he just held me close. There was really no need for words, for they would have only disturbed the peace and completeness of the moment. And so we drifted off to sleep.

****

As expected I woke late the next morning, around nine o clock. Raymond was already in the little sitting room with the wireless. I called his name and he was by my side.

"What's the news?" I asked sleepily.

"Not good at all. There's fighting in Holland and Belgium and there seems to be no effective counter attack. The march is going on unchecked, and the Nazis are parachuting troops in Holland and taking over bridges and airports. They're pouncing upon Belgium and it looks like total chaos. The British Expeditionary Force has been a singular disaster, and I think, soon, the much vaunted Maginot Line will become the saddest joke in history."

"Oh dear," said I, but my mind was elsewhere.

"Were you able to check about Camlin?" I asked. The first thing I had thought of on waking was the disturbing incident I had stumbled upon in the dead of the night.

"Yes, your suspicious were right. There's none by that name on board."

"So what does that mean? I wish we could find out who this Curly Locks is. That could give us a hint of the business he might have had with Mr Delatres."

"I don't think we can find that out without arousing suspicion. The best we can do is to stay in our cabin today. We can rest and sleep and listen to some good music. That way we make sure our presence remains concealed from Camlin and his cronies. Let's be amongst the last to disembark when we reach Gibraltar tomorrow. Then we can see whether those two are together, whether they show any familiarity or whether they pretend to be strangers. If they had to wait till two in the morning to discuss their affairs, in all probability they must be pretending to be strangers. Let's wait and see."

Tom Camlin was now a confirmed criminal or an undercover man in my mind, and after all my efforts, I hoped in Raymond's too. Raymond was brimming with energy this morning, and I could see that his mind was working only on Gibraltar and reaching home. That was indeed a blessing, for now the burning, humiliating memories would remain unsprouted and buried; the instinct for survival would see to that. And the strange puzzle which I had chanced upon last night would keep us further occupied.

The day passed quickly and quietly. We didn't budge from our cabin and I remained utterly lethargic and lazy, reading, sketching and dozing. We sat and strolled on deck after dark, hoping for a continuation of last night's adventure, but nothing happened. We strained our eyes and ears but there were no signs of Camlin or his curly headed friend.

The next morning the valet brought in the breakfast and stayed on to pack our bags, while we sat on the deck under a huge bright umbrella. The journey was coming to an end and we would soon be removed from our secure little cocoon, and would have to face the fearsome, bloody reality of wartime Atlantic. And we really had no idea how things would take off from here.

It was almost midday and the Casino Royale was reaching Gibraltar. We could see the giant size rock from our deck, and the little town sprawled around it. But we were too preoccupied with the unpleasant possibilities that we had yet to undergo, to enjoy the sun or the panoramic view. The ship inched towards the harbour, dropped anchor, and the passengers were getting ready to disembark. We told the valet that we would like to leave after the rush was over. From a certain position on our deck, we would keep a watch on the gangway leading ashore. We got a glimpse of the curly haired man. He seemed to be in a hurry to leave and was travelling very light. Our eyes traversed the entire length and breadth of the gangway but Camlin was nowhere. Had he also like us decided to leave last, for the same reason? The valet seemed to be getting impatient. Almost everyone on the gangway had already left. We were mystified and started moving slowly down the passage towards the gangway, but before we reached there, we finally saw him. He was wearing a tropical suit and a Panama hat, and I saw again the same puffy, alcoholic face, the salacious eyes. I saw Raymond staring hard at him and I choked the sharp, resigned pain which travelled through me, thinking of what he must have had to endure. I thought of a ruse of how not to get to the gangway, and more importantly, to distract him.

"Raymond, I think I've left my ear tops in the bathroom. I'll just run up and get them. Wait for me here, please."

The valet looked exasperated. Raymond took shelter behind a pillar. I ran up to the cabin, stayed there for a few minutes, and dashed down again. By then, Camlin had already left.

"So sorry for making you wait. I seem to be getting so forgetful." I smiled at the valet graciously.

We walked in silence through the exit, and saw Richard just outside.

"Welcome to Gibraltar," he said, shaking hands with us. Gibraltar had given a military preciseness to his speech and movement, and he was no more the dapper, backslapping, colonel we had seen at Nice. The midday sun was hot as we drove off in his car.

"This is absolutely amazing," I cried in disbelief, as I stared at the famous rock. It dwarfed the one at Monte Carlo so completely.

"So it is," said Richard. "It's about one thousand five hundred feet high, solid limestone. And it is this promontory which gives Britain complete control of the fourteen mile strait between the Atlantic and the Mediterranean."

And it would be Gibraltar's ships and guns and planes which would later protect us on our way home.

"Well, our lives are getting more and more dominated by great rocks." Raymond looked at his cousin and smiled. "So what's up Dick? Obviously this must be an extremely busy time for you. And it's dashed nice of you to take all this trouble for us." Raymond seemed relieved that we had a dependable ally close to us at this dangerous and unpredictable time.

"Thank God we met you. It's only because we knew you were here that we didn't panic, and thank you for all your help while we were at Nice," I said.

"Yes, thanks awfully Dick."

"Don't mention it, old chap. There's suddenly a whole lot to be done, naturally, with the situation at the European front. The Nazi army is marching unchecked. They appear tough, their artillery and air force. A lot of fiascoes can happen in the near future. I only hope that my assessment is proved wrong. "

"I suppose there must be a lot going on here, both militarily and otherwise," said Raymond.

"Yes, first and foremost, the civilians have to be evacuated, either to England or the Azores. Security is a constant concern here. Spain is riddled with German agents, and the construction labour here is almost entirely from La Lince, the neighbouring Spanish town. And now with France so vulnerable, there are so many defence and coordination arrangements to attend to. I do hope the French manage to put up a good fight."

The car reached the Army base, and Dick took us to his quarters. The beer was tantalizingly chilled and we had a quick lunch of salad, cold meats and tropical fruit.

"After lunch, I'll ask the driver, to drop you off at your hotel. Most hotels are empty. This is a small place as you know, just about three miles long and three quarters of a mile wide. If times were different you could have stayed with me. But now everything is restricted."

There was so much activity apparent. Army vehicles were moving about, planes could be heard taking off and landing, and it appeared as if most of the town was already evacuated. Other than soldiers and sailors in tropical dress, I had hardly seen anyone else.

"Dick, how soon can we get a ship to take us home?" I asked almost pleading.

"I think we'll just wait for a few more days to see how the war in Europe goes. Presently, the Atlantic is a good deal calmer since the U Boats are mostly operating in Norwegian waters. We have now decided that ships should only move in convoys with armed escorts. We're expecting a convoy to leave shortly, and I give you my word you'll be part of it, but you won't be travelling in the lap of luxury, I assure you." He looked at me and smiled.

"As long as we just get home, that's enough," I said gratefully.

"That should be soon enough, I'm sure," Dick said quite definitely. "Raymond, you'll have to excuse me now, I have a lot of little jobs to attend to. Maurice, that's the driver, will see you to the hotel and you could rest for a while. I hope you weren't sea sick," he said looking at me.

"No, not at all, the sea was very calm and as usual, blue as turquoise."

"Well Raymond, I'll call you around six in the evening, and perhaps we could dine together. Let's see how the European front is doing. That has a very direct bearing on your impending journey." He started looking a little anxious as if he had an awful lot of things to attend to. "So, shall see you around eight, I hope. Oh yes, blackout is very strictly observed, so try and finish whatever sightseeing you want to do before dark.

We walked out and the sentries on duty clicked their heels for a smart salute. Maurice was asked to take us to our hotel. I was hot, sticky and exhausted and thought longingly of the cool greenery of England. This place was so terribly brown and brutal, besides which the heat and the fatigue had made me irritable. I suddenly remembered Tom Camlin, and wondered what he was doing here.

We reached our hotel, a Victorian masterpiece of colonnade design, surrounded by beautiful green manicured lawns and trees planted artistically. The building squarely faced the Atlantic sea shore. We were taken to a suite of cool rooms with high ceilings and solid walls and pillars. Wire mesh doors and windows ensured a cool cross ventilation right through and ceiling fans lazily circulated the air. I was utterly exhausted and as soon as the luggage was brought in and the doors closed, I collapsed on the soft white sheets and experienced the deepest sleep that I have ever had. When I woke up, it was already five o'clock, and the sun was still blazing. I felt heavy and dull; possibly the weather and tropical sea air wasn't very good for me. Raymond was reading the bunch of English newspapers that Dick had given him, and he looked cool and fresh in white trousers and shirt.

"Raymond, this is not fair. You look as if you're in the midst of a nice, lazy holiday, and I'm feeling so terribly horrid, so clammy and hot and dull. I'm going to have a cool shower, and also dress in white like you, and then maybe, I'll feel better."

I did what I said. There's nothing as refreshing as a cold shower on a heated body and mind. I wore a cool white linen dress but no stockings, and felt decidedly more comfortable and easy.

Raymond had asked for tea and sandwiches in the verandah. Neither of us was really hungry, but the ritual of tea was such a rigid fixture of the day that one could really never breach it.

The phone rang. It was Dick. He said dinner appeared quite impossible as the evening for him had taken an unexpected turn. I gave the phone to Raymond.

"That's a pity old chap, we were so looking forward to seeing you...I'm absolutely okay...she's a little droopy; it's the heat I think...I'll tell her so...thanks awfully, that's splendid. Fine...take your time, whenever you're satisfied. We're prepared to move at an hour's notice...we'll just go over, send a few telegrams to England, and generally take a look at the place. Thanks awfully again. Good-bye Dick."

"Well, a pity Dick can't come this evening. He's caught up in too much work. But he's sending Maurice with the car, so we can take a little outing in town. I'd like to send a telegram to Henry and Rupert and to inform them of our latest situation and plans."

He must have noticed my lack of enthusiasm. "Come on, I'm sure an outing will make you feel better. Oh yes, Dick says we must drink a lot of fresh lemon juice with water, salt and sugar. It's supposed to compensate for the salt we lose through sweat. Let me call for some."

"Raymond, what's in the newspapers? Anything of note?"

"Generally depressing. The war is going badly for the Allies. I didn't realize it but there have been enormous tonnage losses for Britain. Passenger ships are being sunk in total disregard of international law. The Nazis have authorized the sinking of every kind of British ship, passenger, cargo, merchant, anything. I believe the British Navy is now organizing convoys of ships with armed escorts, and it appears this measure is bearing some success. Another positive development from our point of view is that most of the German offensive navy is deployed in the Norwegian waters, and that definitely makes our voyage safer."

The lemon juice arrived, and we sipped it slowly, as if it were a dry white wine; it was cool, refreshing and pungently sweet and sour. I felt it revitalize me almost immediately.

"Oh, by the way, the Surrey eleven are playing Sussex next Sunday."

I smiled. Dear Raymond. No war or heat or fatigue could distract him from news of cricket.

"I wonder where we'll be next Sunday," I said wistfully.

I was feeling a little better. What I wanted foremost was a brisk walk in the fresh, green downs, in pure English spring. I hated this brown, barren, country with its dreary monotone. Or maybe I was here at a wrong time and in a wrong season. I wished I wasn't so irritable.

Dick's car was waiting for us and it was a mere five minute drive to the centre of town. We went first to the telegraph office and shot off telegrams to England. Maurice took us to some usual tourist spots of Gibraltar which were still open to the public and then to a view point to catch the majestic sunset over the Atlantic just in the nick of time. We saw the fiery golden orange orb sink lower and lower into the water. There was a spread of gold, then vermillion over the horizon, and then a sad kind of orange bidding goodbye to the world, as the ocean drowned the sun completely. And finally the traces of the sad orange and pink started to disappear and a violet and dusky blue took its place, and then as if by magic, there was a burst of stars in the clear, darkened sky. Congratulations, I thought, you have finished another daily chore, and will now be illuminating some other part of the world. What if you should decide not to rise tomorrow? What an absurd thought, reflective of my general irritation and ill temper. I was now getting more and more angry with myself for becoming a prisoner of my own foul mood.

We drove into town, and I thought I'd like a quick, bracing walk in the main shopping street to pep me up. We saw little shops with curios, some Spanish, some English, bright coloured scarves and an amazing variety of leather craft. There was a large bookstore in the middle of the street which was bustling with customers—soldiers, sailors, local people were browsing through books and magazines, or buying greeting cards, stationery or pin ups.

"Let's look through the bookstore," said Raymond. He always had a great love for browsing through bookstores in unusual places, hoping to discover some rare publications or something which he had been looking for but which had gone out of print in England. "I'm sure we'll find something interesting. One usually does in these kind of places. I realize it is getting late, but we could just take a quick look, and if it holds promise, we can come back tomorrow. We must also collect some good reading material for our journey ahead, which I hope doesn't turn out too unpredictable."

I must have looked unenthusiastic. "And we might even chance upon something to brighten the mood," he smiled with a tease in his eyes.

I really wasn't in the mood for book browsing but I agreed for his sake. He wanted to pick up the English papers and journals he had missed in the last few weeks.

The bookshop was well laid out and spacious, with topics indicated on the tall shelves. I thought I would stroll around the store and see if anything interested me, and Raymond was right, it might lift my spirits. I stopped by at the Art Section, and started leafing through some work on Picasso and Dali, whose treatment of lines and cubes interested me a great deal. This part of the store was almost empty; there was just another person with his back turned who seemed to be examining some thick leather bound volumes quite intently. He left shortly after placing them back in their assigned positions. There was a mirror near the entrance, a decorative sort of a mirror with an arched top and gilt frame and my eyes inadvertently went to it. I caught a glimpse of him from where I was standing. His face was bent downwards as if deep in thought, and his wavy hair which was brushed backward seemed hard to manage, for it kept falling over his face and his spectacles.

It was nearing seven now, but the bookstore seemed to be getting more and more festive. People were laughing and talking loudly, some in Spanish, some in English, and it appeared to me that this was a regular evening haunt; not surprising, since everyone must have been hungry for news and reading material at a time like this. I was tired and wanted to go back to the hotel and rest, and perhaps we could come back here the next day and sift through the store in a more relaxed manner. Raymond was standing near the billing counter with a pile of papers and magazines. As soon as he saw me, he turned as if to go once again to one of the shelves to his right. My companion from the art section had picked up a newspaper and a magazine and was waiting to pay.

"That would be two shillings, six pence half penny. Would you be here long?" The proprietor was trying to be friendly. The man nodded with a mechanical smile, paid, and left the shop.

I went to join Raymond in his corner still looking at the books on the shelves. He made a gesture cautioning me to be quiet.

After checking the main entrance door with his eyes, he said in a hushed tone, "Did you see the man who just paid his bill and left?"

"Why, yes. I got a glimpse of him in the mirror. He was browsing through the art section like me."

"Did he pick up anything to buy?"

"Yes, I think he just bought a magazine and a paper."

"Any books?"

"No, I don't think so. I think he put them back on the shelves. Why do you ask Raymond?"

"Can you guess who he was?" he asked with an interesting expression which I could not make anything of.

"Anyone I know? I really didn't take too much notice of him," I said rather disinterestedly.

"Well, I got a good look at his face while I was near the entrance. As soon as I saw him I knew it was someone I had seen in the last few days. I racked my brains, and it didn't take me long to place him, sans beard and all. You see, I had got a direct look at his face when I opened the cabin door in the Casino Royale. You were further off in the cabin. And I couldn't mistake those eyes even through the glasses he now wears. I got a glimpse of them when he was talking to the proprietor. And as soon as I realized who he was, I ducked to this corner. I don't think he saw me, as his head was lowered when he was walking. My dear, this is none other than whom you call Curly

Locks, our mysterious visitor at the Casino Royale whom you saw the other night with Camlin. He has obviously shaved off his beard and whiskers, cut his hair shorter and is wearing glasses. So your instinct seems to have been right after all. Something is certainly not right in this whole affair."

"That's right. What a fool I am. I did find him familiar, but then I rebuked myself for finding everyone familiar of late. You're absolutely right—the same blue eyes even behind those spectacles. But what on earth is he doing here?"

"I think I can venture a safe guess. Are you in the mood for a little adventure?"

"Depends on what you have in mind," I said, pouting. I was still tired.

"Let's pay our bill and I'll tell you what I have in mind. And try and keep your back to the door."

I did as I was told. Raymond paid the bill and asked casually,

"Could you please tell me your working hours? Its late now, but we'd like to come again first thing in the morning and spend some more time here. You have such an unusual collection."

"Thank you sir. We're open nine to eight, with a break between one thirty and four. Thank you and good night sir."

"Good night. We hope to be back tomorrow."

"My pleasure, sir."

We walked out of the shop. There was a café on the other side of the street, not directly opposite, but so situated that we could if we wished keep an eye on anyone leaving or entering the shop.

"Let's go to that café, and I promise you, I think we'll see some action. The bookshop is open for another half hour. Remember, speak very softly, because at a time like this everything animate or inanimate has very sharp ears."

I was a little flummoxed, but I had by now started getting a little involved in Raymond's sense of anticipation. He looked as if he had something very definite in mind, and I got the feeling it was important. I wished I hadn't been so pernickety and irritable, as I so wanted to be part of what now looked more and more like a cloak and dagger affair.

We sat down in a place where we could see people entering and leaving the bookshop, ourselves remaining unseen. Raymond kept an eagle eye on the door and we ordered our coffee which came almost immediately.

"Now, here's my hypothesis. A French speaking man with beard and whiskers knocks at our door asking for a Monsieur Delatres who is probably the Monegasque bureaucrat who cancelled his booking. Then you see the same fellow and Camlin at an unearthly hour talking on deck. They disembark at Gibraltar, but not together, and we know that Camlin is travelling under a false name. That evening we see Curly Locks without his beard and whiskers, a different haircut and with spectacles, browsing through leather bound books in a bookshop. This, my dear, seems to have all the makings of a classical wartime story of subversion. Our advantage is that we know of their presence on the ship, we have seen them pretend as strangers, and now we see one of them trying to change his general appearance and meddling with books in a bookstore. My best bet is that Camlin will enter the bookshop before it closes."

My heart missed a beat. The name of Camlin churned again all the hateful emotions I had tried to extinguish. And I smelt danger. Camlin was unscrupulous, mercenary and absolutely amoral. I could quite visualize him in the role of a criminal or a spy—he would do anything for easy money, be it blackmail or treason.

"Isn't this getting dangerous Raymond? Shouldn't we tell Dick about it? He did mention something about the town being riddled by espionage agents."

"Yes, we should, but unless there is something concrete to report, we would end up looking a little absurd, and would unnecessarily put Dick through a lot of trouble at a time when he can ill afford it. If Camlin does come here in the next few minutes, then we have a hard amount of circumstantial evidence to report, and not just that, it would be our duty as British subjects to do so."

"But what makes you think Camlin will come now and not tomorrow morning? He could easily come tomorrow, and I'm not looking forward to sitting in the café all day tomorrow waiting for him," I said, already weary at the thought.

Raymond continued convivially, "Elementary, my dear detective. If Camlin comes now, he can secure whatever he's looking for or has been concealed for him there, and work upon it tonight. Otherwise, he must waste another day, and anything can happen between now and then, both to him or to his material."

My heartbeat was racing with fear and suspense. I couldn't bring myself to believe that I was becoming a star witness to what could possibly be an espionage plot threatening the British military or navy. It seemed so dramatic and farfetched. But even at this unreal moment when treason and espionage were likely to unfold before me, I thanked God for giving Raymond an antidote to the memory and associations of Tom Camlin. It was the question of possible treason against England which engaged his entire mind right now, and he appeared oblivious to everything else.

I had spoken without much thought last night on the Casino Royale when I had wished that Camlin were a spy and would be hanged. And now that I was actually being confronted with such a possibility, I must say, I was completely confused and unbelieving.

"Well, what have we here?" Raymond said softly. His jaw was taut, lips tightly pursed, but in his eyes there was exhilaration; his wits had been put to test and his forecast had been accurate. There was that particular glint of satisfaction in his eyes such as men have when they've been proved right.

The last rays of light were adequate for me to recognize the huge, ox-like torso moving heavily towards the shop. In tropical clothes he looked even more indecent. His walk was a bit unsteady; it was as if he had already downed half a bottle of whisky. What kind of secret agencies were these, I wondered, that hired such unsteady, inebriated parasites.

Raymond's jaw was clenched in tension and suspense. We saw Camlin go into the shop. It was nearing closing time and the shop windows were being shut. Within five minutes he re-emerged with a package which appeared to contain a thick volume within it. He adjusted his hat and walked down the street just as the curly haired man had done.

Raymond was rapt in concentration. "I think this clinches it. The number of coincidences is getting a little too suspicious. We should now tell Dick.

We'll ask Maurice to take us to him and this brooks no delay. It may be dangerous."

We paid for the coffee, almost ran to the car, and asked Maurice to take us to Colonel Bromley urgently, as it was something extremely important.

It was now quite dark. But no street lights came on; houses and shops were bandaged with black, and the few motor vehicles on the road moved stealthily with veiled headlights. Only the moon couldn't be blackened. Defiantly and brazenly, it kept shining and sending light into this war torn world.

"I'll do my best, sir. You know its restricted area. I'll call the Colonel from the sentry post and ask him what he would like me to do."

We reached the sentry post, and Maurice got off. We could hear him speaking to Dick.

"It's okay sir. Colonel Bromley is just finishing dinner and he's asked me to bring you to the Officer's Mess."

Maurice gave the password, the gate opened, and we drove through the grounds to the Officer's Mess. Dick greeted us very military like in the main hall, and in the dim light I could sense its martial grandeur. There were trophies of war from the many campaigns fought by the British armies, stuffed tigers fiercely standing by, antler's horns and tiger skins decorating the walls, and some marvellous paintings of British forces in different parts of the world.

"So what have we, Raymond. Hope you've had a good day. Sorry about not showing up for dinner but there's such an awful lot going on. Looks as if I'll have to go into the wee hours of the morning, if I want to finish all that I have to."

"Awfully sorry to bother you Dick, but there've been a series of events which we think you should know about." And he recanted the entire tale starting from the change of bookings and Curly Lock's knock, the episode on the deck and the events at the bookstore. Dick listened like a professional without the slightest change of expression, his eyes alert but impassive, his mind absorbing every detail.

"Now Dick, there's something I must tell you...this Camlin happens to be a sort of uncle of my first wife Charlotte...."

The world stood still for me. Raymond continued speaking in a matter of fact manner. His words came like an echo from far beyond. "...his record as I know it is bad...he's totally unscrupulous, and I believe he doesn't do anything in particular for a living... as a matter of fact, he had been trying to blackmail us ever since the circumstances of Charlotte's death went before the coroner...."

Was all this necessary, I wondered, my mind numb but my defenses intact. And yes, I also couldn't help but be overjoyed by the unfazed naturalness of his voice. The last time I had heard Raymond utter her name was on that final grim night at Lanverndel when he had bared his soul to me, when we were a hair's breadth away from ruination. And though it seared my ears now as it fell upon them, it seemed less forbidding, less frightening. The war, its exigencies and compulsions, had extinguished the base, primeval fear of her name, just as it had broken our unspoken covenant of silence.

His voice kept echoing "...no, we checked the passenger list. He's obviously travelling with false papers."

"That's happening quite frequently. We have at least six thousand people crossing the Spanish border both ways every day, for construction work and other day to day activity. The Abwehr is extremely active in Spain, and naturally it is trying to penetrate into Gibraltar. Now let's see what we can do about this."

He picked up the phone and called up his Adjutant, Captain Beck.

"Tony, can you get the files on the Abwehr suspects ready? I think we might have some work to do. I'll be there shortly."

And turning to Raymond, "Thank you for informing me. Let's start with the elimination process. I'll show you some photographs, and let's see if you can identify anyone."

I wondered whether my anxiety and apprehension were visible. Of course, I was in an unsettled state, but also creeping very slowly was a frisson of exhilaration such as one feels when a demon or an evil thing is being destroyed.

We walked to the office nearby. The camp was bustling with activity even in the moonlit darkness. Army vehicles were moving about, soldiers were briskly attending to their responsibilities and guarding the perimeter. By the time we reached the office, past several sentries and guards, Captain Beck was waiting for us ready with his papers.

Dick introduced us and we sat down at his table where a bright table lamp focused on the centre of the desk. Everything else was dark. Captain Beck looked curious, but didn't say a word. Raymond leafed through the photographs in the dossier files, and kept putting them away. He scrutinized one for a longer time and put it aside. By the time he had finished with the lot, there were three files kept aside. He studied them for a while and turned to Dick.

"If you notice, these three photographs are somewhat similar, receding foreheads, aquiline noses, thin lips. The facial bone structure is also more or less the same. With some camouflage, our curly haired man could be one of these."

"Right," said Dick very professionally, "we'll do a check on them. Could you please give us a description of Camlin?"

"Of course," Raymond was absolutely impassive. "He's about six feet tall, heavy, weight may be about two hundred pounds plus, blue eyes, reddish hair, and a reddish skin, heavy thickset neck, and heavy features." The adjutant was noting everything.

"Now we'll start our side of the drill. I'll have someone posted at the bookstore; it seems to be some kind of a clearing house or rendezvouz. Tony, I think you should get on with whatever information we have. It could be serious. Any questions?"

"No sir, I'll be at it right away, I'll keep you informed of the progress."

"Good." Captain Beck left with his dossiers.

"Well, Raymond, I must be off too." Dick stood up, and tried to tidy up the papers on the desk.

"How's the European front, Dick?" Raymond asked as we rose.

"Bad. The Allied Expeditionary Force has been an utter failure. No coordination at all, and too much bickering. The Germans are advancing by the hour into Holland and Belgium, and who knows what's to happen in France."

He lapsed into silence, into his own confidential, military thoughts, a frown gathering on his face.

He turned towards us. "Incidentally, I meant to tell you this tomorrow, an armed convoy is leaving for England very shortly, and God willing, you should reach home within about ten days. Strictly confidential, of course. You'd appreciate that I can give you the exact time of departure only a few hours in advance. So just be prepared to leave at any moment."

Looking at me he said, "You must be exhausted. Do try and stay indoors and conserve your energy. The voyage ahead may be difficult and not very comfortable. I'll do my best though," he said with a smile and the worried frown still on his face.

"Thanks again Dick, and now we'll take leave of you. In any case, I don't think I can do anything except stay indoors tomorrow. I'm so exhausted." And I wished him good night.

"Well, I'm certainly not going to miss my visit to the bookshop, same time." Raymond couldn't resist adding.

"Can't stay out of mischief, eh? I'm reminded of the grand old days." Dick gave a comrade's pat on Raymond's shoulder. "Well, well, I'll be in touch tomorrow. Let's hope we have some developments by then. Call immediately if you come across anything new. And now, I must get on, the evening has just begun, I suppose. Maurice will drive you to your hotel. Good night." He smiled and showed us to the door.

"Good night Dick, hope things are not as bad as they look. And thanks for everything." Maurice was waiting and took us to the car.

We arrived at the hotel through the dark roads and were dead with fatigue. The coffee had killed my appetite and I didn't feel like any dinner. Raymond settled for some soup and we helped ourselves to the delightful Mediterranean fruit—succulent grapes, tangy oranges, and honey sweet figs. We were grateful for the meagre quota of light permitted in the room. How different this was from the spurious blackouts of the *drole de guerre*, which had blazed with lights as if in vengeance. But then Paris would always be Paris. Raymond was immersed in thought. He must have been thinking of the journey back home, dangerous and unpredictable as it appeared, and beneath it, disquieting and real, must have loomed the spectre of Tom Camlin and what lay ahead.

"I wonder what will happen." I was ruminating aloud absentmindedly. "And I'm so tired and so cross and I don't want any more high drama in my life. I wish we were back in England in the peace and quiet of Lanverndel. And I'm so terribly sleepy. I'll be out in a second, I'm sure. Are you worried, darling?" I asked Raymond on impulse.

"I'm not as worried as I'm tired. Yes, we've had more than our share of adventure, that's undeniable, but this Camlin and Curly Locks affair does seem serious. I get the feeling that it won't be long before they're nabbed. Our trump card was that they neither individually nor jointly knew what we knew or had seen, both on the ship and out here. This is what they call the X factor, something which cannot be foreseen even in the most carefully conceived plan—the hand of fate almost."

"Raymond let's sleep, and I'm sure I'll get up only around lunch time," I gave a lengthy yawn and lay down.

"Good night my sweet, sleep well. I'll try and catch the wireless and see what's going on in England and the Atlantic."

Much as I had thought that sleep would overtake me instantly, in actual fact it eluded me completely. It would beckon to me gently like a siren, but every time I came close to it, I would receive a pounding rebuff and my thoughts would start drifting again in confusion. Something was troubling me, riveting something unpalatable and disturbing somewhere in my mind. I tried to search for it and after some effort I saw it...I would take the plunge and ask him...but suppose he became angry or resentful and unforgiving? Nevertheless, I had to ask I decided, for our sake and to give relief to ourselves by talking about things we were both avoiding.

I went to him and said softly and unsurely, "Raymond, please don't be upset, but I'm asking you this because I love you and I don't want you to suffer alone and in silence. Tell me, that this damned Camlin affair is not distressing you too much. Tell me please, as I don't know how much more we still have to see of him, and I won't have you experience another hell in solitude. Please don't be angry at what I've said."

Raymond stopped arranging the newspapers, and looked at me with gentleness and gratitude. He took my face in both his hands, "Why do you say this? Why do you expect that I should be angry? And what is there left to conceal from you? You have known the worst and have loved me in spite of it. You have shared with me for better or for worse just as the vow commands...if it wasn't for you, your innocence, your purity, your loyalty and love, who knows what would have become of me...I might not have even been alive today. Let me be quite truthful, I'm not worried about Camlin or anybody. I've been learning from you too...there's a good bit of defiance that has sprung in me too. Yes, fearful memories sometimes get stirred, but that can't be helped...there are blessings too that I can count. I have you, we've survived and are happy, and we'll make a life together somehow. Yes, there are things I want to forget, but there are also things I want to remember, and I do so, happily and gratefully.

So it evens out really...But I'm not resigned, I'm full of hope... for the future which will deliver me from the past, I'm sure. No, I'm not worried about Camlin. I'll deal with him as one man deals with another. Go to bed now. I'll just catch up on the news and join you. Good night, my magic talisman." He kissed me with protectiveness and a sense of peace, and we were still and silent as if we had just discovered the creation of the world.

My head touched the pillow, and after a while I started floating in the streams of mid consciousness. I saw Camlin laughing loudly and lasciviously, and Charlotte, whom I had never seen in person or in a picture frame, alive or dead, her eyes becoming snaky, slithering out of my mind. I saw the Eiffel Tower and ships being bombed in the Atlantic...and then Camlin was being interrogated in a cell which I had seen once in the movies...I saw Lanverndel, black, charred and orphaned, beckoning me to take charge of it, and I kept drifting further and further into the woods, into the sky, into the sea, and then into black, dead sleep.

Chapter Ten

A blaze of sunlight entered the room as I parted the curtains next morning on waking. The sun seemed almost overhead as I lethargically started to enter the day. I was beginning to get a little annoyed with myself for no real reason. There was a note by my bedside. "Have had a summons from Dick. Don't know what time I'll be back. Have your breakfast and call me at Dick's office. Love, Raymond."

Why did I feel so irritable this morning? After such a long and deep sleep I still did not feel refreshed. I had a cold shower. This Mediterranean heat was really sapping me. I thought I'd order breakfast, but my stomach recoiled at the thought and I felt no appetite. My mind drifted to what Raymond had said last night. It was really the first time since leaving England that he had spoken so explicitly about himself without reserve or reticence, and also

I think with a sense of definitiveness and purpose. A feeling of pride and accomplishment lifted my spirits, and I smiled secretly to myself.

I was now getting quite curious about l'affaire Camlin. I called Dick's office, told them who I was, and asked for Raymond. A strong male voice was saying, "Mr de Villiers is not available right now. I will inform him you called, ma'am, and he'll call you back."

The feeling of dullness and listlessness came over me again and I found the humidity getting unbearable. Overhead, the fan hummed monotonously. I dressed in a light cotton dress and thought I would sip a cool lemonade in the verandah and do some sketches of the Atlantic and the rocks. We were to leave shortly and I was not coming to grips with anything. Our stay at Gibraltar lay under the shadow of Camlin and his partner, and what was to become of them was in a way quite material to the days before us. Would there be one last confrontation between Raymond and Camlin? I hoped and prayed that it would truly be the last, after which he would be out of our lives forever. From the way Raymond had spoken last night, I concluded he was quite prepared to face whatever lay ahead. It would be man to man, he had said, and I felt fairly certain that the fight was back in him.

It was getting to be lunch time. The jug of lemonade was empty and my sketching was disastrous. The lines appeared artificial, contrived, without any natural flow. A parody of the wild rocks and the placid ocean. I put them away in disgust. There was still no word from Raymond. I wondered if he was somewhere where he couldn't use a phone. I kept imagining Camlin and his partner being questioned in a cell. Perhaps Raymond was identifying them. The cell kept flashing before my eyes. I wished he'd come back soon—I felt so lost without him. I couldn't read and I didn't want to turn on the wireless and hear more bad news about the war. I started feeling groggy and limp again, and I thought I'd darken the room and just lie down and shut my eyes. The infernal heat and humidity were sapping me.

Finally the phone rang. It was Raymond. "Darling, it's me. Sorry about rushing off, but you must have guessed why." His voice sounded springy, vibrant and totally in command. There appeared to be a lot going on there.

"Not really. Is everything all right? Are you okay?"

"Yes, I'm fine. I'll explain everything later. I think you'll have to come over here. Maurice has been sent to bring you. I'll be waiting." And he hung up.

Oh dear, I thought to myself, would I also have to identify someone? Had Dick tracked and apprehended both of them so soon? Well, thank God for that if it was true—then we wouldn't have to hang around in the bookstore and ruin our evening.

But that was only the evening which had been saved. What about now? Was I to face that debauched beast again and see the leer in his eyes? There would be obscene innuendoes, bawdy insult, and I would have to countenance it all and stoically do whatever I owed Colonel Bromley.

There was a knock on the door. Maurice had arrived but I didn't open the door, I don't know why.

"Who is it?" I asked.

"It's me, Maurice, Madam. I have been asked to bring you to the camp."

"Could you please wait a minute?" I tidied up and was out in a moment and soon we were speeding away to the camp at the base of the great rock. I didn't like the rock, I decided. In fact, I hated all rocks. They were always a burnt purple or a burnt brown or a burnt grey and brought no joy to anyone's heart.

I was taken inside the office after all the guards and sentries had cross checked my identity at least half a dozen times. For a while I sat alone in the office, and then Raymond joined me shortly.

"It seems we hardly meet these days," I said, and crafted a smile. I had to say something smart. I hadn't the faintest idea about what had transpired and whether the confrontation was over. His face looked composed and quite unfazed, but that really meant nothing.

Raymond bowed to me, and kept the charade going, "My apologies, Mrs de Villiers, but all my attempts to seek your company seem to come to nought. This time it was the call of duty." But it couldn't sustain long.

"Okay, now serious," he continued in a lower tone, with that vigour in his eyes, "I'll tell you everything later. Camlin and the other fellow have been arrested. They're being interrogated and your identification is necessary for the record. I've already done my bit and told them all I know."

"Did everything go off all right? Are you all right?" I asked, looking at him directly in the eye so that the meaning would not be lost.

He understood and did not duck. He looked at me steadily and answered quietly, "Yes, whatever had to be done has been done. And don't worry about me, I'm absolutely fine." He shut his eyes and nodded gently, to reassure me that he was not scathed.

Without a doubt, even in this situation, Camlin would have spared nothing to defile us. But it would soon be over and would never happen again. And the secret prayer in my heart that this should be the last of Tom Camlin would be answered. He was hoisted on his own petard and inching closer to his own end. Perhaps there was some retribution in this world after all.

Colonel Bromley and Captain Beck joined us. "Good afternoon," Dick said with a businesslike smile. "Well, it has been quite a chase since we met last. We got our men on the job. They have their own methods, you know. The descriptions of both men were very useful, and combining this with some incidental information we had from other sources, we were able to connect up events and draw a line through them—the result was quite an emergency. We're still interrogating, but there's this little formality of your identification just for our record. It's necessary even in a summary trial. Hope you don't mind."

"Not at all," said I.

"Will you please take Mrs de Villiers to the Z room?" Dick told Captain Beck. "That's the interrogation room," he said looking at me.

I rose, but Raymond sprang up, "Dick, would it be okay if I accompany my wife? I'd like to be with her."

Dick looked thoughtful. He probably understood, "Yes Raymond, you may go with her," he said without expression.

Actually I had wanted to be alone. I had wanted to uncork the anger and rage that had been bottled up in me for so long, with nothing to inhibit me. And most of all, I had wanted to save him from any further humiliation.

We walked down the straight, narrow corridor and entered the interrogation room. I was mysteriously calm, without fear or nervousness at what I had yet to endure for the next few hours. In fact, I waited in anticipation, for it to begin so that it would end.

And then I saw him—the same lurid face, the eyes that now looked bleary, not with alcohol but with lack of sleep. But the ravages of alcohol were all too visible on that derelict, puffy face. He was handcuffed and bound to the chair on which he sat, and I noticed he had a dark bruise near his right eye.

He saw me and his face showed some interest. "Ah," he drawled, "so you're here at last to sign and seal my death warrant. Hmm, let me see how pretty you look—you were always pretty, pretty and young, young enough to be Raymond's daughter, incestuous old bastard. Anyway, glad to see you're still alive. He hasn't killed you yet has he, my angel of death." He bellowed with feigned and vulgar nonchalance.

"Shut up, you scum," my voice had a sibilance, an unnatural violence. "This time I will not allow you to get away with your evil."

My better judgment cautioned me not to talk. Talking implied a kind of equality, and I didn't want to give him the satisfaction of that in what was probably our last meeting. But I wanted to rub it into him with all my strength that he had not succeeded in destroying us, neither he nor Charlotte. I didn't know yet whether his final destination would be the cell or the firing range.

A uniformed man sat at a desk writing away. Raymond was impassive and the Captain looked embarrassed. I addressed him fearlessly, brazenly.

"Now tell me Captain, what would you like me to do?"

"Mrs de Villiers," he asked, "do you know this man?"

"Yes indeed, I do."

"How many years have you known him?"

"I have seen him three times in the last one year. Sorry, four times if I include the Casino Royale. I did not know him before that."

"What name do you know him by?"

"Tom Camlin."

"Do you know him by any other name?"

"No."

"You must also, my dear, brave Mrs de Villiers, not forget to mention how the honourable Raymond de Villiers murdered my niece and your predecessor Charlotte, and sank her body in the sea. The only reason you've missed the rope around your neck, my good man, is your classy old boys' bloody network. What Raymond, murderer's luck, huh," Camlin's voice interrupted, coarse and sneering.

"Silence, or we'll gag you," the Captain warned.

"Tell me about the night of the tenth on the Casino Royale when you say you saw Mr Camlin."

"Well, I woke up around two on the night of the tenth or rather the morning of the eleventh and I felt very hot. I opened the cabin door and I thought I would get some fresh air on deck. My husband was sleeping. I walked out to the deck, and after a while I saw two men on the deck below. I thought nothing unusual about it, but I found one of them very familiar, the shape of the head, the general figure. They had obviously finished talking and were leaving. When they turned, I saw their faces in the moonlight. One of them was definitely this person, Tom Camlin, and the other was the man who had knocked on our door earlier that evening thinking that Mr Delatres was the occupant."

"We'll talk about the other man later. Could you hear anything they were saying?"

"No, nothing. Some sounds, but nothing more."

"When did you see this Tom Camlin again?"

I narrated the incident of him leaving the Casino Royale and of our watch outside the bookshop.

"Do you know anything about the background of this man? What he does in England, his occupation, his sources of income?"

"Ah, tell them my dear, tell them how I earned a living. Sometimes by exposing murderers, perhaps." He looked at me with a lascivious smile, "And, my word, we've become quite a little tigress, I see. No more hiding behind doors, and trees, huh?"

I stared at him with intense loathing. "I don't really know how he earned a living—all I know is that he was a drunkard, a no gooder and a bum."

I continued clearly and calmly, "I also believe he is a relative of my husband's late first wife."

"Who was murdered by the noble Raymond de Villiers," he shouted trying to rise.

"Silence, you traitor," the sentry held him down.

I looked at the Captain squarely in the face with clear, untroubled eyes.

"Well, you see, that's how he makes a living. You heard it yourself. I believe, Captain Beck, he was a parasite, with no real sources of income. Perhaps my husband would have more details."

"Yes, he has told us all he knows."

"What I do know is that he tried to blackmail us after my husband's late wife's body was found, and not having succeeded in that, he was probably an accomplice to the person who set our home on fire, but we have no direct evidence of that." I drilled every word into Camlin with my eyes.

"Thank you, Mrs de Villiers, do you know if he had any German connections, friends, or business?"

"No, I'm afraid I don't know."

"That'll be all, thank you. We'll just spend some time with Mr Bertolini, after which you may leave."

I dared not look at Raymond. I didn't know what memories had surfaced in him, what devils had risen. But I don't think anything could have stopped me from revealing myself as I did today. I had decided to be intrepid and violent and I had succeeded. I had trespassed into unspoken territory definitely, but I was determined to pierce it into Camlin's head and to scream at him triumphantly, 'You haven't been able to wreck us, you embodiment of evil—neither you, nor Miss Portner nor Charlotte.'

But instead, I heard him shout devilishly, "Damn you, damn both of you. May she haunt you always with her blood upon your hands. Aren't you content with what you've done? Why are you hounding me?"

"You see the background of this man now, Captain. He is the scum of the earth," I spoke softly with a cold, lethal sting.

And then I had my last look at Camlin. The leer, the swagger, the mask of the braggart had all gone; he looked pathetic with the bruise near his eye and the terror on his face. It was the face of naked fear, the fear of death. I held my head high, and with great hauteur and disdain, gave him one last look of contempt and left the room. I knew I would never see him again.

I still did not have the courage to look at Raymond. I wished he could read my confusion and somehow break the ice. I felt his arm take mine as I was leaving, and only then did I have the strength to look up at his face. It was tortured in a way that only I could discern, not the Captain, nor the sentries; the peculiar light in the pupils, but the rest of the face was impassive. It could have been one of those magnificent oil portraits that hung on the walls of Lanverndel.

He looked at me and very faintly said, "Thank you." The rage had still not left me; it had enervated me, and I could say nothing.

I weakly rested my head on his shoulder and felt his warmth and closeness giving me comfort. Despite the turmoil and the strain, a weary sense of victory was washing over me, a euphoria in exhaustion, like a cold steam. I had resolved and I had conquered. I had perjured for him and we would win. We were bound even stronger now, and no one would ever destroy us, not Camlin, not Charlotte.

Identifying Carlo Burtolini, as his name turned out to be, was far quicker, and so impersonal. I merely told Captain Beck what happened at the Casino Royale and at the bookshop. He remained completely silent during the entire interrogation, and quite frankly, I didn't give a damn about what happened to him. All I can remember about him at this point is his shorn curly hair and his deep blue eyes, and that he and Camlin were involved in an Abwehr plot to bomb the anti-submarine base at Gibralter, and the entire ring had been busted in the nick of time by Colonel Bromley and his men.

Our responsibilities in this affair being over, the Captain led us again to Dick who was busy dictating at his desk.

"So, is everything over Tony, and can Mr and Mrs de Villiers leave now?"

"Yes, sir." Captain Beck left the room.

Dick looked up at us, "Well, we do try and follow the rules of natural justice even during war. Though this is a summary trial, we still want to be as fair as possible. Oh yes, I meant to tell you, the convoy is leaving sometime soon, as scheduled. I promise I'll try and give you a few hours notice, but it won't be much. So you should start getting prepared for it, and I repeat, this is absolutely confidential. As for this Camlin business, it's over as far as you're concerned. And I suppose just begun for us." He lapsed into thought. "Well, I'll be in touch with you off and on."

I was so terribly tempted to ask Dick more details, but I knew the information would be secret. Raymond may have pieced something together, or Dick may have told him something. Perhaps he would tell me after we reached the hotel.

The compulsions of the morning being over, I suddenly felt exhausted and utterly drained. Camlin's impact was beginning to show itself, now that the test of self-preservation had passed. I was ravenously hungry too. It was already late afternoon and I realized I hadn't eaten anything since last night.

We returned to our hotel and said goodbye to Maurice. I felt so tired and listless, and didn't want to leave the room for the next few days. I asked Raymond to order a large tea, whatever was available—sandwiches, scones, cakes, savouries, lemonade, as soon as possible.

"Did you have any lunch, Raymond? I'm famished," I asked.

"No, but I had a huge breakfast this morning while you were still asleep. I didn't want to wake you, you seemed so terribly exhausted. I've never seen you so tired before. Are you well? Or is it just the travelling and the heat? And today's events are certainly not going to help," he said ruefully and abstractly, his eyes focusing nowhere.

"Yes, that's true, but I'm glad for today. I'm glad I saw that beast, and even gladder that I said what I did. Just feeling brave and making grand resolutions is not enough. It's when you carry them out and pass the test that you really feel good and confident."

"You've not just passed the test, darling. It's much more than that and you know it. And all the while, my burden of guilt keeps mounting."

"Why Raymond? I also had to do my bit. But I'm all confused. I don't know whether I'm glad or relieved or both, but I think this will be the last of Camlin who brought so much misery to our lives. And he really brought this upon himself, didn't he? Did Dick give you any details about what happened?"

"Only a very guarded gist. I can understand the information must be very sensitive and secret. But I could gather that yesterday after we spoke to Dick, the Intelligence got active. They had already been processing some information about Abwehr operations in Gibralter. There's some very strategic naval and military activity going on here right now and the Abwehr are supposed to have strong bases in Spain and Italy, from where they probably operate. There had been bits and pieces of information coming in, but I believe we gave them quite an important lead."

"So, that business of spies that we kept hearing about all over the place was obviously true."

"Yes, but that's expected at such times. Now, apparently Bertolini, that's your Curly Locks, had been doing a lot of gun running in Spain for the Fascists during the Civil War, and there was quite a dossier on him. The description tallied, so they were able to trace some leads to him, and I suppose they were lucky too. They were able to get him in his hiding place and found a wireless transmitter and receiver there, and that's how they got to Camlin. The usual practice in such a case is they just wait around until some message comes in. That's how they get further information and more leads and so it goes on. In fact, they often give a decoy reply to a wireless message to obtain more incriminating information or documents. Perhaps Camlin sent a message and fell into the trap like this. But the Intelligence was able to round up quite a little network I believe. The objective was to dynamite the anti-submarine base through the vegetable and fruit supplies to the camp. This was all that I could piece together. Naturally, Dick has to give out as little as possible at a time like this, but Camlin's goose is cooked, I think."

I couldn't believe what I was hearing. And all of it coming out of two coincidences that happened on a ship and in a shop. "What will happen to him?" I asked with a savagery despite my stomach growling with hunger.

"The interrogation will go on for some days, I suppose, so that they can gather as much information as possible. Depending upon how serious the evidence is, if it is established that he is involved in the dynamite plot, it could mean execution for treason. Sometimes, the agent turns a double agent, and if that is in any way advantageous to his captors, say for getting more sensitive information, they may take the risk. But judging from Camlin's background and temperament, I would consider that highly unlikely. In fact, I spent most of the morning telling them what I knew of his social background and character."

"I was told that the Germans are very efficient. They really couldn't be that efficient if they employ men like Camlin."

"This business is different. If an individual is of use even for a few minutes, regardless of any other flaws, he is used. But in Camlin's case, luck was not with him right from the Casino Royale. We were really not supposed to be on that ship, and they would only have boarded after checking the passenger list and making sure that it was safe. But they were obviously not able to keep abreast of the last minute cancellation, or perhaps the message didn't reach them. To make matters worse for them, we of all people were present on the ship. And as if that were not enough, you decide to roam the deck at that unearthly hour and see the two men together. After that, I don't think they stood a chance."

"What about the Monegasque bureaucrat? Do you think he is also involved?"

"I don't know. They will probably be doing a check on him right now. Maybe after the war is over, we'll invite Dick over to Lanverndel and ask him to tell us the whole story. Till then, I suppose it will have to remain top secret."

"Does Dick have a family?" I asked.

"His wife died about five years ago, just before he went to India. She was a wonderful woman but always very frail. They have two children. His son is presently in India, just entered the civil service, and his daughter is married to a solicitor in London. Poor Dick, he was shattered when Angela died."

The tea finally arrived, a large two tier trolley, and the waiter started laying it on the table in the adjoining room.

"Raymond, I am famished. Don't watch me while I eat. It's going to be one big attack."

"It's all yours, my sweet."

It was probably the first time in my life that my greed was bigger than my stomach. I heaped my plate with all the goodies—chunks of wispy cake, crisp savouries, assorted sandwiches, piping hot scones. They were simply delicious. I had a second helping of everything, by which time Raymond had already put his plate away. I was eating at breakneck speed but I just couldn't stop myself. I now swooped upon the tangerines and grapes and ate them alternately, a segment of tangerine followed by a couple of grapes. The tangy sweet sour sensations excited my taste buds and I started feeling like a naughty school girl at a midnight feast.

"Well, I hope you've enjoyed your tea, Mrs de Villiers, 'To a hearty appetite'," he toasted me with his tea cup.

"Don't tease me," I pouted. "I know I'm being a perfect glutton. It's these strange hours we've been keeping the last few days and disturbed sleep patterns. Oh Raymond, I can't tell you how much I long to be back in England, war or no war. Just think of it, we'll be leaving in a few days."

By this time, I had started getting a queasy feeling in the stomach, and there was something disagreeable going on within me. I thought I should move about and it would settle. I cursed myself for eating like a pig, and so fast. Fortunately, Raymond was busy trying to get up to date with the wireless and couldn't see me. I tried to breathe deep to stabilize the queasy feeling but nothing seemed to work. The unpleasant pressure was building all the way up to my neck, and I had to rush to the bathroom. It was uncontrollable, and in no time all the goodies that I had glutted went down the drain, literally. On and on the spasms shook me, until finally there was nothing left inside.

What a mess, I thought. I shut the bathroom door and cleaned up. I gargled, but the metallic taste wouldn't leave my mouth. As I came out of the bathroom, I saw Raymond waiting for me.

"Now tell me what exactly the matter is. You've not been feeling well, and for some reason you're not telling me. What happened just now? I'm wondering whether I should call a doctor."

"No, no, really. I think I was just too greedy and ate too much on an empty stomach, and all that lovely stuff just went down the drain. What a pity."

I worked up a little giggle, and tried to sound facetious, but deep down I was a little concerned too. I hoped I wasn't heading for any major illness. Perhaps I had contracted trypanasomiasis or filariasis. After all, we were pretty close to Africa, and I remembered my father telling me that these diseases were rampant there. Perhaps that was why I was always so groggy. On second thoughts, I decided it may be wise to see a doctor, more so in view of the impending journey home.

"Yes Raymond, perhaps it would be better if we call a doctor. I'm feeling a bit run down, a little ill. I only hope I haven't contracted any infection. We have such a long and uncertain journey ahead of us."

The manager of the Hotel was asked to send for a physician. He arrived, a stodgy, elderly gentleman, a Dr Gordon who had a kindly manner and spoke to me as if I was a little girl.

"Now, what's the problem, my dear?" I tried to be as coherent as I could. I told him about my tiredness, my drowsiness, my lack of appetite, and finally what happened just now. He asked me about my digestion. I told him it was just fine until now.

He opened his briefcase, and pulled out his thermometer and stethoscope. He took my temperature, checked my pulse and my heartbeat. So far, he seemed satisfied about everything.

"Now let's see the colour of your eyes and tongue, my dear."

I stuck my tongue out at him. He stared at it and then pulled my lower eyelids down. He nodded appreciatively and said, "Hmm, no jaundice, as I can see. How long have you had this lack of appetite, my dear?"

"Actually, I'm not quite sure, perhaps three or four days, but I thought it was on account of the travelling we've been doing. We have to sail for England very soon and I just want to make sure I'm not going in for any serious illness."

He asked me again about my digestion, and I assured him that everything was perfectly normal. He asked me some other personal questions as most doctors do, and then told me to lie down to do the usual abdominal check. I obliged grudgingly. Finally, he looked rather thoughtful and rubbed his cheek as I rose.

"Hmm, I think there's no need to worry about anything my dear. Congratulations. All your symptoms seem to suggest that you may be with child. Of course, we have no way to confirm it so soon, but everything seems to point that way."

I turned motionless for a moment. I couldn't believe my ears. The doctor's words were not settling down anywhere. My heart was flooding with a warm golden happiness, and it was overflowing on to the rest of me, warming me, making me touch the sky. In my semi-dazed state, I could see Raymond spring to his feet and come behind my chair and place his hands upon my shoulders. He remained silent for a while.

"Doctor Gordon," his voice sounded so different, slightly stunned and terribly earnest, "I hope she's all right. Please tell us what to do. We have a long and uncertain journey ahead of us."

"Dear Mr de Villiers, there's really nothing to do. It's a perfectly natural state for any woman to be in."And turning to me, "The only thing to do is whatever nature bids, my dear. If you are sleepy, then sleep. If you feel like eating, eat whatever you wish. The first few months can sometimes be disagreeable, but that's no reason to be alarmed. It passes off. Try and drink as much milk as possible and eat whatever pleases you. Mint and citrus fruit can sometimes provide great comfort, if you're not feeling too good. Eat slowly and at short intervals. No strenuous exercise. Try to eat light, dry food like biscuits, nuts, fruits, but do try and take in as much milk as you can."

I was still in a pleasurable trance. Raymond would take charge and do all the listening. Dr Gordon addressed me again.

"Sometimes, you can be a little ill in the beginning. Sometimes, it can go on for a few weeks. Just take it easy, and continue leading as natural a life as possible, my dear. And also remember a positive attitude helps greatly. Don't be afraid or nervous. If you're a religious person, spend time in prayer; if you're an artist or a reader, dwell upon your favourite themes, and think only good, positive thoughts." I could hear everything the doctor was saying, as if in a dream, with the words still circling, giving comfort and warmth.

"We have to take this voyage to England in rather uncertain circumstances. I think we'll come to you tomorrow for a regular consultation, so that we know what to do and have all we need for the journey." Raymond's voice was still coming from afar, with a tone I'd never heard before, a mixture of intense happiness and anxiety.

"Most certainly. Whereabouts do you live in England?"

"Near Salcombe, about ten miles from Dartmouth, a country house called Lanverndel."

"I think I know the place, I've seen pictures of it. A truly magnificent manor." He said no more. Did he know the rest? I didn't care. Let him know Charlotte or her ghost. I was expecting Raymond's child, something she could never do. And we were going home to Lanverndel. Our baby would be born at Lanverndel, like his father was, and before him his father. I was beginning to understand what the good doctor was saying about positive thoughts. Yes, I promised myself, that's how I would be. I was already feeling marvellous.

The doctor took Raymond aside and said something to him, and I saw Raymond blush for a moment like a schoolboy. Some male exchange, no doubt.

"Before you leave, Doctor Gordon, we must have a little celebration and drink a toast to the most beautiful new mother." He pulled out a bottle of cognac and three glasses from the sideboard and started pouring. I, of course, couldn't even think of it.

"Water for me, please, Raymond," and I poured some into my glass.

"Fair enough," he said to me happily reaching out for my hand and giving it a squeeze, and then he handed the cognac to Dr Gordon.

"To my beautiful wife. May we always have good fortune and happiness."

We clinked our glasses and drank. Events were racing too fast for me. But for the first time Raymond had called me beautiful.

He showed the doctor to the door, then closed it behind him and looked at me. He looked different, like a boy, radiating great pride and joy. He walked over to me, picked me up in his arms and kissed me repeatedly, on my face, my eyes, my lips, my neck. "Thank you, thank you, for everything," he kept whispering. His eyes held mine between kisses, and we laughed together with happiness.

I remembered it was the first time for him too.

He rang for the butler and asked him to bring warm milk and biscuits and nuts for me. He forgot the war, the wireless and

Tom Camlin. He was listing out things to be packed, things to be bought, food to be taken along for my well being.

"What was the doctor telling you which he didn't want me to know?"

"Ah, nothing much," he said with a twinkle in his eye. "He was just giving me a list of my responsibilities."

I looked dumbly, and then I comprehended, a wide smile flooding my face. I was always told that motherhood brings out a special beauty and mellowness in a woman. Fatherhood, it seemed to me made men look more youthful and boyish, beaming with pride at the accomplishment. That is exactly how Raymond appeared that evening.

The remaining days at Gibraltar passed off peacefully, considering so much had been crammed into the previous ones. I took it easy, woke up leisurely, tried to drink as much milk as I could, and discovered that my appetite had disappeared. The good doctor was right. Citrus fruits and mint tea were extraordinarily helpful and I discovered a delightfully soothing night cap in chammomile.

Raymond was as wonderful as could be. He treated me like a piece of delicate bone china, while I spent my time between the living room, bedroom, verandah and the lawns. I tried to follow Dr Gordon's advice to the hilt and thought only positively about going home, about Lanverndel, about the baby. Of course, it would be a boy, and his father and he would do all the usual things together, cycling and riding, cricket and football. Ah, what happy dreams these were! I remembered someone telling me when I was a little girl that when the Lord shuts a door, he opens another somewhere. How many doors had opened and shut in the last one year, I mused. I decided I would do some sketching before leaving for England. I hadn't been fair at all to Gibraltar in my sketch pad.

Dear Raymond, other than fussing over me, he was busy firming up arrangements for our departure. Dick had apparently assured him that my present status entitled me to the most comfortable cabin on the ship. He had a sitting with Dr Gordon and procured all the provisions to be carted along. The voyage would last anywhere between a week to ten days, depending on how friendly or hostile the seas would be, and Raymond wanted to take no chances. There were cartons of exotic teas and spices bought from an Indian shop to pep me up, hampers of fruit in various stages of ripeness so as to last the journey, cans of milk powder, chocolates, and an enormous amount of reading material.

Dick was able to spare some time to see us the next day. We had a cozy drink together and I made him promise that he would visit us at Lanverndel after the war was over and give us every detail of the Camlin affair. Other than this, we never spoke of it at all. News from the battle front continued to be grim. Holland and Belgium were falling, their defenses crumbling and Rotterdam had been bombed senseless. French military judgment had apparently gone wrong and already three German armoured units had penetrated the Ardennes and were on the Meuse between Dinant and Sedan. The road to France was open and the Maginot Line had become a tragic irrelevance.

A day before leaving, we had a telegram from Henry informing us that there was a communication from the county office that Raymond was to be appointed Commandant for Civil Defence for the County and his presence was urgently required. Using little brevity, Henry spent many words welcoming us back, saying that Lanverndel was quite presentable, and he felt sure we would be pleased.

Raymond took the news of his appointment in quite a matter of fact manner, but I could see his mind was already working on it. An agreeable distraction, I daresay, from fussing over me. He sent a reply telling Henry that we'd leave as soon as circumstances permitted, and to explain our present predicament to Colonel Osmund. We were not quite sure when and where we'd land, but we would contact him and the Colonel as soon as we reached England.

The wireless blared forth news which was getting worse and worse by the hour. The French armies had been pounded to silence by the stukas and low bombers, and were now being sliced by the

Panzers as the Germans started crossing the Meuse. The RAF had suffered crippling losses in a fruitless counter offensive.

Raymond tried his best to look calm, but I knew he was worried and there were plenty of things to be worried about. My pregnancy, and a voyage totally unpredictable and fraught with danger. The war doing so badly for the Anglo-French Alliance, with every passing moment making it certain that the extremely professional and well equipped German army would have an easy run through France. And who could tell what repercussions all of this would have in England. He must also have been worried about Lanverndel—what he would see there, the memories and the pain. I thanked God once more for giving us so many other worries that re-entering Lanverndel would be the least of them. And I was grateful that there would be new responsibilities awaiting him in England, even though I had no clear idea what they would be. But at the end of the tunnel was home, with its verdant gardens, its rivulets and woods to soothe our souls.

At last, we got the summons we had so anxiously been waiting for. It was around ten o clock at night on 23*rd* May when the phone rang. Dick was on the line telling us that we should be at the wharf in an hour and board HMS Olympia. A vehicle was coming to pick us up with someone to see us through the formalities. He wished us luck and god speed.

We had rehearsed the drill so often and had been in a sort of permanent state of readiness for so many days now, that it didn't take us very long to settle our dues, check our papers once again, collect our bags and rush under cover of darkness.

Thus, armed with everything that we could possibly require, with plenty of hope and confidence in our hearts, we departed from the purple rock and the heat.

Gibraltar would always be invaluable to me, just as it was to England.

Chapter Eleven

When I look back and try and recollect our voyage, fraught with danger and risk as it was, I find my memory plays tricks with me. Some events appear clear and fresh as if they happened just yesterday and their images are sharply etched in my mind. Others are blurred and foggy and difficult to focus, however hard I try.

I remember the early hours of the morning in which we set sail. The sea would be calmer then, but more importantly, we would be sailing the treacherous northern waters during daylight. There were fears on everyone's minds—of German U Boats, wolf packs, marauder ships which we had read about, roaming lawlessly over the Atlantic, destroying and sinking at will.

We drove through a maze of little roads and reached the guarded entrance to the harbour in complete darkness. Corporal Jones, our escort, showed his identity papers to the guards under a minute shielded torch, and we were allowed to enter the heavily fortified shore. Our suitcases and luggage, mostly hampers of food, were taken over by another set of guards, and would be sent to our cabin later. I could now clearly see, even in the hazy, dim moonlit night, the large number of ships, some stationary, some slowly moving into their slots in the convoy. There was so much activity and movement all around. The atmosphere was packed with tension that was rising with different kinds of unfamiliar sounds coming from inside and outside the ships.

The Corporal guided us to the HMS Olympia, a walk of about ten minutes. As we stood at the gangway, he showed his papers to the officer on duty, took him aside and spoke a few words, then gave him a smart salute and bid us goodbye.

We held out our papers and passports to the officer. He scrutinized them, looked at our faces and flipped a few pages in his file. Then he looked up and smiled at Raymond. "Welcome aboard, Sir. Someone on the deck will take you to your cabin. The Captain will be meeting you sometime later."

"Thank you," said Raymond, as we started to walk up the gangway.

"This ship is truly beautiful, even with its martial trappings." I gasped at her size and elegance. The night was getting darker and clouds were stamping out the dim moonlight.

"Yes, it certainly is a beauty. During its heyday, this was one of the most luxurious ocean liners, sailing mostly between Southampton and New York. I think it can carry around five thousand people. Today, the poor lady has a most unglamorous name—DEMS. That's a defensively equipped merchant ship. Except that now there are no merchants on it. Only troops or their families and stranded people like us." He smiled, but even as he was talking, I could see that he was studying every detail of the anti-aircraft guns mounted at various positions on the deck that were now becoming visible, and rows of other heavy guns facing upwards and downwards.

"What's all this?" I asked, pointing towards them. "It's almost like a battle ship."

"Yes, it is," said Raymond. "The low angle guns are meant to protect us from surfaced U Boats, and high angle ones from enemy air attacks."

I shivered. We had reached the deck. A uniformed person standing there asked us for our papers again. Then he led us to our cabin.

"Sir, the Captain has ordered 'darken ship', so no lights. All portholes on the ship's side have been shut tight, and you can see that every window and other openings on the superstructure have been covered with thick black paper," he said. "A precautionary measure that we must take at night to avoid visual detection. Enemies lurking all around. But it's not all that bad. We all manage," he turned to us and smiled.

"Yes, of course, this is absolutely necessary," Raymond replied.

I looked around me. There were at least fifty ships in formation, with a few ships still moving towards their allotted places in the convoy. The Armada looked grand.

"Goodness, I never realized that the convoy would be so huge," I exclaimed.

"There must be a great many ships wanting to reach their destinations safely on all sides of the Atlantic—Canada, America, maybe the West Indies, and, of course, England. There are probably a large number of oil tankers, cargo ships and troopships, and definitely warships and patrol ships for protection."

I could see some other beautiful, elegant ships, also converted into troopships, bringing men from all over the Empire to fight for Britain. Civilians, some alone, some with their families were returning home to feel safer with their own folk in their own homes.

The convoy had a simple rectangular pattern of about five lines of ten ships well spaced apart by at least about five hundred yards, and ten rows of ships of various kinds spaced little more closely. Our ship was somewhere in the middle. I suppose that meant that it was well protected, surrounded by tankers and the valuable cargo ships, which Raymond told me were loaded with tanks and planes and God knows what else. And hardly a mile away from the four corners of the convoy, and at the front and rear of it were our protector ships, called Corvettes.

We entered an almost pitch dark cabin and waited for our suitcases to arrive. It felt so claustrophobic, and Raymond was already getting restless and impatient.

"Darling, please take care of the suitcases and all that. I'll try and see when I can meet the Captain. He must have his hands full, poor chap. But I must check on all the details of the ship, the facilities, the emergency drills, life saving measures, life boats, and anything else. They'd anyway be giving us all the safety information sometime soon, but it's good to see for oneself."

"OK, but come back soon."

I still didn't feel too good, but the sheer risk and imperatives of the moment had taken over. I was possessed by one thought and one thought alone—we just had to reach home safely, and our child should be born at Lanverndel.

The hampers and suitcases finally arrived. In the dim light shed by a tiny bulb hanging from the bulkhead, I started opening the one with articles of immediate use, and arranged them on the table and chest of drawers.

Raymond returned about half an hour later. "I was lucky to be able to meet the Captain, and ask him about the ship's safety measures. They'll be having some mock drills tomorrow for the civilians, after they're a little rested."

"When is the convoy starting?" I asked.

"I didn't think it proper to ask, as I know these things are kept very secret. But I expect we should start in another hour or so. Wouldn't you like to get some sleep now? "

"Let me take my last look outside. After all, I have to tell our children stories of all our adventures." I smiled, and went towards the deck.

Raymond joined me and held me close. Together we stood side by side, watching the ships and the gentle waves in the dark night. My eyes scanned the coastline and caressed it. "I will visit you again, not like this in anxiety and apprehension, but in peace and blessedness. You have vanquished one foe, and the other will be vanquished too," I said to myself, and bid goodbye to the great rock which had brought us so much good luck.

We returned to the cabin, and I simply collapsed on the berth. Raymond was there covering me, sitting by my side, and taking care of the rest of the world. Before crashing into the dark unconscious, I had remembered in a confused sort of way that I had another life within me, and that we had to survive whatever happened.

When I woke again, I had no idea where we were and what time it was. As my sleep broke, I heard the waves of the sea, gentle and dulcet, and I thought I was in Lanverndel. Had we changed our rooms to face the sea, I wondered. But these were not our rooms, I reminded myself, they belonged to Charlotte. I saw in my half sleep the emerald lawns meld into the sea. No, I told myself, we were not in Lanverndel, we were in Nice, on the beach. I must have muttered something, for I felt Raymond's cool, strong hand on my forehead, smoothing my hair gently.

"There, there," he almost sounded like a nurse, "would you like to wake up?"

"Darling, I've been in all kinds of places. What time is it? What's going on?"

"Well, it's nearing noon, and so far it seems good. Did you sleep well?"

"Yes, very well. I just passed out, and until now had no idea that I even existed." I smiled at him, "I'll just keep lying down. Let me see how my system behaves."

"Would you like anything to drink? Tea, coffee, ovaltine?"

"No, Raymond, thank you. Let me just take stock of myself. Whereabouts are we?"

"We should be in the waters around the south of France, which I think is really the deadliest bit. My own feeling is that now the convoy will take a wide detour and sail towards the Irish waters. You're not seasick, are you?"

"Not at all. In fact I seem to be feeling better than usual. What a strange thing this human body is. You give it all the comfort and it does nothing but complain, and when you have to rough it out, it behaves splendidly."

He smiled, "Glad to hear that. Now, I'll mix some milk and ovaltine for you. Would you like to have it?"

"Actually I wouldn't mind some. Is it all right if we go on deck after I get dressed?"

"Of course, if you should feel like it."

I washed and dressed and felt quite well. Before leaving Gibraltar we had heard over the radio that the Nazi march into France was progressing unchecked. We kept our fingers crossed that we'd have reached home before they came near the French coast.

"Raymond," I asked, "do you really think there are U Boats lurking around nearby? And how would our escort ships be able to tell?"

"Well, Dick's information was that most of the enemy U Boats have been ordered out of the Atlantic into Norway. Let's hope that is true; there'll be less danger from wolf packs. But you can never tell. As far as detection is concerned, I was given some sort of a hint that our ships have some very modern and secret detecting devices which can locate a U Boat under water. That is why it is safer for us to sail over these waters even during the day. The U Boats cannot surface since then they'll be seen, and if they remain underwater, they'll be detected by the new device. That's what I could pick up from Dick and the ship's Captain. But that's the theory part. How much of this actually works, we will know only later."

He looked at his watch, "It's about eleven o clock. Well, let's see where we might be right now, even approximately. I'll just take a look at the sky and see where the sun is, and try and work it out."

He went out and returned after a while. "I think we just might be around thirty seven or thirty eight degrees north by now, probably approaching the waters most prone to U Boats and marauders. That's when we really need luck. Feel like coming out on deck? "

"Yes, of course." We walked on to the deck. The waters were calm, and the ship sailed majestically, all the columns moving smoothly at similar speed in perfect formation. If only the weather would remain fair, and we would reach home safely.

There was a merry gathering on deck and I breathed the fresh sea air which was getting cooler and gentler as we kept going north. Ours was the officers' and civilian deck, and we had for company several English families coming home from their assignments in the colonies. There was a young couple, Major and Mrs Henderson, with a small boy of about four, on their way home from India. For the next few days, Jennifer Henderson and her little son were by my side always, whenever I was scared or sick. There were also several single ladies, some with children, some without, whose husbands had joined the front.

The ship was moving with grace and speed, leaving a foamy wake behind her. All around us was an endless expanse of gently undulating blue green waves. I kept drinking in the air and scanning the grand scene around me of all the convoy ships steaming ahead in neat formation. As we were entering deeper ocean waters, the swell increased and the roll and pitch of the ship started making me feel very uncomfortable. It was the beginning of the worst bout of sea sickness that I ever experienced, which lasted right through the voyage. I fled to the cabin and never left it again. Doctor Gordon's words were no longer convincing or comforting. I was so badly shaken that the farthest I would leave the cabin was till the door, and that too, with my back turned to the sea.

Raymond was perplexed and helpless, and couldn't understand what to do. He begged Mrs Henderson for help, and almost immediately all the ladies on the ship were pooling in their experiences and knowledge to help me through. They were marvellous and reassuring and kept repeating that this was really nothing to be worried about, that they had all gone through it, that it was perfectly natural, but it was unfortunate that this business of war and U Boats was exacerbating my nervous condition, quite understandably so. Jennifer Henderson made me an infusion of weak tea, cinnamon, honey and lemon peel, and for the remaining days on the ship, most of which are smudged in memory, it was the only drink I could retain. The hampers of fruit and food were given away and I lived on biscuits and nuts. I read whatever I could, though I cannot remember what, and went through all the mock drills. But what I can still remember with great clarity and gratitude is the care and consideration shown by all our fellow passengers whilst we shared those moments of peril.

Raymond was like a rock. He never left my side, and I knew he was pleading with the powers above to see us through this safely. He was my nurse, my companion, my friend who put up with my strange, new condition without the slightest trace of impatience. He organized bridge evenings, read and discussed books with me, and tried everything that he could to entertain me, and help me pull through. I had only one goal to achieve, and that was to remain in one piece, come what may.

And then it happened. What we had all feared secretly, but had not dared to express, after each peaceful day had passed by. It was on the night of May 30, when we were awakened by a shattering explosion, and sounds of continuous gun fire.

Raymond and I scrambled out of our bunks. We hurriedly dressed and wore our coats, gathered our papers and valuables in a bag, and stepped out of the cabin. The dark foggy night was ablaze with a huge cloud of flame reaching high into the sky. Clouds of black billowing smoke, shaped like mushrooms of changing size, were forming a huge cloud over the sea. There were shouts and screams, and in the light of the flames, we saw that a ship just two columns away to our right was on fire and listing badly.

"Damn. The U Boats have done it." Raymond's face was distraught and furious. "Don't panic, darling. We have to get over this. We don't know how this will go. Just don't lose your nerve."

"No Raymond, I won't, I promise. I'll follow whatever they told us at the mock drills."

The bow of the stricken ship had now lifted clear off the water and it was rapidly sinking, stern first. Lifeboats from neighbouring ships were making way towards it in an effort to gather survivors who had managed to stay afloat in the sea. Flares were being fired to light up the area to help locate those crying for help.

Suddenly our ship swerved violently to the left, and after a while to the right again, and kept repeating these movements. I almost fell, and clung to the door. It was chaotic, the ocean churning violently and all the ships zigzagging. We had been told at the mock drills that this was a maneuver meant to confuse the U Boats in locating the ships above, so that their torpedoes miss target. But the ships were coming so dangerously close to each other, almost on a collision course. It was terrifying.

There was frenetic activity all around. Members of our ship's crew were guiding agitated passengers to go below deck, so that no one was lost overboard due to the violent movements of the ship. Officers with their team of sailors were checking the status of the lifeboats and preparing for any contingency if we got hit and had to abandon ship.

All around us, we could hear loud booms of exploding depth charges. We could see frightening vertical spouts of foaming sea water wherever underwater explosions had broken the surface of the sea. I turned cold with fear. Would we be the next target? Was the U-boat still roaming wild beneath the sea? In panic, I tried to recall the instructions given to us about lifeboats and life jackets. Where were the life jackets kept? Where were we instructed to assemble, if 'abandon ship' was ordered? Which lifeboat had been assigned to us? Were there enough lifeboats for all of us?

I couldn't remember a thing. But Raymond was at my side. He would know what to do.

"Raymond, what should we do? Remain here or go below deck?"

Before Raymond could reply, our ship suddenly swerved to the left, and it's speed picked up. All the other ships were also going left, with very short distance between them.

"There's a torpedo coming at us," we heard a shout from somewhere.

That's when all hell broke loose. I could see many of our companions still on the upper decks running helter skelter to any part that they thought instinctively was safe. But we stayed where we were.

Our eyes were riveted on the approaching shark-like object that raced beneath the surface of the sea towards our ship, leaving a stream of massive bubbles in its wake.

There was a shattering explosion and our ship shook violently. I almost fell but Raymond caught me in time. He held my hand tight and put his arm around my shoulder. He was watching the scene around him intently.

"I think we've been hit by one of those damned U Boats," he muttered. I went weak with fear, and clung to his arm, praying with all my might.

He was silent for some time, alert, watching, listening.

After what seemed an age, he spoke, "Doesn't look like we've lost any speed or maneuverability. And we're not listing. I don't think we got a direct hit. It's probably just grazed the hull." He was straining his eyes towards the sea. "The damage to the hull can be patched up quite effectively. The ship's damage control crew must be already working at it. They are trained for such a situation. I'm sure the ship will survive this attack. I think it's been a bloody lucky escape."

By now, our ship was speeding away northwards along with the remaining ships of the convoy.

Suddenly there was another underwater explosion. Our ship heaved upwards, and then fell back upon the waves, and we saw the ship next to us go up in flames, with the same mushroom cloud of black smoke and the flames reaching up to the sky. We were barely a hundred yards away from it. The U Boats had done it again. The ship had been hit by torpedoes and was going down.

We could see the lifeboats and their crews all around the stricken ship, doing their best to ferry survivors to our ship, as we were the closest. How many had perished was a question on all our minds, but couldn't reach our lips. We could see our ship picking up badly shaken survivors, many of them injured. They were the lucky ones. Then the ship suddenly veered west, turned east again, and zigzagged like this for at least an hour.

Occasionally, we heard the deafening explosions of depth charges being dropped by our convoy ships on suspected U-boat positions, and there were sounds of intermittent gunfire. The air was full of acrid fumes emanating from fired shells.

This had gone on for about four hours, with us watching from the upper deck. Suddenly, we saw that dawn was breaking. The light had changed and the sun was peeping out from a hazy place far away, on a foggy horizon.

It had become quiet, and we heaved a sigh of relief, as if a nightmare had ended. The grey light was gradually getting stronger. It was gently brushing the fog aside, and giving us some strength. Our eyes got back their full vision, but remnants of the black smoke were still visible, reminding us that our peril was still not over, and we had no idea of what lay ahead.

It had been quiet now for quite a while, but Raymond said that meant nothing. "U Boats can stay deep under water for quite a long time, and escape detection, while they have devices to detect the path of ships and attack again," he said. "And now that it is daylight, their periscopes are enough to do that."

His words were prophetic. This is exactly what happened.

We were both trying to catch some sleep, which seemed impossible. The sounds of explosions were still reverberating in my ears, and the flames over the ocean took me back to the night when Lanverndel stood burning. Images of the sinking ships came before me. God knows how many people must have died. I could feel our ship still moving quite fast towards the west. But sleep still wouldn't come.

Instead, there came another thunderous blast, followed by series of explosions.

We jumped out of our beds and went out. Another ship just a column away had been hit. It was bobbing up and down, but the flames were much less than what I had seen earlier.

"This time the torpedoes seem to have missed. The Captain must have taken some smart, evasive action. It will survive," Raymond said, "but I'm sure the attack will continue. No U Boat would like to think it has failed."

We could see the corvettes rushing some distance behind us. They had made a huge circle, as if they were laying siege to the U Boat's location. They pummelled the sea with depth charges. There were sounds of muffled explosions and the sea was spotted with the accompanying water bursts. Our ships were determined to destroy these underwater demons.

Thank God they were successful, for a few minutes later and not too far from us, we saw something emerge from the sea.

"That's the periscope, the conning tower and the nose of the U Boat rising out of the water." I could sense the relief in Raymond's voice. "It seems to be positioned at an extremely awkward angle. I think, that means it is been severely damaged, thank God."

A group of sailors were scrambling out of the conning tower. They were assembling on deck with their hands up, and our ship's Captain ordered the boats to be lowered. We could see an armed party of sailors picking up the captured crew of the rapidly sinking U-boat and transferring them to a corvette stationed nearby.

"I think this should be the end of the attack for the present," Raymond said. "The German Naval Command would by now know that they've lost a sub, and the crew has been captured. They would probably not try anything more right now."

I wanted to ask so many questions, but was exhausted and weak. I just hoped to God he was right.

Raymond continued, "It's been such a terrible night, and day. We've lost two ships and at least two are damaged. God knows how many lives have been lost, and how much tonnage gone under the sea. But they've lost a U Boat. Our navy has at least that to its credit."

Our ship was speeding away towards the west, at about 18 knots. The convoy seemed so much smaller. Many of our companion ships bound for the Caribbean and America had parted company and taken different routes. The sea had a natural calm. The islands of oil and the black clouds of smoke were left far behind. I was exhausted and numb and felt an unbearable urge to sleep.

****

The next day, the Captain announced that our ship had been hit just below the waterline in the aft section in a compartment that was used mostly for storage. The shipwrights on board had patched up the small jagged hole in the hull, and the Captain was confident that there was nothing to worry about, that the ship was completely sea worthy, and would reach home soon. I was relieved and thanked God, but was still too shell shocked to understand anything else.

The days and nights passed—the sound of the waves, the changing rays of the sun, the falling temperatures, all of which I witnessed from within our cabin.

We were skirting around Ireland to avoid the treacherous areas. The weather was fair and our convoy was getting closer and closer to home.

One day we heard sounds of an aircraft flying above. A wave of panic hit us all. Was this an air attack? But soon there was an announcement informing us that there was no cause for alarm, that these were our own RAF planes giving us air cover. A roar of applause went up, bringing great joy to our hearts.

That evening, when Raymond was organizing my supper, strangely enough my appetite stirred. I thought I detected a different gleam in his eye, and I could tell he had some special news to give me.

"Well, I have a surprise for you, my dear. Would you like to guess what it is?" He sounded happy.

I smiled. It would either be some interesting information he had picked up from his bridge group about the war, or someone would have sent some special food for me. I suddenly thought of the huge and bright red strawberries from the Lanverndel gardens, the sweetest I had ever tasted.

"I know. You got me something special for my supper."

"Sorry to disappoint you, dearest, but perhaps we could think of that tomorrow. Guess the surprise for the day."

"Raymond, do stop teasing me. Tell me quickly. I've been so patient, not that I'm not grateful. I thank God every day that somehow we've survived it all. But I can't bear it any longer. I just want this to be over. I want to go home."

"And so you shall, my dearest. Tomorrow morning, if all goes well, we should be dropping anchor at Liverpool."

I screamed with joy and disbelief, almost hysterical. "Raymond, tell me you're not joking, tell me you're not saying it just to comfort me. I can't believe it. I just can't believe it."

"Yes, yes, the Captain announced it officially this afternoon. You were asleep. There's still about a hundred miles to go, but we're in safer waters. We've crossed the dangerous zones and there's not much chance of the enemy lurking this close to the British Isles. And the closer we get to home, the stronger is the air cover we have. So there, did you like the surprise?"

I was delirious with happiness. I hugged him and there were tears of relief pouring down my face. Raymond whispered, "Thank God you pulled through, thank God both of you have pulled through." I sobbed even harder. "Yes, yes, he'll be born in Lanverndel."

Next morning, a large formation of sea gulls overhead escorted us to Liverpool Port.

****

I stepped out on deck after what seemed like ages. We were finally safe and I took a deep breath. There was happiness of seeing again the shores of England, the chimneys puffing smoke, the hustle and bustle at the port, the hectic activity of the Royal Navy. I did not notice the jubilation on deck; I was only marvelling that we had completed the journey without mishap. I was in one piece, though thin and famished, but the life within me was intact. There was singing, clapping, dancing, praying, all around, and there were tears of thanksgiving.

We went through the usual port formalities, and headed straight for the Hotel Metropole, exhausted with relief and happiness. A pair of gas masks was neatly placed on the study table, something mandatory for all citizens, as a precaution. While I was examining the clumsy and slightly intimidating object, I could hear Raymond asking the hotel manager to arrange for a physician, which I didn't really require. But there was no harm in putting his mind at rest.

I wanted so badly to go home, to Lanverndel, however ill prepared it may have been to receive us. The thought lifted me—the blue sky and sea, the green lawns, the tall stately trees, the gold and blood red blossoms. It was so glorious to breathe good English air again and to know that the saga that had begun with our journey to France eight months ago was about to end, and that we hadn't done so badly. It had started on a particular note, and was ending on a totally different and unexpected one. We had started our wanderings with a private battle against destiny, and we were ending them with at least a quarter of the world embroiled in battle. How small and inconsequential our private afflictions appeared now, even the stare of death on the Atlantic, and how easily they were being eclipsed by the predicaments of people and countries which had suffered so much in the past few years. I suppose this is usually how private misfortune and calamity is mitigated. Miss Portner and Tom Camlin appeared so distant and tame. What seemed real and dangerous were bombs, invasion, occupation, and what was even more alarming was that no one could fathom or predict the course of events which were to control our lives for so many years hence. Perverse as it might appear, I would be lying if I didn't admit that I was grateful privately for all the exigencies which were making our private burdens seem so much lighter.

I was deep in this reverie when Raymond arrived with the doctor. I went through the drill of pulse and heartbeat and blood pressure.

"Nothing to worry about, Mr de Villiers. Everything seems quite normal. Naturally, the poor lady must be exhausted after what you have been through. A lot of fresh air and fresh food, rest and some moderate exercise are the only medicines."

Raymond telephoned Henry and Rupert and announced our arrival. They were overjoyed and relieved. He asked Henry to get a set of rooms prepared for us at Lanverndel, in whatever shape they were. We would not live elsewhere. From now on there would be no running away from home. Only now did I notice that every pane of glass in our suite was covered with thick black paper.

It was wonderful to see Raymond totally immersed in all the matters on hand. I hadn't seen this streak in him for a very long time, possibly not since the early Lanverndel days almost a year ago. But there was a welcome difference—the face that had once, not so long ago, been so opaque, detached and inscrutable now had a boyish openness and involvement. And there was no denying the fact that he looked at least ten years younger. I wondered how such transformations took place so invisibly. Suddenly you just saw them there one day.

Lanverndel and its scorched shadows were the least of Raymond's priorities. He was to immediately take charge as the Civil Defence Commandant for the county. I wasn't quite sure what exactly this would involve, but it made me very happy and relieved that he was already so absorbed in it.

I could hear him shouting over the phone telling Colonel Osmund that he'd be assuming his responsibilities as soon as he reached Lanverndel in a couple of days. At last, his calls were over and he came to me. "Well, I think I've finished all that I had to do. I don't want to turn on the wireless. The news is only getting worse. Paris will be falling, if it hasn't already, and the Allied Expeditionary Force must be making preparations for evacuation. What a terrible story. So at your service now, my dear Mrs de Villiers. Tell me, are you feeling happier, better? How's the appetite? And what, pray, can I do for you?"

"Oh, Raymond, I can't tell you how much better I'm feeling. It's almost as if a huge load has been lifted from me. Just the fact that there are no more journeys, that we survived the terrible voyage and are safe, and we'll be going home. And to know that you're well... that's the most important. And I suppose you are going to have an enormous amount of work ahead of you with this war. I presume I will too, getting Lanverndel started again. I almost feel superstitious saying it, but I feel so happy and so hopeful."

"You must rest now, and try and eat to make up for whatever you have missed. I get a little nervous seeing you get frailer day by day." He kept himself busy pampering me with whatever fresh, appetizing food he could lay his hands on. And in my new found psychological ease, my appetite was better, and I was both physically and mentally much fitter to undertake the last lap of our journey, the train to west country.

Raymond had initially suggested we hire a cab, but I thought such extravagance quite unnecessary, especially at a time like this, and besides, the doctor had preferred the train from a purely medical point of view. So train it was, and Raymond asked for the car to meet us at Exeter. It was with great excitement and anticipation that we set forth through the beautiful meadows and fields for our home in the west.

Returning to Lanverndel had always been encrypted deep somewhere in my subconscious ever since I had left. I had imagined it over and over again—sometimes in triumph, sometimes in fear, sometimes in joy. But now that the moment was drawing near, there were none of these things, only a sense of immense relief at being back, and a sense of worry about what the war would do to us and our country.

The train hurried on, and the landscape grew more and more familiar. What a glorious summer this was. The impact of the war was still not noticeable; the only difference I could see was that there were a lot more military vehicles visible on the roads. But otherwise, everything else seemed just the same as before. The sun was golden in a sky of clear blue, and the fields of barley and rye took in every ray of sunlight. Here and there were patches of yellow mustard, adding richness with their colour. The orchards were clothed in blossom, and nature seemed totally oblivious of the apocalypse that awaited it barely a few months away.

We sped onwards to Bristol. My excitement, childish as it may have been was getting more and more uncontrollable, and I must have been an awful nuisance, for I kept asking Raymond repeatedly how many hours we were away from home. I realized I had neglected him so much the last few days, poor darling, and it was he who had been doing all the caring. He was intently reading *The Times*, and now and then he would give me a reassuring look and smile. That taut look of anxiety which had branded him on the ship was gone. We were to reach Lanverndel in a few hours, and I was bringing to Lanverndel what belonged to it—an heir who would possess it as generations before him had, something Charlotte could never do. And I felt proud and superior.

But we both knew that we were at a threshold, as yet another moment of truth awaited us. We had still to face those stone walls with their secrets, and the avalanche from the past. I was anxious, desperately hoping that our hard earned healing and catharsis would not be lost, and I wanted so much to tell him that I was by his side, and he was not alone. I was about to start sinking into despair and helplessness, but I caught myself just in time.

"Raymond," I said somewhat tentatively, "tell me truly darling, you are happy, you are at peace, now that we're returning. You must promise me...you must tell me...I know I'm not much help, I say the wrong things and I'm clumsy...but I love you, and I don't ever want you to suffer alone, please."

He looked up at me a little startled, and then he smiled, a spontaneous, natural smile. "Since you ask me, I must tell you the truth," he said. "Naturally, I'm happy to come back to Lanverndel, and I sincerely hope it is looking more presentable than when we saw it last, considering the amount its cost. But what I'm most happy about is that you are well, after all the risks and discomfort and travel that we've had to go through, and that we bring back a precious gift to Lanverndel. But be prepared, there's going to be such an awful amount of work awaiting us. This war will be bad, much worse than anyone can foresee." He lapsed into thought again. "I don't think there's going to be any time at all to be unhappy." He held my hand and smiled at me.

How like him! He hadn't answered anything I had asked, but had spoken his mind. These were good symptoms, I suppose. His mind was working, not with associations or memories, but with the war and civil defence; not with Charlotte or Camlin, but with Colonel Osmund and county administration.

It was now past midday and we were approaching Somerset County. Finally we reached Exeter, the last hour stretching for ever so long. And then I saw Henry, good, loyal Henry whom I was straining my eyes to spot. He was standing with John, and then I saw Patricia and Rupert, and my heart was flooded with joy. Little by little, the familiar world was reconstructing itself. I realized then how much I had missed it, even though I had known it for such a short time, and had never really belonged to it.

My happiness was uncontrollable. I hugged Patricia, then Rupert, then Henry. Even Raymond, usually so formal and undemonstrative couldn't prevent himself from hugging his sister hard and kissing her.

Patricia gave me an affectionate look. "It's so good to see you again. Welcome back. But you're so gaunt and pale. I know you've been through a terrible time, but thank God, you're back, safe and sound."

She turned to Raymond. "Now, you are looking another Lawrence Olivier. What's the mystery?" Patricia laughed, throwing her arm gently over my shoulder and pulling me close.

Raymond continued smiling with his favourite fake frown. "No mystery at all, my dear Pat, all explanations will be forthcoming. Yes, we've been through sleepless nights and bombs and torpedoes, and its sheer providence or luck, call it what you will, that we've returned safe. But I assure you I have not ill-treated my wife or willfully deprived her of food, though I suppose in a sense, I am responsible for the way she looks." Everyone looked a little interested, wondering how seriously to take Raymond. Our luggage was deposited in the station-wagon and we set off with Henry and Patricia and Rupert for Lanverndel.

"Thank God, you've arrived safe. We were so afraid after we heard the stories about the Atlantic, the U Boats and the horrifying destruction. We were terrified when we read about the losses of the convoy coming in from Gibraltar. We tried to get more details, but it was difficult. So we just prayed hard and kept our fingers crossed." Henry's voice still seemed so worried and concerned, with us right before him.

"Yes, we were definitely lucky, but it really was one of the most terrible times we had to endure. So unexpected. But we pulled through alright. Let's be thankful for that. Incidentally, how's Lanverndel doing?" he asked in the same tone.

"You shall see," said Rupert heartily, "and the credit goes to Henry entirely. He has spared no effort to ensure that when you see it again, you won't be able to tell too much of a difference."

"Thanks awfully, Henry. I can't tell you how wonderful it is to be back with all of you again, and once more thanks for everything you've done, Rupert and you."

"Don't mention it, old chap. We must lunch together soon to hear all your adventures," Rupert said with his usual good humour.

"Yes, we must, and there's so much to tell you. We've been through a rather risky adventure over the Mediterranean, and then the most terrifying voyage over the Atlantic with U boats and torpedoes. It's quite a miracle that we survived after seeing two ships so close to us hit by torpedoes and sink. Anyway, thank God, we managed to reach home safely, even though our ship was hit and damaged. Raymond will tell you all about it," I added shyly.

"But first, we shall have a drink at Lanverndel, and I have something special to tell you which is far more important than all of this, something you'll be delighted to hear."

Patricia looked at me and held my hand. I think she instinctively understood and knew the reason why I looked so pale and thin despite my good humour. But she said, "Well, I am curious, and something tells me it's going to be wonderful news."

I noticed that Raymond had, in such a short time, and quite imperceptibly, donned again his county role, something I must confess I found somewhat alien, after what I had become accustomed to during our long wandering sojourn. He seemed happy and content amongst the people he loved. And he had promised them an announcement. But before that we needed all the strength to enter Lanverndel.

It was getting dark and the blackout was gradually making itself felt. I saw the depressing difference of dimmed headlights and blackened glass everywhere, emitting not a ray of light, in the villages, in the homes, in the shops. Only the half-moon cast a dim glow through the nebulous sky, as if it too was finally being smoked out by some wartime regulation.

At last the car slowed down and I saw in the dusk the great intricately crafted wrought iron gate; the drive that had been steered with such dexterity, that at every curve or turn, the beautiful landscape was never lost; the trees forming an archway above, like the impenetrable canopy of tropical forests which I had seen in pictures. We crossed the dainty rivulets, the deep woods, the flaming cherry blossoms and golden daffodils, my eyes straining to confirm my memories. They were exactly as they were in my memories when I had entered these gates for the first time. And finally I saw Lanverndel. Was there a sense of déjà vu? I was a little confused. No, I told myself, I was not the reticent, diffident bride coming here for the first time. I was the legitimate mistress of Lanverndel, and Charlotte no longer possessed it, not the grand sea wing, not the Honey Vale, nor the creek; the last remnants of her, the wisps of lingerie, the enameled mother of pearl brushes, the lace and satin were now particles of ash, lying god knows where, and there were no dark secrets anymore shrouding the massive walls.

I looked at Raymond's profile from the back seat where I was sitting. His face seemed rigid. I reached over the seat and touched his shoulder, and rested my hand on his neck above his tie. I moved it to his mouth, and I felt his hand move up and hold mine and then he kissed it repeatedly. We had reached the porch, and once again I saw them all there, though hazily—Bede, Jane, the maids, the cooks, the gardeners, all of them. This time the porch was dark, and it would see light again only years later after the war had ended.

****

Lanverndel was the same and yet looked different; the study familiar, but not quite; it looked new but in some indefinable way lacked sparkle. And then I knew why. Every inch of glass on doors and windows was clothed with heavy oiled black paper and the lights were dimmer than candles. Pluto darted out, excited and feverish; he smelt us to confirm, and then was uncontrollable, his nose and eyes and yelps asking all the questions. It was so good to be back.

Bede brought in the drinks, scotch and soda, and Raymond was in charge again, master of his world. My eyes tried to scrutinize every detail of the furniture, the upholstery, the furnishings, the curios, some familiar, some new. I wondered where Henry had produced them all from, and I noticed for the first time with conviction that the building looked quite whole again, though a little unfamiliar.

I asked for apple juice. Patricia looked at me, "I would have thought a spot of brandy would be good for you."

I smiled and shook my head. Raymond proposed a toast. "To returning home," and then looking at me, he continued, "with something, sorry, someone new, and to everybody's health." I felt myself blush. Patricia came and kissed me on my cheek.

"Congratulations," she said. "I'm so glad for you and may you have all the happiness in the world." She went to her brother. No words were exchanged between them as they quietly embraced each other. Rupert and Henry raised their glasses and we all followed.

"This is perfectly delightful, old chap. Wonderful news." Rupert guffawed happily. Henry proposed a toast welcoming us and we raised our glasses again and drank to everyone's health.

They left early knowing that we were tired. "Patricia, just let me get familiar with Lanverndel again, and we'll meet here for lunch soon. There's so much to tell you," I said to her, and we bade them good night.

Raymond and I were now alone. We looked at each other directly, our eyes clasped together without fear. He held out his hand to me, and we climbed up the stairs to our rooms. They were the same rooms we had used earlier. The staircase was new, so were the carpets; some familiar paintings were absent while some new ones hung on the walls—men and women in period dress, ancestors retrieved from some store or basement, I presumed. We went up the stairs noiselessly, holding hands, and stood outside our rooms. Raymond turned the knob and we entered. I refused to look around or to compare it with my memories. He shut the door, and we were in each other's arms, tears streaming down our faces, tears of happiness that we were still together, that we were still alive and at Lanverndel.

We had an early supper, and I ate reasonably well. For the first time in Lanverndel I slept like the chatelaine of her domain, confident that it was finally hers.

Chapter Twelve

The next few days were a swirl of activity. They were slightly unsteady to begin with, but I worked very hard to familiarize myself with my role in the new Lanverndel, with as much confidence as I could muster. Raymond, I seldom saw. He was so completely occupied with so many things, and spent long hours away from home. There were the accounts and affairs of the estate that he had to take care of, and there were his new responsibilities of the war. He would leave early, sometimes even before I woke, and leave a note by my bedside. I missed him intensely, but on the other hand, there was nothing more gratifying for me than to see him throw himself so completely in his affairs. He had taken charge of his new post, and spent all his mornings at the County Office with Colonel Osmund taking stock of facts and figures and plans and strategies.

I, meanwhile, was not doing too badly myself. I took charge of the menu and trimmed it down drastically. I didn't care what the servants would think. There was, after all, a war on, and food couldn't be wasted. Besides, expenses had to be brought down, and it mattered very little to either of us if there were only two courses for lunch instead of five, or two snacks at tea instead of a dozen. In any case, I had never really been able to discover the final destination of the mountains of food that used to be cooked earlier. And I firmly decided that I did not want another housekeeper or a replacement for Miss Portner. I would try and handle everything myself.

It took some time getting used to the infernal blackouts and stumbling along in semi darkness. It made simple chores appear so cumbersome and complicated, but this was to become our way of life for the next five years without respite. My health was improving, and gradually my appetite and strength were returning. I inspected the changes in Lanverndel and established a routine for myself. I would spend some time in the morning with the gardeners seeing the grounds and lawns and the flower beds, and would give instructions, or make changes or try new experiments. Then I would spend a few hours going through various areas of Lanverndel that I had never seen before—the basements, the lofts, the stables, the little lodges all around. I realised Henry had done an absolutely marvellous job, and it would suffice until the war got over. I still did not feel mentally prepared to inspect Lanverndel from within. One day I would have the strength to do it. After that, I would decide if I wanted any further changes.

Henry had thoughtfully assembled a functional wardrobe for Raymond; he knew Raymond's taste and style and what he would need. As for me, I felt comfortable with whatever I had.

The newspapers were full of the fall of France and the evacuation at Dunkirk. But it all seemed so distant now. Not at all as threatening and frightening as it had felt when we were in the Continent, or in Gibraltar or over the Atlantic. Now safe and secure in Lanverndel, the war seemed none of my business.

My days, though pretty full, were long and lonely, for I was away from Raymond after so many months of physical and emotional closeness. I missed him unimaginably. I had grown so accustomed to his presence, the rustle of his papers, that peculiar aroma of male paraphernalia, the silent whistle between his teeth, a good natured tease now and then. How much more substantially I had grown to love him, not just in childish adulation or in hero worship as before, but with much greater understanding of his character, his strength and generosity. We had experienced so much together and the world outside had changed so drastically. I remembered again what my father had told me years ago, that we emerge so much stronger after struggle, but only if we've given a good fight, and haven't buckled. I think my father would have approved of me.

I never felt any nostalgia for the old Lanverndel, nor for the priceless objects d'art and furniture that had gone forever. Perhaps deep within me I had always acknowledged that they were all Charlotte's, and that the Lanverndel which I had entered for the first time, almost a year ago, really belonged to her. Well, I shrugged, that was the past and it was over; every trace of it had been burnt. Nothing in Lanverndel was hers anymore. Was I secretly glad that the past was now mere ashes? I bit my lip and cursed myself as I felt a stab of guilt.

I still could not fathom what Raymond was feeling, and I worried a great deal about it. It was his home that we had reentered, his memories going beyond a generation, to his parents, his childhood, his trophies, and then to the gruesome chapter of his life with Charlotte. But I have always held the belief as I do to this day, possibly as a backlash to the tragedies I saw so early in my own life, that speaking about something traumatic or painful with someone who loves you and tries to understand, heals as it unburdens. One day there would be time and I would talk to him.

Raymond would come in for a hurried lunch. He was always busy and preoccupied and had to travel continuously. There would be meetings in London which would keep him away for four or five nights. He spoke little about them. I presumed they must have been extremely confidential, and frankly, I was not at all curious about them. He would go often to Plymouth and all along the coast to Land's End.

One day after he had returned late in the evening from London, he announced quite abruptly, "You know, I think I'll be starting flying again. Its years since I last flew a plane, but I'll have to start practice soon."

I was shocked and was turning increasingly insecure and adamant. "I had no idea that you were interested in flying." I found my voice getting a little sharper. "Wouldn't it be better if you waited until the baby is born before you start such risky hobbies?" I said, trying my best to keep my tone normal.

He gave a loud laugh. "My dear young lady, do you realize there's a furious war raging in Europe, of which you've had a pretty traumatic experience yourself? I assure you, I don't mean to fly for pleasure. My country needs my services, and that's all there is to it."

I felt so utterly foolish. "Oh dear, how stupid I am. Of course, it's such a serious situation and I am so ignorant. But what am I going to do? You are going to be away more and more, and I'm so lonely, and I hate this awful war, and I won't have anyone to turn to when the baby is born." I burst into tears, and they wouldn't stop, as hard as I tried. I sniffed and snivelled like a guilty schoolgirl and as usual had no handkerchief.

Raymond was beside me in a second. He held me close, and pulled out his handkerchief. "Forgive me darling, I've been such a brute. I hadn't given a thought to what you're going through. You've been so brave and patient and I've behaved like a cad. I know I haven't been able to spend much time with you lately, and I can understand you must be nervous. Now, dry your eyes. You must listen to me. I know it's no excuse, but I've been frightfully preoccupied these last few days. Finances are not too good, and I've had to borrow quite heavily. Lanverndel has cost us an awful lot, but I'm glad we did it. Someday, I suppose, land prices should go up, and then we can sell the Devonshire land. Anyway, I'm sure there'll be some solution."

'Raymond, forgive me, I'm truly sorry. I feel so terrible," I managed to squeeze the words through my foolish sobs.

"No darling, it's not your fault. It's I who has been a brute. And yes, I must tell you, I will have to do a substantial amount of flying, noncombat, but generally on call. And now, prepare for some more changes. We'll have to convert the basement into an air-raid shelter for the village. We can expect a lot of action in our parts, once the Germans take over the French coasts. A major part of Lanverndel will also be used for other purposes by Whitehall. I know all this will be a strain on you, but we must do it—we owe it to our country. Now tell me, would you like me to arrange for a nurse to move in? An elderly, retired person, since the ones nearer your age would all be in some service or other by now."

I felt so ashamed of myself. "No, no, this is so foolish of me. It must be the strain and tension of the last so many months. No, I don't need anyone. I just have to adjust to this horrid war. The fact is that I miss you so much, and I'm so afraid when you are not here, not of anything in particular, but generally about you and the baby."

Raymond chuckled. "I simply cannot believe that you are afraid. Don't you remember how you risked your life in so many ways the last year? I don't believe it, you can't be afraid."

His words were a boost, and I felt much better.

"I don't know. When I talk to you, it seems so ridiculous, but when I'm alone, I seem to be afraid of so much. Earlier I was afraid of Lanverndel. It all seems so foolish if one tries to explain it. I wonder if I'm making any sense at all."

"But of course, darling, you must be out of sorts, and everything is so chaotic and will get even more so. We must ask Pat to come over. I'm sure she'll give you confidence. I hardly know anything about babies. I'll ask her to come tomorrow. Would you like that?"

I sniffed and blew my nose. "Yes, I would like it very much. I'm so terribly sorry. I've behaved abominably. I should be helping you with your problems. Instead I only add to them."

"Let me see, I'll try and be back early today. Let's have tea underneath the maple tree and we'll go walking to the Honey Vale, and spend a good evening together."

"That sounds marvellous. I have an appointment with Doctor Spencer this afternoon. I'll finish that and will be waiting for you."

Before I could complete my sentence, he was gone.

My visit to the doctor was a great success. He was extremely pleased with my general condition, and more importantly, with the way my appetite was improving. I was now ten weeks pregnant and could feel myself putting on weight. My energy level was improving, and the world had started looking brighter. I remembered Doctor Gordon's advice in Gibraltar. It was ridiculous that I should expect Raymond to neglect his duties and hang around the house just so that I wasn't lonely. Somehow, the reality of the war had still not struck our part of the world in its true, bloody seriousness. Life here seemed not much different in many respects from what it used to be, except for the blackouts.

I considered the idea of accompanying Raymond on his next visit to London. I thought I should take more interest in what he was doing, in what the plans for Lanverndel were. It was just the loneliness and fatigue and my changing body that were making me so peevish. But there was a war going on, and one couldn't indulge in helplessness and idleness.

Raymond was true to his word. He arrived exactly at half past four for tea, and we celebrated this grand ritual underneath the maple tree. I had dressed with care selecting from my French wardrobe that I had acquired in Nice. The French really understood clothes. I noticed my colour was getting better and some of the new weight was beginning to show. I went towards the drive as soon as I saw him, and he took my hand as we walked to the tea table.

"I'm so glad you were able to get away, and I want to tell you, I'm very grateful that you've done this for me. I'm sorry about my terrible moods. I'm sure they have something to do with being pregnant. By the way, the doctor says he's pleased with me."

"Next time I must come with you. I wish I could scrape some more time to spend with you, but it seems next to impossible. Oh yes, Pat is coming tomorrow for lunch. She'll probably stay on till tea time."

"That's lovely."

John poured the tea and the ritual began.

"Raymond, did you have to take a lot of trouble to do this for me?" I asked.

"In a way, yes. I postponed a lot which should have been done today for tomorrow. But that's okay. Being with you is also important, and while there's still time to postpone, one might as well do so." He smiled.

"I don't know what happened to me. But I'm picking up, and I've decided I should start becoming a little more useful. You said something about air raid shelters. What was that?"

"Well, it appears certain that Lanverndel will be billeted and used quite substantially for various war purposes, definitely an air raid shelter. We'll be firming up everything when I go to London next. But be prepared to have very little of Lanverndel for ourselves."

"Raymond, can I accompany you to London on your next visit?"

"But of course, if you should feel like it. I'll probably be there for two or three days. The civil defence plans have to be discussed. But I won't be able to spend very much time with you. You wouldn't mind that, would you?"

"Of course I would," I said very definitely, "but I'm patriotic too, and quite prepared to sacrifice my time with you for the sake of the country. After all, I too must contribute somehow." I smiled.

He returned my smile, "And incidentally, I don't think you'll have too much time to spare very soon. Once the real activity starts in Lanverndel, you'll have your hands quite full."

"You know, in a way I'm looking forward to it, whatever it is. It will protect me from imaginary fears."

"The roles seem to have reversed, I see. If you remember, not very long ago it was I who had to be protected from imaginary fears, and what a marvellous job you did. I must confess I'm rather clumsy and ineffective in this field."

"You are teasing me as always. Shall we now go for the walk that you promised me?"

"Yes, indeed, we shall."

We changed our shoes. He took my arm and we set forth for the second time together for the Honey Vale.

I didn't want to think, I didn't want to remember, and I really didn't want to see anything. I just wanted to be with him and be conscious that we had transcended our memories, our jinxes, and the past. That was victory enough for me.

"What are you thinking of, little girl?" he asked almost tenderly.

"Do you want to know the absolute truth? I was thinking of you and how wonderful it is to walk with you here again after so many months. We've survived, and Honey Vale will always be beautiful."

We stood still in the woods. Of course, I didn't expect a response to that. I was supposed to read his silence and understand. He took me in his arms, and I felt the world stand still and a magic spread everywhere. He kissed me with tenderness, a quiet passion, as he hadn't done in a very long time.

We continued our walk in hushed silence, having only our closeness and our peace to comfort us. The mysterious beauty of the woods, the riot of the flowers and blossoms, the lengthening rays of the sun were a fusion through which we airily walked on. The magic was ours alone and words did not belong here, they would have been like noisy intruders. I was determined that we should walk to the sea, just to prove to ourselves if nothing else, that we were not losers and had survived. We kept walking towards it, completely overwhelmed by the vast blue sheet. We saw the fire of the sun drown in her, the burning molten orange sinking deeper and deeper into the placid waters and then disappearing without a trace.

Words would still not come. Miracles can hardly be followed by words. We turned around after watching the horizon, and headed for home. We could feel each other's breath, but we still did not disturb the silence. We walked on, looking at each other now and then, acknowledging to each other that we had not suffered in vain, not fought in vain, that life with all its beauty and wonder still lay before us.

We decided to dress for dinner, dinner with wine and flowers and candlelight. It was perfect, the courses one after another, I scarcely remember what. He, the master of his world, and me looking quite elegant I thought in my blue dress. And then we went to our rooms. I brushed my hair and wore my nightgown and when I returned to the room I saw Raymond standing with an extremely preoccupied frown on his face.

Oh dear, what could have gone wrong on a day as perfect as this? Had he remembered something he oughtn't to have postponed? Was it another visitation from the nether world of memories?

I trod gingerly and with great trepidation asked, "Darling, what is it? Is something wrong?"

He looked at me, still serious and deep in thought."Actually, I was thinking of Gibraltar—of Doctor Gordon and his prescriptions. I'm not quite sure. Am I still in the celibate zone or am I out of it? "

I burst out laughing. "Of course you are. I was waiting for you to remember."

Chapter Thirteen

We visited London in early July, after France had fallen and Dunkirk was over. My health was better and I had recovered admirably from the aftermath of my Atlantic adventure. Raymond grew more and more involved in his official duties and flying missions, and I tried to absorb myself as best as I could in my household affairs and in the special experience of motherhood. There was no such thing as a routine—timings were chaotic and sleep irregular, and sometimes I would not see Raymond for days together.

I tried to put our last visit to London out of my mind—that had not really been a visit, but a last ditch stand against fate, and we had in a way carried the day. No, I would not be shadowed by it, and would enjoy London with the spirit of excursion and try and gain insight into the culture and history of this great city, something I had never had a chance to do earlier.

The ambience of London appeared to me quite schizophrenic; feverish hysteria side by side a casual nonchalance. It seemed to me that people walked differently, talked differently, and they appeared to have a great enthusiasm about everything they did. But underlying the activity everywhere was a visible patriotism which cut right across all barriers of class and community. At night, the city which was famous for the glitter of a million stars, became a sheet of black beneath which the bustle went on unperturbed.

London was full of the new Prime Minister. Day after day we heard his fine speeches, and we grew to love him, his indomitable courage and his cigar. London too, like Paris, was a city of speculation and rumours, though not quite so racy or spirited, and a Nazi invasion was the most popular subject of discussion. I thought everybody appeared a little confused, or was it because there was a kind of novelty in the threat of invasion. The papers spoke of Operation Sea Lion and observed that it was the first time since Napoleon, that England was facing a threat of invasion. Most ordinary Britons wondered in a disbelieving and nonchalant way that if this were indeed true, how on earth they would ever handle it.

But no one could miss the spirit of ardent patriotism all around, even in restaurants which declared proudly that they served only English food. Strangely, there were no road signs in the city. It was only later that we learnt that they had been removed to confound possible invaders. Of course, it was only out of towners like us who became victims of this measure. Lamp posts were painted white to help navigate the nighttime traffic moving around with blackened headlights. But what struck me as most exhilarating was the presence of so many young girls and women in almost every walk of London life. They were doing all kinds of government duties, in the postal and defence departments, working in all kinds of factories, in active service. Perhaps, I too would have been one of them, had I not made that decision to be au pair to Mrs Kappelhoff, a decision which so changed my destiny. And while girls of my age and class were risking their lives for the country, I was expecting a child in the lap of luxury, and this seemed to be the extent of my input during this troubled period.

We stayed at Raymond's club, a comfortable place just off Knightsbridge. He liked the service and the privacy, and as for me, I found it equally convenient, as I was planning to be a full time tourist, and one couldn't ask for a better location for that. Raymond was practically incommunicado all day, so I would be off on my own—visiting art galleries, museums, the famous shopping areas, and generally feeling the frenetic pace of London life. We would meet at the end of the day and I would excitedly narrate my adventures and discoveries to him.

On our second day in London, he asked me, "How would you like to have about twenty-five children at Lanverndel?"

I wondered what he meant. "What do you mean, Raymond? How on earth will you produce twenty-five children at Lanverndel? All I know is that with great patience and some difficulty, I'll present you with one next year."

Raymond kept looking at me, but his thoughts were elsewhere. "Then that would make it twenty-six. You see, my dearest, the government has decided that it would be better if the children from the cities are moved out to foster homes in the country. They're of the opinion that this would help their parents to contribute more completely to the war effort, in the sense that they wouldn't have to worry about their children's lives or safety."

"Oh, is that so? Of course Raymond, I'm sure I'll manage. Lanverndel is so huge. All the rooms and lodges can be used. But we'll have to get extra help and nannies."

"Yes of course. I was wondering whether the entire line of lodges near the stables can be converted into little dormitories for the children. There'll be enough room for the maids and nurses. The basement, as I told you, will serve as the air raid shelter for the village, and a lot of Lanverndel is going to be billeted by the government."

"Oh, really," I was quite baffled. "What on earth for?"

"That, my dearest, we will never know, at least not till the war is over."

I wasn't listening. I was thinking in the privacy of my mind. Let Lanverndel be billetted, let it be occupied by aliens. The remnants from the past would be exorcised faster, the shadows and associations would be erased by sheer circumstance, and we would have fresh, untainted insignia on it. There would be the Plymouth Children's Wing, the London Children's Wing, and heaven knows which other cities the children would come from. Then there'd be the Billeted Wing and the Air-raid Wing. Old fearful memories and associations would fade away faster and be replaced by fresh ones, and the present would silently obliterate the past.

My little mental pirouette over, I returned to terra firma. I found Raymond watching me with a puzzled amusement. "Where have you been? You seemed to be on a very private planet."

"Yes," I smiled. "I was in Lanverndel. Lanverndel with children and not ghosts."

I could have killed myself for being so tactless and insensitive, and I turned hot with shame. How could I have made this slip which must surely have pierced his soul and hurt him.

"Raymond," I tried to make amends, stammering, "I was thinking ...the children would drive away the... the...whatever remains of the past...even faint shadows...and it will bring us peace."

"Yes, I know. I was thinking of the same thing."

I was glad there would be so much to occupy me; I was glad we'd be sheltering children, for I suddenly felt a very intimate inquisitiveness about them. I almost felt I had never known them before. Why was my mind playing such tricks with me? For some time now I had been noticing how things around me would change perspective with an unnatural suddenness; one minute they would look familiar, and the next, things would become completely alien and I would not know them, however hard I tried. Did this happen to all women in my state, or was it that I had absorbed too much experience in too short a time?

When the children did come to us, poor dears, some of them lice-ridden and frightened, many with no knowledge of hygiene, and others who had never seen the country before, my maternal feelings sprang to the fore. I wanted the children to feel safe and secure, and happy, and I would do everything to make them feel so. For, I knew what it meant to lose one's home and be without one's own folks.

We spent four days in London, and as I joked with Raymond, I spent them in London and he in Whitehall. He met up with several of his classmates from Eton and Oxford, now seated in various departments in Whitehall, and before we left we were invited to a dinner at the Savoy, something of an old boys' reunion, so to speak.

I wasn't exactly brimming with enthusiasm at the thought of spending an evening with an assembly of highbrow bureaucrats, even if they had been Raymond's contemporaries at school or college. To nurture confidence and to try and exude it in impersonal Nice or Gibraltar was one thing, even if the beau monde there had remotely heard of us or the tales surrounding us. But this was different. These were Raymond's personal friends, people who cared for him, people who knew the various turns his life had taken.

And then like a knife it cut me—they would have known Charlotte, they would have been her guests at Lanverndel and been enchanted with her beauty and charm. And they would compare me to her and feel sorry for Raymond.

I wouldn't meet them, I thought. I would tell Raymond that I wasn't feeling well and that he should make the usual excuses and regrets for me. I sank lower and lower into despair and weariness and the warm glow of self-pity extended its grey, comforting embrace, and for a moment I was tempted to succumb.

But I gave myself a violent shove instead. Was that all there was to my brag, to my hard fought determination? I tossed my head upwards to one side coquettishly and sang a tune. I may not be beautiful or educated, but Raymond loved me, and I was carrying his child. So why was I allowing her to crush me, her beauty or her brilliance or her accomplishments? She was just another chicane, a masquerader, a hoax, and Raymond did not love her; he had never loved her.

I dressed with care and tried to look chic and well groomed. I must hold my head with self-assurance and do Raymond as much credit as I could. I scrutinized myself critically—yes, I would be confident and natural and not allow myself to show any diffidence or despair, and his friends would not feel sorry for him.

The party was a success, and the gentlemen and their ladies were utterly gracious to me. No one looked at me more than what was socially necessary, and conversation was centred upon the men recalling their college pranks, and the eccentricities of their tutors—how a technique had been developed to purloin examination question papers, and how successive classes had perfected this technique. There were a phenomenal number of A's in these years naturally, until one of the porters stumbled upon the entire operation quite inadvertently, and reported it to the tutor. The game was up, but there was nothing anyone could do about it without compromising themselves. The only apparent result was that the number of A's plummeted mysteriously that year.

No one spoke of Lanverndel and no one spoke of the war. It was like a group of school boys getting together and recalling their camaraderie and the good times they had enjoyed within or outside the bounds of school law. They spoke of many of their friends gone forever in the trenches of the Great War. All the men present seemed to be on the other side of forty, and I was the youngest wife present, from a different world and not quite belonging, but I realized clearly for the first time what class and breeding truly meant. There was no condescension, no curiosity, only a lot of kindness and interest in our experiences on the Continent, and over the Atlantic.

Finally, it was I who braced myself and spoke of Lanverndel and how we were expecting a lot of children from the cities, and how when the war would be over, we would meet over a weekend at Lanverndel and repeat this evening which had been indeed so enjoyable. I was quite pleased with my performance. I may not have been glamorous or an intellectual, or even moderately erudite, but I had demonstrated some measure of poise and élan which I had always envied others for, and most importantly, I had not embarrassed Raymond in any way.

Back in Lanverndel, Raymond became invisible again. The basement was being converted into an air raid shelter for the estate and the village, to spend the nights and days whenever there were alerts. Access points, exit points, toilets, water facilities were being constructed. The lodges were being prepared for the children and whatever Lanverndel possessed now, which was very little, was placed at their disposal. No longer were there rooms filled with linen and curtains and covers, no longer presses overflowing with delicately embroidered linen and damask, the rare, subtle broderie which strained the eye to merely see their intricate designs. They were gone, gone with the flames that had swept the shadows away. However, the neighbouring industries, philanthropists, and families contributed generously and we managed to get enough furniture and linen, clothes and shoes for the children. Nurseries and dormitories, bathrooms and toilets were improvised, heating and water arrangements hastily made, and space for the nannies and maids organized.

One day, I asked Henry to take me on a tour of Lanverndel, something I had been thinking of for a long time. I felt ready for it and I thought I must do it now. Not merely on account of curiosity or proving to myself that I would pass the test, but I simply had to take stock of the space I had at my disposal, for God knows what kind of demands would be made on Lanverndel in the coming months and years.

We started our tour in right earnest beginning from the suites and guest rooms on the ground floor that I had never seen before—altogether six of them, forming an eastern arm extending from the central core of the house. I didn't pay too much attention to how the rooms were furnished, or what artifacts stood in them and what paintings adorned the walls. My main purpose was merely to assess the space I had at my disposal for the unknown contingencies which would surface in times to come.

We returned to the porch and stood there. Henry was watching me quietly. I thought he looked a little nervous, God knows why. After all, he too knew how changed our lives were. He kept looking away from me, as if he was not able to tell me something.

"Mrs de Villiers," he said, "would you like to see the upstairs also? It's more or less the same." He looked away towards the lawns. It was a bright sunny day. I saw a pair of fat, fluffy squirrels scamper across the hedgerow. They had found some nuts and were now sitting on their haunches, gnawing away, trying to reach the kernel.

Yes, I did want to see the upstairs, I wanted to see the grand sea wing. It was childish, it was inquisitive. But I wanted to see if Charlotte's last imprints had dissolved and vanished. And I wanted to see it alone, so that I would not be self-conscious, so that I was free to look at whatever I wanted, for as long as I wanted, open any cupboard or drawer, examine any decoration, and finally bury the last of the ghost forever. I knew I would do it.

"No Henry, not today. It's already late. Maybe sometime next week. In any case, as you say, it's more or less the same as downstairs, and I am so much more familiar with the rooms upstairs."

Henry looked relieved. He still wouldn't look me in the eye. "OK, if for some reason I am not around, too many visits to the county offices and solicitors, the keys are always available with Bede."

"Thank you, Henry", I said, "you are a wonderful friend."

I decided to visit the grand sea wing one morning, about a week later. I prepared for it meticulously; as I was determined it should be my last rite of passage, my last battle to evict forever the remnant lingering shadows of the past.

I consciously played back my last furtive trespass there and recalled its great beauty, the ornate ceilings and bed posts, the persistent scent of gardenias... how foolish and clumsy I was then, so immature.... I remembered Miss Portner invisibly following me, trailing my every move...silently, politely undermining me with her freezing superior attitude, wishing me to disintegrate, to collapse... intimidating me, making me feel inferior, inadequate...by her fabled evening gowns, furs and lingerie.

I entered the room, my mind concentrating upon itself. I looked around, my eyes focusing on the window. And then, for an instant, I saw a huge ornate ***C*** flash past me from the window overlooking the circular, terraced lawns reaching the sea. I saw the ornate ***C*** now etched powerfully in the air in the middle of the room, a shaft of sunlight piercing through it like an arrow. My eyes couldn't move away from it—I seemed paralyzed. With great effort I moved my hand, then my arm and then my head. I saw a magnificent painting on the wall. It was Raymond's father, looking handsome and aristocratic. It was a formal portrait; he wore a suit of the early twentieth century style, with a deep grey cloak. His eyes were looking straight at me, with approval I thought, and then I saw the huge ornate ***C*** shrinking, fading and disappearing out of the room. The grand sea wing had been swept clean, cleansed of all the shadows. I heard the sound of gentle sea waves splash against the shore.

I smiled at Raymond's father, my hand moved upwards on its own, and rested upon the swelling on my stomach. I returned to the library, feeling light and airy and victorious. A huge weight had lifted from my shoulders.

Raymond asked me which part of the ground floor I would like to keep. I told him I wanted only the hall, the living room, the dining room and the study, and the rest was his.

"Remember, the whole area and the access will be cordoned off completely, and not even you or I will be allowed inside without permission."

"Raymond, if it's so secret, then why choose a place like this which will be buzzing with activity?"

"That's the whole idea, to have it in a place buzzing with activity so that it's least suspect."

I just gave up—these men and their war. So, my morning room, the billiards room, the bar, the spare guest rooms, six suites in all were handed over to Whitehall, and I saw them again only many years later when the world had changed beyond recognition.

One morning Henry came looking a little anxious and unhappy.

"Mrs de Villiers, if you don't mind, could I have a word with you? It's a little personal. Could we sit in the study, please."

"Of course, Henry. What's the matter? Nothing serious, I hope."

"No, no, it isn't serious, but it's something you must know, and something I've been putting off, quite unnecessarily."

He came to the point straight away, "You see, when we were getting the grand sea wing together, we came across a safe, which we were able to somehow open with great difficulty. Well, I don't want to disturb your peace of mind, just when you and Raymond are settling down again, and God knows I've been putting it off long enough. But I just didn't want to put it to him, especially now that his hands are so full. You could handle it so much better."

"Yes, but what's the matter?" I asked with an impatience bordering on fear. What apocalypse was going to hit me in the next few seconds? I started getting more and more panicky.

"The safe was full of extremely valuable jewels. I've made an inventory of everything. What would you have me do with them?"

I must have turned pale, for my heart stood still for a moment. So that's why Henry was so ill at ease the day he took me on the Lanverndel tour. Easy, easy, I counselled myself. I have to take a practical, rational decision, and I mustn't buckle under the shadow of her jewels. And Raymond should not know anything. I would tell him later after many more years had passed.

One thing I was completely sure about—I wanted to have nothing to do with her jewels. But how would I know which of them belonged to her and which were de Villiers heirlooms? I would have to ask Patricia, I reasoned. So far, my logic was progressing fine.

I told Henry that I would talk to Patricia and let him know what to do in a day or two, and I repeated that Raymond should know nothing about this. I phoned Patricia and presented the problem to her. Would she be able to identify what belonged to her mother or the de Villiers family, I asked. A strange thought crossed my mind. There was another de Villiers who was also a rightful owner of these jewels, but alas, he couldn't be consulted, and I couldn't speak for him.

"Yes, I think I can tell you what belongs to the family and what doesn't. Viewing mother's jewels was a special treat she would inveigle me with whenever she wanted me to do something against my will. The last time I saw them was just before I got married and was asked to take my pick. Yes, I think I'll be able to tell the family heirlooms quite easily."

"Patricia, do me a favour please. Could you come over as soon as possible and help me separate them from the rest?"

"Yes, I'll come." There was a longish pause. "I'll come tomorrow." And again a pause. "What will you do with the rest?"she asked, without mincing words.

"I don't know. I don't want to even look at them."

Patricia came the next day, true to her word, and Henry produced the whole array of jewels and laid them out, almost in a military formation—diamonds the size of little rocks, rubies and sapphires finely set with exquisite craftsmanship, emeralds, the colour of the Lanverndel lawns, amethysts with a twilight haze, turquoises, rich and raw like little pebbles, topazes, chains, rings, bracelets, all blazing and mocking me with an evil, hypnotic brilliance. I felt ill and looked away.

"Patricia, please do what must be done. I can't see this anymore."

"Don't worry. Why don't you just sit down? I don't think I shall take much longer. I can already see the familiar objects."

I sat down, and Henry asked me whether I would like some tea. I suddenly felt like tea.

"Here we are. This belongs to the de Villiers. This doesn't. I'm quite sure." Patricia had performed her duty with utmost sincerity.

"Patricia, I realize I'm nobody to say this, but please take whatever you want from them. They're as much yours as they are Raymond's. Forgive me if you think I'm being crass."

Patricia took my hand. "But of course, I'll do so with pleasure. Now let me see, I always liked this ruby ring and pendant, and this bracelet." She tactfully put the rest in the casket. "Now this is yours and may you have all the luck and happiness wearing them." She kissed me and asked, "Have you decided what to do with the rest?"

"I really don't know. I don't want to tell Raymond. It would be like flaunting the very things that would hurt him. But yet I cannot decide anything without his knowledge."

"I think you should simply hand them over to King and Samuel's at London and ask them to sell them off. They've been with the family for ages. You could use the money to help you out with Lanverndel."

An idea flashed across my mind. "I'll do better than that. We could contribute the money to the County Civil Defence. I don't want Lanverndel to have anything to do with it. What is your opinion Henry?"

Henry looked impassive. I think he was more worried about Raymond and me rather than the jewels. "No doubt, Raymond will have to agree, and then I'll ask the solicitors to handle it."

"Oh no, isn't there some way this could be done without Raymond knowing? And why should the solicitors come into it? Can't we just hand them over to the jewellers and put the proceeds with the county as contribution from an anonymous source? I'll tell Raymond later, when I think the time is right."

"Okay," he said quietly. "Would you like to keep the inventory?"

"No, Henry. I don't want it, and I don't want to ever see them again."

How he handled it I never asked him, but about six months later there much excitement at the County Offices, and Raymond told me that an anonymous contribution of seventy five thousand pounds had come for the County Civil Defence from someone in London.

I decided I would tell him about this little intrigue only after the war was over, when our children would be romping over the lawns, and the past would be even more distant than now.

Chapter Fourteen

The children from the cities came to us in early August. They came, not twenty-five, but fifty of them, ranging from the ages of four to twelve with their identification cards, gas masks and five nannies. The lodges had been prepared with double-decker beds, cupboards and little chairs and tables. A kindergarten for the infants, and classes for the older children based on their literacy, which was in any case indifferent, were organized by the ladies of the neighbourhood. Each of the lodges housed ten children and a nanny, and Jane's two sisters were brought in to help. The local doctor gave the children a check up, and though many of them needed cleaning up and skin ointment and lessons in hygiene, there was really nothing wrong with them. One of the lodges was converted into a dining place and kitchen, and after a month or so everyone seemed to be settling down. Meals were prepared and dishes washed, rooms cleaned and linen laundered; it was almost as if there was another little world pulsating with a life of its own within Lanverndel, a world of babies and baths and nurseries and excursions.

The children were perpetually hungry for the first few days and piles of food would virtually disappear at each meal, much to the chagrin of the servants. But I counselled patience; the children had come to us hungry and it was only a matter of time that their eyes and stomachs would experience the security of food. Cleaning them up took some time. At first they resisted baths and there would be long bouts of screaming and yelling, but gradually with the gentle firmness of the nannies and the maids, the children settled into a routine and before long they were adjusting to their new life. I would sometimes organize special treats for them—apple pie or chocolate cake. They stayed with us right through the war and I grew to love them very protectively as my little wards. Many of them have done very well and have kept in touch with us to this day.

Soon after the children came, the bombs came. I shall never forget the first bombing, around the end of August, on the twenty-fourth to be precise. We had gone through mock air raid drills quite a few times in the village, but when the real thing happened, it was something beyond the pale of imagination; blood curdling was the only word I could think of to describe it—it was like the end of the world.

We heard the siren, and the children were rushed underground. People living on the estate and in the nearby houses, and the household staff used the shortest routes, and before we knew it, the sounds of the explosions started, sometimes seeming close and sometimes far away. Raymond had told me that the radar stations on the coast, at Plymouth, Falmouth, Land's End, the Isle of Wight, and so many other names which I cannot remember now, would most certainly be bombing targets. He was at his office, and I hoped he was safe. Some children screamed, and others went white with fear. The sounds became more and more terrifying and continued endlessly for twenty minutes without a break. In panic, I suddenly wondered whether my baby was getting injured by the lethal vibrations and noise. In future, I must smother them with a pillow.

Then finally, there came a terrifying silence, almost deafening, and after a while the all clear sounded. We scrambled out of the basement, all of us shaken and the children terrified. But we stayed faithful to our instructions and continued to attend to our chores wherever we had left them off, as if everything was perfectly normal.

"Why are they burning such loud crackers? It's not Guy Fawkes," asked a very concerned little boy. "I'm scared they'll hurt us."

"No, they won't hurt us," I said very firmly. "Our planes and soldiers will destroy the wicked people, and won't allow them to hurt us. But you must remember, every time you hear the siren, you must run over here."

I hated the blackouts that we had to endure; but there was no escape. Sometimes they would become unbearable, especially when I was alone, and then I would wait desperately for dawn to break. I would play a little game with myself, a fantasy game, that I was living in a castle in the Middle Ages, and no better form of light existed anywhere in the world.

The older children had been placed in charge of groups of smaller ones to help the nannies, and we became quite an experienced group of civilians as the air raids were repeated during that terrible year, learning also how to get on with day to day life. We read in the papers of the hellfire London was enduring with such good humoured resilience and defiance, and only then did we realize that we were being let off rather lightly.

Of course, I would never see Raymond on air raid days. He would be on the roads, supervising fire fighting with scarce resources, medical and first aid, arranging urgent repairs of water and sewerage pipes. The main targets would be the air fields, the harbours and radar stations which stood as our all weather guards. Then there would be deaths, and even though he never told me about them, I could always tell by the look on his face.

Life continued like this right through 1940. It was a life of bombs and fires, wreckages and deaths. Air duels became part of the sky, and there was hardly a patch on the coastline from where they were not visible. Giant vapour trails, the dog fights going on thousands of feet up in the air, sudden explosions and red flashes of flames, and the thunderclap of a plane as it blew up in the air. The dead were mourned, but the determination and will to fight grew stronger, and stoically we braced ourselves to do whatever was required for king and country.

The children were progressing satisfactorily and by now their routines were fairly well established with hours for study and play and outdoor activity. In October, some parents came to see their children, and it gave me a strange kind of happiness seeing perfect strangers fill my home with tears of joy.

I was getting heavy but had to be fighting fit out of sheer necessity. I had a full day with administering to household affairs, the children's affairs, running Lanverndel and coordinating with Raymond. We donated many of our vans, trucks, cars to the county authorities to be converted into mobile canteens and ambulances. The kitchens, old and new, and pantry were emptied of all the thick huge iron and steel utensils and age old ovens and hot cases. I always imagined them finding new life as Spitfires or Hurricanes—Lanverndel's contribution to the war. The kitchen was refurbished with lighter aluminum ware, just the very minimum, so as to keep the household going during the war. One day surely the war would be over, and then I would equip the kitchen according to my wishes, just as I would Lanverndel. Fortunately, I had not become sentimental about anything in the hidden kitchen area. In fact, I had never even seen its massive treasures until they were being removed for handing over—ovens the size of little rooms, large enough to bake for an entire army, pots like little ponds which had fed soldiers during the Civil War, so Raymond told me. Nothing was mine. What had been Charlotte's, I would never know, but now they were all gone, and in a strange, contented way, I felt light and cheered. Slowly, almost as if by an unseen hand, Charlotte's Lanverndel was dissolving and vanishing. I wondered whether it was following a deliberate pattern as it seemed to, and I was glad.

The bombs continued falling and people kept dying. Sometimes I was convinced that this was the last chapter of the Bible, and that we would all perish. At these times I would turn morose and demoralized and would start sinking into a mindless kind of torpor. I remembered my father telling me once, it seemed so long ago, that this was the luckiest century to be born in, a century where science and reason would reign supreme, where the devils of disease would be conquered and the mysteries of the universe be unravelled for the benefit of mankind. I was glad he was not alive today to witness the age of science reaching its high point of glory; how it had enabled men to kill and devastate with unprecedented accuracy and proficiency; how it had become enslaved to the hecatombs of destruction.

I sighed. Our baby was to be born in another two months, and I had organized nothing. I didn't even know where to begin. I had only myself to depend upon or at best I could ask Patricia for help. Raymond was so busy, and it would not be fair to expect him to be part of this. I called Patricia and asked her for some tips on how to go about the whole business. She sprung the most beautiful surprise.

"Don't worry, my dear. I have the entire layette ready for you, including some of Howard's things for luck. Raymond had also mentioned something about a nurse moving in. I've already fixed it, Mrs Walters is her name. She's an elderly person and will stay as long as you want her to."

"Patricia, thank you, thank you so much; you are my fairy godmother. I don't know what I'd do without you."

'Anytime, my dear. Now, your job is to get the nursery ready, and a place in the basement prepared, just to be on the safe side."

Dear Patricia, she was always so thoughtful and kind to me, and how much trouble she was taking on my account.

"How's Raymond?" she asked.

"Frankly, Patricia, I hardly see him. Sometimes we manage to see each other late in the evening, but we're both so dog tired. And he's travelling so much. But he seems well, and frightfully busy."

"Listen, I'll come over next week. Meanwhile, don't worry too much."

"Yes, do, Patricia. I'm truly looking forward to it."

Our basement was now quite a lively little place. There were games for the children, tables for cards, some music instruments, dining tables, some crockery. Mattresses had been stacked for night raids, when we would normally be houseful with the nearby villagers and our staff settling in for the night. A separate corner would have to be enclosed for me, if the time came here.

Henry was like a pillar. He ran the estate as best as he could. He attended to his duties as the Civil Defence Warden for the area around Lanverndel, and he was my greatest support and strength, now that Raymond was hardly here. Worry about Raymond I often did, especially since I knew he was flying over Occupied Europe, off and on, on some kind of secret missions. Sometimes in the darkness, I would turn irrational with fear, but something in this dreadful war had generated enormous reserves of courage and resilience in all of us. We would hear of deaths of people we knew, we would hear of destruction of homes we knew, but we would cast everything aside and go on mechanically with our lives. We would see dog fights in the skies above us, occasionally an enemy plane would be shot down around Lanverndel, and the entire gruesome business would be brought to our doorstep; yet we kept pretending that it really didn't affect us.

Our coast was taking a savage battering. Plymouth and Southampton were blitzed repeatedly, and all through the year the pounding continued unabated. Many of our children were from those parts, and before the terrible year was over, three of them had lost a parent each, two had become orphans and several had lost their homes. I can still remember the chilling dread that would come over me each time I had to break the tragic news to the unfortunate child, and the misery we would all undergo trying to console what we knew deep down in our hearts was inconsolable.

Everyday brought fresh news of horrific destruction—Coventry, its historic Cathedral smashed; the parachute mines in London destroying everything they touched without discrimination; the beloved dome of Saint Paul's which was somehow saved by round the clock firefighting by volunteers who snuffed out every live bomb which hit it.

And then fortunately the weather turned foul and the Luftwaffe was forced to slacken its pace.

Christmas was quiet and solemn. There were simple presents for the children and tea with them and the Lanverndel staff. I was now heavy in my movements and getting more and more uncomfortable. The nursery had been furnished, and Mrs Walters, the nurse sent by Patricia had already taken residence and was getting familiar with the house.

I was getting tired, irritable and incredibly lethargic. Doctor Spencer had warned me that the baby may come a little early and that I should be prepared.

I had only one wish in my heart, that Raymond should be home when the baby came. Mrs Walters inspired confidence and Patricia said all she needed was a telephone call and she would be by my side. My daily routine was quite altered now. I rested in the afternoons, knitted now and then with my feet on a pouffe. Raymond's routine was as unpredictable as the bombs. On days without mishap, I would see him at least once and then he would be off on his covert sorties to France or wherever, about which I really knew nothing, and I did not want to burden him further with my curiosity. I would only pray feverishly that he should return home safely. He did tell me once in a very circumspect manner that he was in contact with Yvette la Casas. The French Resistance was getting powerful and I suspected she must be an active member. On days or nights of bombings, I scarcely saw him at all. He had set up a moderately self-sufficient room at his office, and by now had visited almost every home in the county, grieving with the bereaved, helping the hungry and homeless, very often through his personal generosity.

Jane had taken over the myriad household chores and proved an intelligent and able girl. We had great shortages of food—tea, coffee, sugar were hard to come by, for England had suffered heavy shipping losses. Meat we hadn't seen in years, but fortunately the dairy and poultry at Lanverndel supplied not only all of us with adequate milk and eggs, but also the hospital and the orphanage. Lanverndel also managed to give us a reasonable supply of vegetables. Our harvests of grain and fruit had mercifully been good this year, and the household staff had preserved large quantities of jams and jellies and juices. Raymond had made it a rule that anyone who came to Lanverndel for shelter, poor or rich, was to be given hospitality, and I secretly hoped that their good wishes and gratitude, especially of the poor, would bring us luck and a healthy baby.

The winter was getting colder and the weather persistently worse, particularly over the Channel. That gave us some relief from bombing raids, but the demand for fire wood and electricity kept increasing. Dr Spencer checked me up and was quite satisfied, but repeated that the baby would come earlier than expected. He preferred the confinement to be at Lanverndel. It would be safer, he thought, instead of driving around on dark, bomb prone roads, with no one in a position to predict exactly when and where bombs would strike. Raymond and I agreed, and I was gloriously happy that the new de Villiers would arrive in his own home, as had his ancestors before him.

Raymond used every possible excuse to be at Lanverndel these few days, but he appeared tense, both for me and for whatever he was postponing. Yet, I could see that he was waiting with as much excitement as I was, except that it was manifest so differently, the indifferent kind of excitement that only a man can have. He waited for four days and there were still no signs of anything happening. So after making sure that all arrangements for the confinement were foolproof, that the chauffeur would be on the premises round the clock, that Dr Spencer and Patricia would be ready to receive my phone call, he left for his assignment, promising that he would be back in a day.

I smiled as bravely as I could, "Sorry, I can't help you out on this one. You carry on. Jane and Mrs Walters will look after me. And I have Dr Spencer and Patricia nearby. No one could ask for more."

"If you only knew how much I want to remain with you." He spoke crisply, but I could see his eyes were moist.

"Darling, don't worry. I have so many people around me. Millions before me have undergone this, queens and princesses and ordinary folk. I'm sure I'll manage."

He said good-bye, but wistfully and regretfully. I smiled. I knew the baby would come in his absence. And I was right. That night, a little after midnight, I felt the violent convulsion. Lash after lash struck me, and no one could save me, not Dr Spencer, nor Patricia or Mrs Walters or Jane, though they kept giving me instructions and courage, and finally after about eight hours of flailing, came the miraculous relief and I heard the primitive cry of a new life on earth.

"Is it a boy or a girl?" the question repeated from the beginning of time.

"It's a healthy bonnie girl. You have been wonderfully patient and brave and now we shall take over from here. Congratulations." Dr Spencer was beaming with pride as if the credit was all his.

"Yes, you must try and rest now, after all that slogging. Ooh...I have the most beautiful niece in the world." That was Patricia, who had stayed by my side all night.

"Why are babies always born at night, Doctor?" I asked, exhausted and drained of all feeling. "May I see the baby?"

She was being washed, her umbilicus being dressed. She was wrapped and shown to me. Even in my numb state, I could see she was Raymond in miniature, the same bones, the same eyes, the same mouth. I seemed to have been left out of the transaction entirely. When would Raymond come? I drifted off to sleep.

When I woke, I had been sponged and cleaned and the baby was lying in the crib next to me.

"May I hold the baby please?" I said to no one.

"Ah, here we are. Congratulations and thank you." Raymond's voice was coming from the adjoining room.

My spirits brightened. "Raymond, darling, thank God you've come." He was by my side, his hands holding my face and covering it with kisses.

"I had to leave at the right time, obviously," he looked at me, "damn this war."

I laughed. "I knew it would happen as soon as you left. Do you like her? She's a spitting image of you."

"Like her? I love her. She's so beautiful. Actually I'm pretty stunned. I don't know what to say. Just too overwhelmed."

The nurse gave her to us—the rose button mouth, the eyes tightly shut, yet the face unmistakably Raymond's. And he was overjoyed, I knew. It was the seventh of January, 1941.

Chapter Fifteen

She was christened Alexandra Patricia de Villiers, Alexandra after Raymond's grandmother, and Patricia after his sister. The household was overjoyed and we had a splendid celebration of sorts. The children and the maids did up the house with spartan wartime resources, the cooks turned out cakes and pies and savouries, and there was lemonade and ginger ale. Suddenly, Lanverndel became festive again with flowers and candles and singing. Alexandra was two weeks old and was a good child, sleeping day and night.

Once again my routine underwent a somersault. I picked up in health, and as Alexandra grew bigger, so did another facet of me. My contact with the other children acquired a new dimension—there was greater empathy. I could perceive their deprivation and experiences with greater sensitivity.

The year 1941 was bad. Food was rationed and was getting harder and harder to come by. Bombings were intermittent but frightening. The month of May saw the worst bombing of our coast and of London, and it reached a peak in June, just before Hitler turned his airforce and armies towards Russia. Even now, I can see the headlines with bold, black letters announcing, "BLITZ OVER. IT'S MOSCOW'S TURN NOW." I hoped and prayed to God it was true.

Meanwhile, each day was a miracle, with or without bombs. The children were cared for, Lanverndel survived, and we managed a reasonable amount of food for everybody. I would dream of my childhood, of the featherlight angel cake my mother would bake for me, the roast and pudding for Sunday lunch. I would remember the meticulously planned menus at Lanverndel in the old days, which were not that old really, when mounds of the most exotic food would remain untouched. I would try and simulate the taste of those tangy Mediterranean oranges, the creamy bananas, the syrupy figs on my tongue, all the things we hadn't seen in an age, and content myself with that. But this human body is after all a miraculous affair, adjusting quickly to anything, luxury, hardship, pleasure or pain. Well, having learnt to survive nature, it had now to start learning how to survive man-made modes of destruction, gifted to us from the age of science.

Alexandra was growing up a beautiful child. Initially, she slept almost continuously for a month, something that made me exceedingly worried, but Doctor Spencer assured me that this was nothing unusual. I remembered reading somewhere that babies grew in their sleep. I went through all the infantile stages with her, the eye movements, the first sounds, the teethings, the crawling. Raymond was fascinated and spent every moment he could spare with her, spoiling her, playing with her, making her laugh. She had the arrogance of a tiger cub, the brightness of the morning star, and the stubbornness of a mule. I think she was born with basic knowledge that continuous screaming would always get her whatever she wanted.

"Raymond," I asked one day, "where on earth did Alexandra get this obstinate temperament from? I can't think of anyone in my family like this."

"From me, I suppose. I remember my mother telling me I was exactly like this. You'd better ask Patricia. She must have borne the brunt of it. And somewhere in my life, it must have died out. You'd agree, I'm sure, that you've not encountered it."

I tried not to laugh. "No, not really. Though sometimes I do think I almost have to use a pair of tongs to extract even a sentence out of you."

"Ah, now you're trying to intimidate me. And I'm sure that's not at all true. Okay, let's observe me, shall we, and I'll prove you wrong." He tried to look peremptory and instead looked quite funny.

This time, I couldn't stop my laughter. "No, no, please don't do that. That'll spoil all the fun."He shook his finger at me in reprimand, and I blew him a kiss in return.

My greatest joy was seeing Alexandra grow, looking like an angel, and behaving more and more like a little tyrant, with the whole household dancing to her tune, exuding irresistible charm to anyone who ventured to discipline her. She spoke her first words at eight months, walked at eleven, and by the time we celebrated her first birthday, she had all the confidence of a two-year old. She seemed to have her priorities neatly charted out. I was indispensable only at bedtime, the nurse and the maids were required for playtime and outdoors, and Raymond for indoor mischief and a general carte blanche for having her own way. She broke all the household rules, and categorically refused to sleep in the nursery. Raymond indulged her to the hilt, and normally allowed her whatever she set her heart on.

"What does it matter? Her demands are so simple, and I would rather she be with you until she is older. I don't want her to be frightened of the bombings—it might leave a permanent scar on her mind, and I would not like that to happen."

"I don't mind in the least. I feel much happier and safer if she's with me, and in any case I'm alone most of the time. And so often in the middle of the night we have to make a dash for the basement."

She would ask about the bombings, and what they were. I answered her truthfully, and after that she ignored them completely, not showing even a trace of fear. What an unusual, fearless, free spirited child she was, so opposite of me. I wondered how on earth I would ever cope with her. I suppose once the war was over, Raymond would take charge; he never seemed to have a problem with her.

The years of war continued to pass, as is the fate of time always, come what may. Birthdays and Christmases came and went, but more than anything else there were deaths, bereavements and funerals, of men at war on the ground, in the water, in the air, of hapless, innocent civilians who faced the bombings and later the VIs and V2s. Patricia's son, Howard, finished school and enlisted with the RAF with all the fire and dash of a nineteen-year old. Patricia and Rupert were proud of him, but I could see that a subtle change came over Patricia's expression after that.

My days were full with Alexandra's growing mobility sometimes bordering on the dangerous, with settling her down in the nursery school, administering to the children and running Lanverndel. How wonderful it was to watch a child grow, especially your own, at a time when the world outside had almost closed up. Alexandra now spoke fluently and seemed to enjoy the nursery classes with the other children, but what she enjoyed most were the little jaunts to the woods with Jane to collect flowers and insects. I would keep a keen watch over her in my own unobtrusive manner, as I wanted so much to figure her out, to find a key to her personality. I was quite reassured with what I saw—she was a considerate child, loved plants and animals, and was friends with the other children. It was just that she was so unusually self-contained and seemed to know exactly what she wanted, something I could never understand. In her movements she was natural and bold, just as she was in the face of whatever little obstacles she encountered in her innocent, unstained world. How would I ever understand how to handle her?

But that, thank heavens was still a long way off. Right now, she was the joy of my life, my creation in whom I tried to see both myself and Raymond. I would sometimes stare hard at her when she was sleeping, and would feel a deep tenderness for this little waif who sometimes seemed so inexplicable to me. In a sense, she was everything I was not—aristocratic, confident, with so much personality and a devil may care attitude. My heart brimmed with joy for that.

The erratic wartime months sped fast at Lanverndel. Though I had plenty to keep me busy, I missed Raymond intensely. The demonic war had by now started wearing everyone out, and I could feel it was taking its toll on me as well. Everyone had only one fervent prayer, that it should somehow come to an end, so we could start living normally again.

We were going thorough 1943, the year Raymond turned fifty. Sadly, he wasn't in Lanverndel on that day. He was away on one of his flying missions which would normally last for three or four days. I had reached a stage when I wouldn't worry if he hadn't returned within that time, but on this particular occasion a week had passed and there was still no sign of him. He had told me more than once that if his absence went beyond two weeks, I should contact a certain telephone number in London. Well, I told myself, it was still just a week, and I shouldn't panic. But the strange coiled feeling at the back of my head kept bothering me.

Alexandra asked about her father repeatedly. She was progressing well in the nursery. She knew so many songs and rhymes, which she mixed up at will, giving them a stamp of her own scrambled tunes. She did the same with alphabets and numbers, and could say quite a few of them, but in a sequence that she chose. She had drawn some pictures to give Raymond on his birthday. She had discovered a new bush full of wild berries, and had 'saved' it as she said for presenting to her father.

I couldn't reveal any of the fear and panic I was feeling. It would surely be infectious, and the child seemed to have such an uncanny intuition. So I kept up the facade and made up a little story of how her papa was helping the king to destroy the wicked people and would return as soon as he had finished his job. She seemed convinced and continued to live her charmed little life spreading joy all around her.

Two weeks were about to close, and I was sick in my heart, sick with fear, terrified about a very definite possibility which I dared not even think about, the pain of it lashing every living cell in me. The only one I opened my heart to was Patricia. I knew she would understand, for she was going through it each day for her son. She promised to come over the next day. As soon as I saw her, I broke down.

"There, there," she said, "I wish there was something I could comfort you with, but it all seems so meaningless. Only we who must wait know what it means." She placed her arm over my shoulder, "Come, dry your eyes, and don't lose hope. That's all we can do. If others see you losing hope, it will demoralize them as well."

I pulled myself up. "Patricia, you are always so brave, so dignified and composed, even with all that you go through each day for Howard. And look at me, behaving so irresponsibly. There must be thousands of women like me. At least I'm lucky, Raymond has always returned, and I always thank God for that."

"Well, we just have to be brave and strong, however trite it sounds. I'm so frightened most of the time, really, but I dare not show it to Rupert. It would shatter him. Hang on for today, if you still don't hear anything, we'll call London tomorrow."So we went on, one frightened woman comforting another.

The fifteenth day broke. I had hardly slept the night before, but had to pretend before the household that all was normal. Alexandra went to the nursery, and I sat down, sick with foreboding and despair. I would call the London number I decided, but in actual fact I was doing everything possible to postpone it. I thought I would first talk to Patricia, and I stood up to go over to the phone. Just then John knocked and announced a visitor.

"Mrs de Villiers?" he asked.

"Yes, what is it?" I went still with fear.

"Sergeant Watson from the county office, ma'am. I've been asked to give you a message"

I was about to collapse; it was going to be bad news. My head had started swimming.

"There has been a change in Mr de Villiers' plans. It may take him another week to be here."

The visitor's words were not registering. A thousand questions were rushing through my head. I finally found my voice.

"I'm sorry, I'm a little overwrought. Could you please repeat what you just said."

The sergeant did so politely.

"Is he all right? When did you say he's returning?"

"Mr de Villiers seems to have run into a problem with his plane, so he's returning by boat. It could take about a week. I've been authorized to say only so much."

"Thank you, thank you so much. But you're sure your information is correct. There couldn't be a mistake, could there?"

"None whatsoever, ma'am."

"Thank you, thank you very much." I was weak with relief, but empty of all else.

"My pleasure, ma'am," and he took his leave. I heard the motorcycle start, and then it was gone.

I had to pick myself up. I had to inform Patricia. My voice and movements seemed alien to me, as if they belonged to someone else. I heard Patricia's relief, but I felt lifeless, exhausted and numb, feeling nothing at all. Then, doubt and disbelief started battering me again. Suppose the information was wrong...suppose the boat was torpedoed and it sank...I would never even come to know until days and days had passed. Meanwhile, there was nothing I could do except wait and have faith.

He came finally, six days later—thin, tired and weather-beaten. I heard a car drive in, and I knew it was him. Alexandra was in the nursery, the maids were doing their chores, and my ears picked up the sound of the car engine in the drive. My heart thumped as I ran to the porch and stood in anticipation. Yes, my heart was right. It was he, and almost automatically, I said a silent prayer thanking God.

He stepped out most naturally and gave me a hug.

"Sorry darling, things went a little out of control."

His voice sounded dull and dead. He was obviously very tired.

"It doesn't matter, Raymond. You're back and you're safe. That's the only thing that matters."

"Where's Alexandra? How's she?"

"She missed you terribly. Kept asking when you'd be back. She's been all right. She's in the nursery. Shall I send for her?"

"No, let her come as usual. Let it be a surprise for her. Oh, for a decent cup of tea, a long hot bath, and a long uninterrupted sleep." He stretched his arms behind his head and yawned.

I smiled, "Yes darling, you shall have all three." I asked John to send up the tea immediately

We went upstairs. I prepared his bath while he waited for the tea. His face had a strange expression, not just anxiety and exhaustion, but a kind of sadness, a fatalistic kind of sadness. Perhaps, he had experienced severe shell shock, or had seen too much death and destruction. Anyway, he was back, and that was all that really mattered to me—the rest would mend itself, just as everything else about this horrific war would.

"Raymond, what's the matter, darling?" I sat close to him and held his hand. "You've been through some kind of hell, I can see that. I can't tell you what it means to see you again. I almost died with fear. But I kept going because of Alexandra."

"It's been hell all right. I'll try and tell you about it later. You remember Yvette? She's dead. It was very tragic," and he sat silent again, trying hard I could see to keep his equanimity while sipping his tea.

I was stunned. People were dying every day, around us, but not Yvette, with her feminine softness and masculine aura. She couldn't die. I tried to recall the last time I had seen her in Paris, with her uniformed escort.

"Oh God, I can't believe it. She was life itself."

"Yes, anyway, I think she went the way she wanted to go; perfectly in command and in the midst of what she was so completely committed to in her heart. Yes, I'll tell you all about it later."

"Raymond, your bath is ready. I'll serve lunch after you've finished, so you can catch some sleep after that. I think Alexandra will be coming soon."

"Oh, by the way, I didn't even ask how you've been. How boorish I've become."

"I've been fine, only worried sick about you, and missed you terribly. As years are going by, I miss you more and more."

He came to me and took my face in his hands. 'Thank God you're well, and Alexandra. I wonder how much longer we have to go on with this infernal war. It's so strange. You know, I would give anything to spend long idle hours with you and Alexandra at Lanverndel, but it seems next to impossible. And I remember, there was once a time, it seems so long ago now, when I had all the time in the world, and all I did was keep running away from here. Well, that's life, and its ironies and follies." He smiled and went to his bath.

I phoned Patricia and gave her the good news.

And then I went downstairs to ask for early lunch. Alexandra had just finished with the nursery class and came running and stamping. I told her I had a surprise for her upstairs.

"Papa's here, I know."

"How did you know Alexandra?" I was astonished. She was beaming with smiles. "Mummy, I knew it. I knew it in the morning."

And she dashed off upstairs with Jane following her. She waited patiently for Raymond to come out, and after that it was one chaotic, noisy reunion with screaming and laughing, and leaping and jumping over the beds and sofas and on the floor. Would anyone have believed that the highly proper and staid Raymond de Villiers was capable of the acrobatics I was witnessing! She was rattling off stories of the nursery, how one of the children had wet her clothes and not with water, giving renditions of songs and tunes she had made up.

Raymond promised to accompany her to examine the wild berry bush which she said she wanted to present him with.

"Alexandra," I said, "how would you like it if we all had lunch together. Papa's hungry and anyway it's your lunch time, and you could sit at the table with us." She screamed with excitement and went thumping down the stairs.

Raymond kept smiling and looking at her wistfully. "You're right, Alexandra is really a very unusual child. She seems so self-contained and confident, never grumbles or complains about anything. And to think she's just a little over three." He was falling into the same syndrome as me—there's no one like ours.

"I'm just waiting for this damned war to be over. Sometimes I feel so exhausted, and to think that all I do is run a home. And Alexandra needs you more and more. Sometimes I wonder whether I handle her correctly. I never seem to know when to check her and when not."

We had lunch, the three of us, with Jane helping Alexandra. It was a treat for her and she made sure she enjoyed it thoroughly. So much so, that by the end of the meal, water was dripping from the table and morsels of food were sticking to her face like impressionist art. By the time lunch was over Raymond was about to doze off in his chair.

I touched him gently on his shoulder, and he opened his eyes with a slight jerk. "Sorry darling, I haven't had a night of proper sleep for the last two weeks."

"Yes, I can see that. Raymond, I hope you're not planning to go to the office. You must catch up on your sleep."

"No, I'm not going to the office. I'll just make a few phone calls and then call it a day until I feel more civilized."

He attended to his phone calls and then just passed out. He couldn't even stay awake long enough to cover himself. I smoothed his pillows, covered him with blankets, and shut the door gently behind me with lightness in my step and in my heart.

Raymond slept through the remaining part of the day, and I had a hard time explaining to Alexandra why he should not be disturbed.

The story of the King's soldiers and the wicked men was repeated, with a happy ending of her papa returning home safely, after defeating the King's enemies. He woke in the evening as if in a stupor, used the phone to make some enquiries, gave some instructions and sank back to sleep.

I told Alexandra that she could give him her gift first thing in the morning. I was so relieved that she agreed to everything without protest. So much energy saved for me. She had made two coloured pictures for him and we had wrapped them up many days ago in shiny wrapping paper. One was of Lanverndel, or rather her perception of it, and another of the sea and the circular terraced lawns with several birds of all colours in a blue sky. There was a lot of vigour in the pictures even for a child of her age. I felt a feeling of some pride that she had inherited at least something from me.

Next morning, Raymond was up and about much before us, and I could discern from the sombre and taut sentences on the telephone that something very serious was happening. Later, I was to learn that the Allies had invaded North Africa and the Nazis had wasted no time in marching into Vichy France. Would it never stop? It all seemed so pointless. There would be more blood and more devastation.

"Raymond, you had better take Alexandra for the walk that you promised her, before you get wrapped up with your work again."

Alexandra came in shyly and handed him his gift, all the while smiling coyly looking downwards.

"Thank you Alex," he said, as he carefully removed the wrapping.

"The pictures are so beautiful. We will paste them and frame them, and I shall hang them over my dresser. And then one day when you're a young lady and become a famous painter and have great exhibitions, we'll remember to place them at the entrance, and then we shall all dance."

He picked her up and swirled her in the air with her laughing and screaming with happiness. "Now, shall we go to see your special wild berry bush that you've been keeping for me."

"Papa, let's go now. Hurry, it'll start raining."

The sky was getting cloudy and grey clouds were descending, enveloping everything. They grabbed their coats and put on their walking shoes and were off.

I remained alone, somewhat exhausted, but contented. My world was complete once more, my prayers had been answered and Raymond had returned. But the last few weeks had exacted their toll—the dread and panic, the sleeplessness, the facade.

Reflection is a state that possesses me whenever I'm alone, as I suppose it does all of us, and the course of my life plays itself back. Today, I felt satisfied and on track. What a wonderful feeling it was to be afraid of nothing, to be independent and secure. The ghosts were dead and even I was hardly reminded of them. Memories and associations had faded and had been replaced several times over. They were gone, some charred by the fire, and others obliterated by the war which had so fundamentally changed our lives. The final healing had come from the elflike magic of Alexandra, and the spell of joy she cast over everything in Lanverndel. And so I went on to proceed with my chores.

There was bloody action going on in the war zones, which meant that Raymond would again be working round the clock. We had hardly had time to speak at length about anything since his return. He had mentioned Yvette's death, and I could see that he had gone through something very traumatic which hadn't still left him.

It was almost a week later when Raymond and I finally found some time to talk, and he gave me an account of his last visit to France. He told me how Yvette had been running escape routes for Allied soldiers and airmen from occupied France all the way down to Marseilles after which they would coordinate with Gibraltar and try and return to England. It was only now that Raymond revealed to me what he was doing and what had been going on surreptitiously at Lanverndel all these years. I realized I was living in the midst of an outfit making identity cards, passports, travel documents for the Strategic Operations Executive, an organization based in London of which Raymond was a part. They were responsible for parachuting documents, wireless sets, money, arms, medicines to British agents in Nazi occupied countries for use by the Resistance.

"You may find it funny, but we're called the Moon Squadron."

"Moon Squadron? Any particular reason for such a romantic name?"

Raymond had a hearty laugh, "No, no, nothing romantic at all about the Squadron. It's just that we fly only on moonlit nights, a few days before or after full moon, for obvious reasons. With moonlight, we don't need any elaborate navigational assistance, as landing becomes easy. And the Lysander, that's the single engine plane that I fly, hardly needs any ground to land or take off."

"Oh really, I wonder how I missed noticing the moonlight bit?"

He continued. "Well, I'd had a fairly long stretch of good luck, but this time the Lizzie gave me problems and I had to crash land. I landed in a ditch, but the wing and propeller had completely gone. It broke my heart to desert my good, faithful Lizzie, so agile and quick, but I just had to do it. I was given shelter in a friendly home nearby, but unfortunately, before the local resistance outfit could dismantle the plane, it was spotted by a German patrol party, and the entire village was subjected to the usual house to house search."

"Oh my God, that must have been so terrible."

"Yes, it was. Then began the running and hiding, until I reached Paris. I spent some time with Yvette. She was running an incredibly efficient escape route and putting herself to great risk. She was involved with a lot of dangerous resistance activity, like blowing up bridges and trains. Dear God, you should have seen the fervor and commitment with which she was working. So energetic and efficient. And what an amazing network of contacts she was running all over France for escorting Allied airmen and soldiers to Spain."

"But what happened to her? How did she go?"

"I'm still not quite sure. She accompanied me to Dijon and put me on the train to Marseilles. She said she'd be staying on there with friends for some other work she had. As soon as I reached Marseilles, I was informed about a massive explosion on a bridge while a heavily guarded train was going over it. The train was loaded with arms and ammunition from Dijon to Paris. I think after that the net closed in on her. Perhaps there was a slip up, or the local outfit was infiltrated, but my host at Marseilles told me that when they closed in on her, she coolly opened her handbag, took out her revolver, smiled at her captor and shot him in the heart. Cynical as it may sound, I think she went the way she'd have liked to go." He lapsed into silence and deep thought.

"How tragic. She was one person who so completely fascinated me. So intelligent, so poised and gracious. And what a personality. I remember when I first met her, it wasn't so long ago, I wanted so much to be like her. In fact, I truly looked forward to spending time with her. I thought we'd invite her here after the war. What hell they seem to be enduring in Europe, and I grumble here merely because I don't have enough tea or coffee or sugar. Anyway, so what happened after you reached Marseilles?"

"Ah, from there I was taken by another guide to Barcelona, and then the British Consulate took over and I reached Gibraltar."

"What? To the great rock again? Good Heavens," I asked incredulously.

"Yes, it was from there that I asked for a message to be given to you. Two weeks were going to be over, and I knew you'd be worried."

"Yes, I really was worried, and so was Patricia. But what a terrible time you've had."

"No, not really, I was quite well looked after. They gave me clothes, food, shelter. But it was after a long time that I had this feeling of being hunted, of running for my life. And believe me, it wasn't exactly the most agreeable feeling. Or perhaps, I've just grown too damned old for it."

"And then you did the same journey from Gibraltar?"

"Yes, except that this time I came home on a battle ship, and wasn't quite a civilian."

"What about Yvette's children? Where are they?"

"You remember that young man Conally whom we met at Nice? Well, Yvette managed to send the girls to America with him. Fortunately, she had no financial problems."

"We must make enquiries about the girls, perhaps call them over sometime. We owe her so much."

"Yes, we do. Poor, brave Yvette." He was deep in thought, in sadness. "There are so many more like her there, who we will never know."

Chapter Sixteen

The war continued, changing its focus and ferocity as the months passed by. The bombings were fewer but Raymond's flying became more frequent. Operation Overlord was launched, but before that there was coordination to be worked out with the Resistance groups, and supplies to be delivered. This went on through all of 1944 when the bloodiest phase of the war started in Europe.

The lists of the dead and missing kept growing longer, and the whole country seemed exhausted. Then came the weapons of vengeance, the VIs and V2s, the terminal attempts of an army sinking in defeat and desperation, and a dictator gone insane. These flying bombs caused their share of havoc and panic, but they had come too late to change the tide of war.

One by one, the countries of Europe were liberated, and there were more bloodbaths, more towns and cities bombed to rubble.

Raymond's flying schedules became nerve racking and erratic, and most of the time I never knew his whereabouts. The year passed into the next which saw the hellish last battle, and then, finally, the guns that had boomed relentlessly since the year I married Raymond became silent. It was over, the bloodiest conflict in history was over, and we in England, bleeding and relieved, for the second time in fifty years, wept again for the flower of our youth lying under crosses in cemeteries, or drowned in the sea, or just scattered in the unknown.

So another period of our lives was over, and I wondered how we would all readjust to what lay ahead. Raymond would soon be relieved of his war-time responsibilities, and would have to take charge of his estates again and sort out the tangles which had been multiplying. And Lanverndel would change too. Whitehall would vacate its offices, the children would leave us, and it would become private again. Nothing frightened me anymore though we would again be starting from scratch. How many times in life did one start from scratch, I wondered. It was hardly Charlotte's Lanverndel any more, shabby, neglected, battered as it was today. But everything was clean and fresh, and the phantoms of the past had been swallowed by this savage war.

Raymond now had more time to spend with us. He too was exhausted, and kept postponing and dodging taking charge of his long neglected estates. His solicitors advised him to sell his lands at Devonshire to clear his debts and taxes, and eventually this is what saw us through.

The happiest, of course, was Alexandra who was now almost five years old. She exhibited a delightful appetite for life and whatever colours of it she perceived in her little world. She loved music, she loved dancing, could draw well and colour with imagination. She rode with confidence and had natural flowing limb movements. I don't know whether my perception had altered or whether Raymond had changed, but I realized that she shared so much of her father's personality and temperament. He was, of course, the love of her life, and I was just the bolster which must always be there, when she was sleepy or distressed or ill.

Slowly, our lives and routines changed to postwar times. Life was still hard, and when I compare our present lifestyle to what it was before the war, I can only say that the drop has been very steep indeed. After Whitehall returned their portion to us, I simply shut it up, thinking I would do it up later when we were financially a little sounder. We had to cut down expenses drastically to make both ends meet, but I didn't mind.

The children left us and returned to their homes; some lucky ones still had both parents, while others only one. Five of them had become orphans, and I insisted that they stay on with us instead of going to some impersonal orphanage. Raymond undertook to finance their education, and they remained with us until they finished school. They have done well in life and every year at Christmas they come to Lanverndel, which they still consider a home.

Raymond seemed happy and busy. He always had a smile on his face, and the silent whistle between his teeth. He too, I think, set his mind only on the present and the future; the past I was certain receded further and further into oblivion. So be it, I thought. After what we had braved, I was convinced that the sunny period of our lives had begun.

Summer was settling in, after battling clouds and mist and rain. The landscape was going through its miraculous seasonal transformation, as it always does during this time of the year, bringing in the special aroma of summer—blue skies, tender green leaves on trees, sprouting plants and buds all around, butterflies suddenly liberated from hibernation, and birds twittering and enjoying the summer air.

It was on one of these bright sunny days that Miss Portner decided to pay me a visit at Lanverndel.

It turned out to be our last battle with the past.

****

My head was heavy and painful. There was something coiling around me and reaching my neck, tighter and tighter, suffocating me. I must stop it, for if I didn't, it would choke me completely and

I would die. I tried to loosen the coils with my hands, but I saw with terror the serpent's head, and the small piercing eyes wishing me death. I started screaming louder and louder, and then mercifully, I felt a cool hand upon my forehead and my eyes. I was breathing very fast, and the cool hand kept comforting me. I tried to open my eyes. It was an unfamiliar room, white, with a strange smell. I was on an unfamiliar bed and was wearing odd night clothes. I tried to move but a peculiar constriction held me back. And then I felt it, a huge bandage below my left hip, and a continuous living pain. Through a haze, I saw Raymond, looking devastated. He took my hand in his. I tried to remember what had happened, and gradually I saw Miss Portner's face come before me.

"Raymond, what happened?... Miss Portner had come...and I was about to tell John to send her away."

I was sedated, and had to make such an effort to speak. The pain was gnawing at my side.

"Hush, darling. I'll tell you everything later. Don't strain yourself now."

"Where's Alexandra?"

"She's with Pat and Rupert. Jane has gone with her. Don't worry about her."

I kept slipping in and out of consciousness for a day, and it took me about a week to be able to sit again. Alexandra would come to see me with Patricia and Rupert. She had been told that I had had an accident, and she insisted that I should return home, now that the accident was finished.

"The doctor says I can come home in two or three days. Now isn't that nice? The only thing is that I shall have to be in bed for some time. That's quite okay, isn't it, Alexandra?"

She gave me her most beautiful smile.

Soon I healed sufficiently and my spirits too became brighter. I implored Raymond to tell me the details of what had happened. All I had been able to gather so far was that I had been shot on the thigh by Miss Portner.

"Quite sure you'd like to hear it all now?" he asked.

"Yes, I'm sure. Please tell me everything."

"Okay, you remember ringing the bell and calling John? Well, he came and you turned towards him. It was at that moment, Miss Portner took her revolver out of her purse and aimed at your heart. Well, it's only through miraculous chance or a divine power protecting you that she collapsed, probably that split second when she pulled the trigger, and that's how the bullet went through your thigh." Raymond kept his voice low and impassive, but the anger was seething beneath.

I was shocked and revolted. "Where's Miss Portner now? What happened to her?" Then almost to myself, I asked, "Why does she hate me so much?"

He was expressionless. "She's dead. A clot hit her brain, cerebral thrombosis, I believe it is called."

So there would have been more police at Lanverndel, the newspapers would again have had screaming headlines, and the entire past would have been exhumed and bared naked once more. But nothing seemed to matter, nothing seemed to frighten me anymore, and that was that. The last of the evil was gone, and we were finally free.

There was one last statement to the police. The wound was healing nicely and soon I left for home. There was to be daily dressing and antiseptic cleaning, for which a nurse came in regularly. The doctor was satisfied, but I had to stay in bed for another two weeks.

I tried to keep my mind occupied during this period but was quite unable to do so. Why was I constantly racked by flashbacks? All I did was lie still and keep thinking about the curious twists and turns my life had taken. Always threats, always phantoms relentlessly pursuing us, always battles putting us to the test. But win them all we did, and strangely enough, after each curtain call there came a bonus of happiness, however tentative. There were always shadows, but then from somewhere a shaft of light would appear and illuminate the chiaroscuro. There was always the bitter, and then the sweet.

Was this the true essence, the essential pattern of life? I would never know, for who can answer these primeval riddles of life. Just when we believe we've wrested one adversary and got him under control, from out of the blue appears another, and the confrontation begins all over again. Did life ever have moments when there were no adversaries to slay, no devils to conquer? I wished so much I could see the future. But then, serious thinking when in poor physical condition is never advisable; one finds the world so much more fearsome, one feels more helpless and even the silver linings appear dull.

I healed fast and walked again, limping at first. But neither my disability nor my disfigurement bothered me. In those silent weeks, I realized again the depth and strength of our bond, Raymond's and mine. Even though we were a generation away from each other in age, and a world away in social class, it didn't seem to matter. He did so much to look after me and make me happy and kept repeating that he should have taken the bullet and not me. Dear Raymond, I don't think he has been able to rid himself of the guilt he feels on this, quite unnecessarily if you ask me. For it was me whom Miss Portner hated, not him. Had we both been present at the landing that day, she would still have aimed at me.

Alexandra, my little cherub, was like my nurse and companion. She dutifully reported every detail of her day at Lanverndel to me and her own adventures in school and outdoors.

Yes, there's always the bitter and the sweet. Exactly a year later our son was born, bursting with vitality and health. We named him after his father and mine, and he was christened Michael Raymond de Villiers.

Epilogue

Years have gone by, seasons have rolled on, and Raymond and I sit beneath the maple tree for tea, as we always do when the weather is fair. Our children are home for their holidays. Alexandra is now seventeen and continues to be as enigmatic and free spirited as when she was a child. She has Raymond's face and an extraordinary vitality inherited from heaven knows where. Raymond says she reminds him of no one he remembers except himself. This he adds only for effect, I know. But there is a certain elusiveness and passion about her which is totally alien to both of us. From some unknown ancestor, I daresay. Her presence exudes life and activity, and her eyes are often more expressive than her words. She has, I would say, a quiet kind of flamboyance. Michael, now twelve, has my face, but is otherwise Raymond all over again. He tends to be reflective, philosophic and is unshakeable as stone. I think secretly Raymond relishes the replication and I find him sometimes watching Michael curiously, when he is fixing an electric toy train or knocking down some other plaything.

Alexandra and Michael don't quarrel often but when they do, the entire establishment is commandeered. The household staff is roped in to take sides, the animals are acquired and prohibited from socializing with the other side and Raymond and I have to listen to charge and counter-charge. Then suddenly everything gets forgotten and there is much civility and affection, and plans made for inviting respective friends, going on picnics, riding or visiting Aunt Pat's farm.

The children are indeed a blessing. They took over from where I left off. I am almost forty now and Raymond is on the other side of sixty. I look older and he younger, though he has greyed and I have not. His walk is still springy and his gait perfect; and though there's a slight cushioning around his abdomen which he is very conscious of and tries hard to wish away, he looks quite athletic even now. His face still patrician, if anything even more so, is lined, but the eyes are clear, and there is a sparkle of happiness and contentment in them. There are no stalking shadows anymore, and he laughs and talks easily. Much of his time is spent on running Lanverndel and on the children's activities. We have a set of good friends, some in London, some nearby—a small comfortable group, people who were in school or college with Raymond, people with whom he played cricket or fought the wars. We visit each other frequently, play golf or tennis in the afternoons, or bridge in the evenings.

Then, of course, there are dear old Patricia and Rupert who have shared so much with us and never stinted in their affection or support whenever we needed it. They have also borne their cross with fortitude after Howard crashed in his burning Spit and is today with an artificial leg and hand. But nothing of the private hell that she must endure ever reflects on Patricia's face.

Dick, our saviour in Gibraltar, met a tragic but heroic end in North Africa, winning the Victoria Cross posthumously. So we were never destined to keep our rendezvouz at Lanverndel, and the secret of Camlin and Burtolini went with him. I can see him even now at the base of the Great Rock, tough and in command, his face brown and decisive, his field glasses dangling around his neck. Dear Dick, how much we owe him and who knows what would have become of us had we not met him so unexpectedly at Nice.

I am now quite a well-known pencil sketcher, not a celebrity, but quite well-known. When we went to Cote d'Azur after our tragedies at Lanverndel, I decided I would keep a sketch pad. It was to become my faithful companion throughout our travels, and now I'm never without it. I have captured some interesting scenes at Nice, Monte Carlo and Gibraltar, but my heart's delight are of course the ones I have done of Raymond, some mischievously, some very sharp and down to earth, and of the children at various stages, crawling, toddling, playing.

Lanverndel, I have sketched from almost every angle, in every season, from every direction. I have covered the grounds, the Honey Vale, but never the creek or where the fishing cabin was. In fact, there is no cabin anymore. When the restoration was going on, I wrote to Henry and asked him to break it down completely. I wasn't concerned about what people would say. So there is no cabin in the creek now. I suppose Raymond has noticed it, but since he has never remarked on it, I have said nothing either.

It is incredible how my sketching has acquired more individuality and force with each passing chapter of my life. I now sketch for magazines and advertising companies and have had some exhibitions at Lanverndel which have delighted our neighbours and friends. I do some honorary teaching work at the local school and Raymond is very proud of me.

The aftermath of the war was difficult and bitter. Almost everyone we knew lost someone. Lanverndel escaped bombing, though it looked shabby and neglected, but we didn't mind. Costs and taxes soared and Raymond had to sell sizeable chunks of land to make both ends meet. All our loyal staff are still with us and we all count our blessings every day.

I have never seen Raymond happier. We are settled in our ways with no pretensions or affectations. I am not the toast of high society like Charlotte was, but I am, in a sense, a self created woman and do not regret anything in my life. I think I look quite elegant and smart and Raymond is proud to escort me around. What a contrast from the day when I first stepped into Lanverndel and wanted to hide behind every column and wall. I have a practical and tasteful wardrobe, mostly from Harrods or Burberrys, and I realize now that chic and graceful clothes add to one's personality—nothing outrageous or extravagant, but merely simple and dignified.

Raymond and I have, what I consider, a very special closeness and understanding. I suppose after what we've been through, we fully deserve it. Sometimes I feel the story of our lives unfolded an age ago; sometimes it seems as if it was just yesterday. Our folders of memory are so arbitrary and capricious. Some memories we consciously snuff out and never want to play again, while others we nurture and guard so tenderly that we never lose them. That apart, as one grows older, whatever falls within the range of recountable memory, I think, we label recent, and only that which cannot be remembered clearly, we say happened long ago. On this issue my mind plays tricks with me frequently.

On the whole, life has not really treated us badly, though we certainly have had our share of tragedy and travail. But the passage of time changes one's perceptions so much. What looked like tragedy or misfortune decades ago appears to be just another unpleasant or exaggerated situation, after it has been left behind. I learnt my lessons about life from all of them, most importantly, that one must not just give battle, but give it repeatedly; and the more afraid we are of something, the more tenaciously we must confront it. I learnt this for the first time, possessed by rage, as Lanverndel stood burning and we watched broken hearted and stunned. It was that rage which unleashed the perennial stream of energy from somewhere that made me grow, and after that there was no holding me back. I wanted Raymond to pick up his life again, I wanted to save our marriage, and for that I took impossible risks. We went to the Cote d'Azur, which was laden with memories of all shades and we faced everyone, our souls parched and searing, making civil conversation and discussing trivialities. From nowhere, I acquired poise and the art of conversation. I started taking decisions, sometimes overtly, sometimes unsurely. Survival, both Raymond's and mine, was the only raison d'etre of my life in those years.

We have known fear and pain, but have also known great happiness and triumph, and we read each other's expressions and gestures with considerable ease. There are times when we both experience that great stillness between us, when neither speech nor expression is necessary, and we acknowledge our silent thanks to each other. The gestures are innocuous, a smile which only he and I understand, a look in the eyes expressing gratitude, a touch of the hands which speaks more than words. After all, we dared the Fates and won, when all hope seemed lost.

The children come racing in with the dogs, with muddy jeans and boots. Pluto the Second is about to knock down the tray. The children have spoilt him so much that unless he is given due consideration at tea he does not settle down. The other spaniel Champagne is very gentle and ladylike and patronizes everybody. The children have tea with us and talk of the highlights of their day and plans for the next. Very soon, the radiogram will be blaring and we'll be subjected to the new sounds of rock n roll and pop, and then will start the inevitable debate—Elvis Presley versus Cliff Richard, a debate which has all the potential of becoming a full-scale war!

We are going to have the traditional County Carnival at Lanverndel next week. Of course, it is not as grand as it used to be before the war, but I insisted we resume it after we had recovered a little. The neighbours and the staff had missed it and there was a popular demand for it. The surrounding villages exhibit marvellous floats, with local people, our friends and neighbours, all part of the parade that starts from Lanverndel. The day closes with a fun fair, and a huge bonfire. Raymond personally supervises it, and it has now become a great event in the county. The fiasco of my first county carnival is long forgotten, and even if I am reminded of it sometime, I dismiss it casually with a shrug.

My left thigh has a knotted scar where the bullet went through. Raymond caresses it whenever he sees it and I call it our talisman of happiness. It was that bullet which swept away the last of Charlotte from Lanverndel and laid the evil to rest. The bullet which passed through me, I think, brought Charlotte's end.